AWFUL BY COMPARISON

Patricia Caliskan

SAPERE
BOOKS

AWFUL BY COMPARISON

Published by Sapere Books.

11 Bank Chambers, Hornsey, London, N8 7NN,
United Kingdom

saperebooks.com

ISBN: 978-1-912786-07-7

PART ONE

Chapter 1

Jennifer

It was the middle of November when things first hit a landslide which slowly gathered momentum. I was ill, absolutely full of flu, but too scared to call in sick as so many branches of the bookshop I worked for had closed during the last twelve months. But on this day in particular, from the moment I woke up, it was as if the universe was trying to tell me something.

After dragging my aching bones from under the warmth of my duvet, I'd knocked a cup of Flu-a-Way down the front of my coat, trying to dose myself up before I left the flat. I missed my train by seconds, just in time to watch as the doors closed on a herd of vacuum-packed passengers, all looking about as cheerful as I felt, and then, in a cruel assault by the hand of fate, I'd fallen *up* the stairs on my way out of the station, instigating the start of a ladder in my new, velvet-look tights, and dislodging the heel of my left boot. A boot, which was one half of The Best Pair of Boots I've Ever Owned, which isn't something you take lightly after four years' devoted service. My heel was now revolving in 360-degree circles all the way down the street, like a faulty wheel on a bad choice of supermarket trolley, forcing me to concentrate on every step, so I didn't end up whirling around like Julie Andrews in *The Sound of Music*.

By lunchtime, my cold had gone into overdrive, I was completely famished and totally frazzled, organizing our new display of Literary Classics. I'd spent that morning in the basement of Brookhouse Books, supervised by Angela, my manager, who had to stomach my failed attempts to do everything she could have done much better herself. A fact she wafted under my nose along with the scent of her expensive perfume. I'd just found out that, with store closures up and down the country, my Saturday over-time was now officially classed as "helping out", and, due to the Flu-a-Way-down-the-coat incident, I'd left my packed lunch in the fridge at home, which not only meant spending money I didn't have, but also that tonight's dinner was most likely to be this afternoon's leftover sandwich.

I negotiated my way around the aisles at the supermarket, until finally joining the procession at the cash register.

And then, there she was. My sister.

Grinning at me from a box of hair dye in the shopping basket in front, looking as beautiful and carefree as ever.

Meanwhile, I had flu-blotches covering my face which, a quick glance on the make-up aisle assured me, looked as sore as they felt.

In fact, if Lara could have seen me, she'd probably have faked a phone call and left immediately.

You mightn't know my sister's name, but you'd probably recognize her face. Laura, or Lara Taylor, as she's officially known, has starred in fashion campaigns for the last 15 years.

Every now and again, usually during a day like today, when it's pouring down and I'm umbrella-less, I catch sight of my sister, joyfully clutching her ankle on a box of moisturizing tights, or winking theatrically from the cover of a magazine.

She's everything I'm not, which is great news for her, but the biological equivalent of "here's what you could have won" for me. Like me, most people have never winked theatrically, or worn moisturizing tights, so that I can live with, but those aren't the only differences between us.

Even if you'd known me for absolute years, or I'd selflessly donated my best kidney to save your life, Lara would still be the sister you'd notice first. Only after a quick double take might your eye fall on the girl standing next to her.

The short-arse with the heavy calves? That's me. The little sister.

The recurring cry of, '*You're* Lara Taylor's *sister*?' isn't just about her having a dream job, modelling clothes and cosmetics all over the world, but genuine shock that I've shared the same bedroom, let alone the same womb, as this ridiculously photogenic woman. Trust me, I spent many a school day leading a trio of jeering kids across the playground so Lara could vouch for our shared paternity. And occasionally, if I hadn't annoyed her too much that day, she would.

We grew up in Ingleford — a place so small that a mention on the weather forecast twelve years ago made it into the local paper, and provided the 'humorous' sign-off at the end of Father Dooley's Sunday Sermon. Even wearing the standard-issue Ingleford uniform of walking boots and waterproof jacket combo, you couldn't help but notice the long limbs, tiny waist, and thick, blonde mane, which set my sister apart from the rest of us.

So you can probably understand why Lara was something of a celebrity in the village long before she was snapped up, winning *The Face of Francesca* magazine when she was seventeen. An achievement which, I don't mind admitting, was thanks in some small part to me.

'I don't even like having my picture taken,' Lara had insisted, standing in front of the mirror all those years ago, while I filled out the application form with a choc-ice in one hand and a biro in the other.

'It's not just about getting your picture taken, it's about being a model!' I'd gushed, aged fourteen, hoping she wouldn't notice the ice cream river I'd just spilt on top of her duvet, as I sat cross-legged on her bed, eager for my sister to be discovered. 'It's about travelling all over the world, being famous!'

'Do you really think I could win?' she asked, sweeping her hair up into a makeshift ponytail, while she assessed the gentle curves of her profile.

'Defo! Everyone fancies you, and you've never even had one single zit, or needed braces, or had psoriasis, or anything,' I assured her, reeling off a list of my latest teen ailments.

So she agreed, and sat answering questions, before getting the tape measure from Mum's sewing kit and updating her vital statistics. I wrote everything down in my neatest handwriting, subconsciously hoping that some of her glamorous good fortune, or even just her ability to eat the same stuff I did without being the same shape, might work its way down the family tree and make me slim, gorgeous, and popular too.

But, of course, it didn't.

Now I know we shouldn't judge the size of our thighs or the whiteness of our teeth by the digital dimensions of the girl on the fashion pages, and on a good day, I know I'm not that bad, but the truth is, I'm awful by comparison.

While I loved how my sister lived in a shiny, more glamorous world, I was just a little sad that she couldn't be bothered showing the slightest bit of interest in my life. Although, I thought, unwrapping my scarf as I limped back into the office on tiptoe, still trying to manoeuvre the heel of my broken boot, I wasn't even that interested in it myself.

'Management meeting in five minutes,' Cliff spluttered, as I unpacked my bag with every intention of pulling up a chair and quietly stuffing my face.

'You're joking? I haven't even had my lunch yet.'

I managed one large bite before it was coats off, downstairs, and into Angela's office. Everyone was already seated when I arrived. I closed the door with my best, 'Oops, sorry I'm late' face, chewing down the last morsel of cheese salad, as I edged along to the seat which Luke had saved for me, trying to pick up the main thread.

'Faced with the current economic climate, we simply can't forge our way past the digital revolution without a few battle scars,' Angela said. 'Publishing has changed and Brookhouse simply has to change with it.'

My mind wandered to the selection of bodice-rippers taking pride of place at the ground floor counter, which I could see now only appealed to a small percentage of our customers. It was then I noticed the pile of envelopes on Angela's desk, just as Cliff cut to what I hoped wasn't the point.

'This isn't change. You're firing us!'

'You're not being fired, Cliff. You're officially on gardening leave. During the next four weeks, Brookhouse shall endeavour to find all members of staff similar positions in some of our remaining branches...'

'Gardening leave?' I whispered to Luke. 'I haven't got a garden.'

'What remaining branches? The ones that have managed to cling on, miles away? At the other end of the country? And are you going to pay for us to relocate, too? As union leader,' Cliff began, with a spittle spray of excitement, 'I should explain, we are now in the official negotiation state of redundancy.'

'Redundancy?' Luke shrieked.

'Yes, redundancy,' Cliff said, folding his arms in one last, grand gesture of defiance, 'which I think might explain those envelopes Angela's about to present us with...'

I couldn't help but think Cliff was enjoying the whole thing a little, despite being out on his jacksy along with the rest of us. The envelopes might have book tokens inside them, I thought, eager to prove him wrong. Some sort of goodwill gesture to acknowledge the extra efforts we'd all been making in the run-up to Christmas.

But even I wasn't that naïve.

I looked around the room. Everyone was as shocked as I was. Everyone except Angela, who had known exactly what was going on, long before she made me stack boxes of books in the basement for most of the morning, knowing I could barely see for sneezing, as I bent and lifted, bent and lifted for hours.

And it was nearly Christmas. *Christmas!* I wanted to say, when you're not supposed to do bad things to nice people, not now, when there's no jobs out there and Jesus died on the cross for us. The least they could have done was let us down first thing in the New Year, when we were already skint and thoroughly depressed by the thought of the long month ahead.

I re-crossed my legs, giving Luke the *can-you-believe-this?* face I usually saved for whenever the cash point censored our Friday night out due to insufficient funds.

'Are we really being made redundant, Angela?' Sue whimpered, on the verge of tears.

'This isn't a reflection of your work,' Angela reassured us. 'It's merely a reflection of the current climate.'

At this point, Sue let out a sob, and Angela took this as her cue to pass out the envelopes, which didn't even have our names written on them, let alone a £5 gift token inside. Cliff had been right. We were sacked.

With the amount of realistic options I had available, I preferred not think about what was lurking around the next corner of my life.

Chapter 2

Lara

The airhostess kept her smile firmly in place as I stretched out my neck, beyond tense and sick of having to play this little game with her. Especially when I was fighting the urge to bleach her moustache before we prepared to land.

'I asked for vodka, not the tears of a unicorn…'

'There's really no need to take that tone, madam.'

'Well, there's really no need to board a seven-hour flight without your HRT patch, but we're having to deal with *your* mood swings, aren't we?'

I turned to the stuffy-looking bloke next to me and tried to share a grin, but he was hiding behind his iPad.

I needed a drink. I was flying home to spend Christmas with the family. Among other tightly woven delusions, they had decided my life was utterly charmed and they depended on me to regale them with tales of my fabulous adventures in Wonderland.

At this point, my parents knew nothing about my fiancé, Silvano, or the fact they were expected at my wedding (my third, but who's counting except my mother) in New York, on January 5th.

I turned back to the trolley dolly. She looked about ninety, which in my own bitter experience, made her far too old to put a smile on anyone's face, surely? Lucky to still be employed as an airhostess, or whatever they called themselves now.

Her features were set into No Can Do mode.

Time for a rethink.

I leaned forward, reading our lovely flight attendant's name badge, '*Elaine*. I'm sorry. I didn't mean to be rude. I'd just be really grateful if you could get me another drink?' I sat up a little straighter in case she rolled out the same old drill. 'My *last drink*. I promise. Pretty please?'

Finally, she doled out the drink that, let's not forget, I was *paying* for, told me to enjoy the rest of my flight and swept past with a new 'bad passenger' anecdote for the team. But, what the hell, I thought, I was happy to let her have her five minutes of popularity with her colleagues, and at this point I was starting to get pretty bored of my own company, so I decided to give the guy next to me another chance.

'We could report her for that, you know?'

He threw me a disapproving look, before he decided to neglect his keyboard for a second.

'Maybe she thought you'd had more than enough to drink already?'

It was obvious life hadn't turned out quite the way he expected and now he got his kicks picking over other people's lives like Thanksgiving leftovers. People were so bitter. Always convinced someone else was having a better time, getting the bigger deal. Talking of which, I thought, nuzzling under my complimentary blanket, I had to try to remember the girl I had to become when I got back home.

Finally relaxing, I felt a delicious sea of nothing washing over me, but then they decided I needed to sit up and put on my seatbelt, we were about to land.

'I only just got on here,' I told Elaine, as she exchanged a withering look with another airhead in a polyester uniform.

'Can I get you some water, madam?'

'What?'

'Water, madam?'

She was practically dragging the blanket off me.

'What are you doing? Get the hell away from me!'

'Madam, can you please calm down?'

The guy next to me decided to lean across at this point, ushering complaints to Elaine.

'She's been like this the whole flight. It's obvious I'm trying to work here. The least you could have done was move me to a decent seat.'

'This is a decent seat!' I said. 'It's me who should have been moved! I don't have to sit next to losers like you!'

I shut my eyes as they carried on peck-peck-pecking and finally told them, *yes*, I'd be good. I was being good right now. Look! I was doing whatever they wanted.

Then I let myself relax and float away again until everyone piped down.

I hadn't spent Christmas with my parents for years. The last time, I'd just split with Travis and realized as soon as I got back there, listening to Mum drone on about my sister's bad dentistry, that the last thing I should have done was go home while my heart was still smashed inside my chest.

Visiting Ingleford was like sitting naked on a park bench and demanding privacy. The girl with the world at her feet. That's what the local paper called me after I got my first modelling contract. I was occasionally reminded of my first bit of press coverage back home when I answered the phone, or bumped into neighbours I'd barely seen since school, because that's how they all remembered me.

Meanwhile, my sister demanded constant attention.

Jennifer would hang herself from a branch by her bra strap if she thought it would keep my folks distracted from me for five minutes. Instead, I knew they'd spend the whole trip wearing expectant smiles every time I walked into the room, wanting to know about all the *amazing* things I was supposed to be doing.

That was the big problem.

They always expected.

They expected me to be happy. They expected good news. They expected me to resemble that girl in the photographs.

What they didn't expect was me. Although, this year I did have big news: I'd met Silvano and for the first and, I promised myself daily, the very last time, I was settling down. I was happy. Silvano 'got' me. There were no expectations.

Chapter 3

Jennifer

Over that first 'in-between-jobs' weekend, back at my old flat with my Christmas playlist on a loop, I had been full of new beginnings and undiscovered talents. I updated my C.V., convinced of my many notable qualities as a prospective employee, and finally got round to finishing Lord Sugar's autobiography, before I picked up the phone and dialled Mum, who, spookily reminiscent of Sir Alan, quickly reminded me, business was a double-edged sword:

'You've been fired?' She barely paused for breath before her hand went over the receiver, announcing the news to Dad. 'Jen's been fired! Unemployed! They've made her redundant,' she said, making sure he got the gist.

Mum was a great fan of synonyms.

'Well, technically, I'm on Gardening Leave until they've officially got nothing else to offer me at another branch.'

'She says she's on Gardening Leave,' Mum called.

'Great. I'll get her job at my place then,' Dad called back.

'This isn't a time for jokes, David,' Mum chided. 'I can't believe it. So close to Christmas? *Terrible.*'

'It's not that bad,' I lied, like I always did when Mum was borderline hysterical. 'I didn't want to end up there forever. This might be the change I needed to happen. You know, to help me change direction,' I added, quoting from George, my ever-optimistic boyfriend.

'Change direction? How can you do that when there're no jobs going?'

As Mum spoke, it was as if my worst thoughts had possessed a warm body.

'I'm sure something will come up.'

'Between now and next month's rent? How are you going to pay for your flat?'

The fact was I wouldn't be able to live there without a new job. I didn't even have a gold filling to sell.

'You've always got your room here, you know that.'

'Thanks, Mum, but I'm sure it won't come to that.'

'Well, maybe not,' she muttered, full of concern. 'Anyway, never mind for now, guess what? I was going to surprise you, but you could use some cheering up ... your sister's coming home!'

'Now?' I'd bleated out, sounding desperate.

My sister didn't do family occasions. The last birthday I'd spent with her was my 21st, when she showed up champagne-flushed, wearing a transparent dress and clutching Patrick, the barely English speaking, French photographer destined to become her first husband. They married a few weeks later in Vegas before she divorced him five months afterwards in a rare display of clarity.

'I thought you'd be pleased?'

'I am. I'm just ... *surprised.*'

And devastated. And embarrassed. And fed up with pretending that I fit in with this family.

'Well, so were Dad and I to tell the truth, but won't it be lovely? All four of us back together again. Your room's ready, and like I said, if you need to stay a little while longer, while you look for a job, it's no trouble at all.'

I made an excuse about spaghetti on the boil, and sat down in the middle of the floor. One call home and my career prospects had been given a headstone. Forget Lord Sugar.

Mum was right, this wasn't good. I had a month and a half's wages to live on.

Why couldn't Lara have come home last year, I thought, back when my smaller jeans still fitted and I could afford to get my hair done?

I stared at my old Brookhouse name badge until emotion fizzed inside my throat. The pin that told me, and everyone else, who I was: *Jennifer Taylor, Customer Order Officer.* I attached it to my pyjamas, scanning the bed-sit I called home, but which was technically my landlord's place. A landlord who wouldn't care less about Gardening Leave or Christmas. Mum was right, I'd have to move out.

I leaned against the couch, pulling a cushion down into my arms. I had no savings, no way of even eating while I looked for a new job. It was a countdown to disaster, with only the faint promise of a flatter stomach to keep me upbeat.

Stop it! I told myself. And my slippers. A pair of fuzzy, fur kittens who always listened at times of despair. Although, between you and me, the right one always looked far more sympathetic than the left, who had one button-eye missing, and looked a little cruel, to be honest.

This was a beginning, not an ending, I thought, reciting one of Angela's platitudes, as the zing of my mobile alerted me to a text from George:

You've prob already seen this, but noticed job might be of interest? Digital publishing on WebJobs.com G xxx

I was almost too scared to look, especially now Mum had reminded me about the job situation, but in an attempt to lighten the mood, which wasn't easy by candlelight, I pondered if 'Googling' had officially become a verb yet, as I scrolled through jobs, kicking myself for not previously having cared for the elderly, never taking a greater interest in credit control, or doing a degree in marketing, until I saw it:

Digital Publishing Assistant. Central London.

My eyes strained to read the details quickly enough. It was me! It was fate! It had to be mine! Before I knew it, I'd be knocking over the alarm clock and cursing the commute like the good old days!

Excellent attention to detail... Bachelor's degree... Work to deadline... Solid grasp of the publishing industry ... discerning appreciation of fiction essential...

Okay, it was a sidestep, but I had the qualifications, and, like George kept saying, more than a fleeting understanding of the publishing industry. It was a dream job, and meant the years spent in Brookhouse, hoping one day to get an actual break in the real world, weren't a complete waste of time.

Just as I'd hoped, they invited me for an interview the following Monday. I texted George straight away:

Got interview for the fab job!!! New start, new life, new Jennifer, here I come! Thank you! Xxx

Things were on the up: my flu symptoms had ebbed away, the man at the key-cutting place had fixed my 'wheel' heel for £7. I'd even managed to get a two-year-old yogurt stain (at least, I hoped it was yogurt) off my suit jacket.

As I got things ready, busying myself around the flat, now that I had time to dust away ceiling cobwebs and remove tea-splashes from skirting boards, I took George's advice, thinking about answers to possible questions, like where I saw myself in five years' time, which obviously, along with everyone else, was a dress-size smaller and earning twice as much.

My old suit still looked quite smart. I'd bought it for my interview at Brookhouse, but it was quite difficult to button, now I'd gone up two cup-sizes, and the trousers were a few inches too long because I'd originally worn them with a pair of sling-backs that had long-since been charity-shopped. Unfortunately, sewing wasn't one of the Personal Skills I'd added to my job application, but I reminded myself interviews were usually seated, and if I got the job, (*Please, let me get the job*), I'd ask Mum to stitch them for me.

I'd called her to let her know about the interview, but she was far more interested in the medieval bird she'd ordered from Hoggs Butchers for Christmas.

'It's a bird, inside a bird, inside a bird!' she cooed, rather appropriately. 'How about that? We've blown the budget!'

'Sounds tasty, Mum,' I lied, thinking it sounded more like something hideous that footballers did at the weekend.

'I want this Christmas to be extra special. You'll have your new job, and, did you know it's been four years since we last had your sister home for Christmas?'

I'd thought it had been longer, until I remembered our last Christmas together had been a blur due to an impacted wisdom tooth, which meant Mum putting my turkey dinner to spin in her new blender. Meanwhile, Lara had hardly spoken as she'd just split up with Travis, husband number two, a country and western singer who wrote a song about her after they split called '*Woman or Wolf?*'

'Don't get carried away, Mum. It's just an interview,' I said, secretly glad she had some faith in my bouncing-back abilities.

'Never mind, *just*! It's half the battle won! Good luck, and remember not to slouch!'

But, as I said, my plans never went according to plan. The next morning, I opened my eyes, sockets aching.

My flu was back. Full-strength. My stomach, empty and weak, felt as if it belonged inside a much thinner person who lived off soup and compliments. Slowly, I dragged the sculpture of my head off the pillow, hair damp, almost stuck to my face.

I wished I was already at home. Mum lecturing me on vitamin C, running a lavender bath, and putting something foul tasting and medicinal in a glass at my bedside. Halfway through this thought I realized I was clearly quite delirious, but no matter how much I wanted to be back under my flowery duvet with Mum playing nursemaid, I couldn't miss the interview.

I trekked towards the kitchenette, head struck down by a lightning bolt, but despite a thorough search involving a thousand takeaway menus and a long-lost phone charger, the painkillers were gone.

George was busy saving the lives of animals, and the only other man in my life was Luke; a red-blooded heterosexual, who lived a 25-minute commute away, and wasn't at all sympathetic to others' ailments. In fact, he regarded illness, misfortune, and heartache in general, as the core components of his existence, and he really didn't like to share his toys. The only other person in the vicinity was my downstairs neighbour, an elderly lady with one eyebrow, who hated me for no apparent reason other than I lived in the same building, and occasionally ruined her day by making eye contact.

I was so feverish that despite feeling the inner-shame of a normally healthy person, fashion and self-respect were hazy recollections of a former life. I pulled my coat over my pyjamas, checking the pockets for change. The shop was only a two-minute walk away, I told myself, as I shut the door, realizing I was still wearing my fuzzy kitten slippers, but far too pathetic to care.

Let them stare! Let them judge!

I was ill and not responsible for my own actions!

The jangle of the newsagents' door hurt my ears, and as the wind picked up, I used my body weight and the power of positive thought to force it open, heaving my way inside. As I did, loose change spilt from my hand, spinning across the floor. Head swaying, I bent to pick it up as a bloke I'd never seen before appeared behind the counter, eyeing me like a security threat.

'Don't worry,' I said, unable to suppress a throaty cough as I scrambled for rogue coins off the dirty, footprint-wet tiles. 'It's my money,' I assured him, wiping my mouth on the back of my hand.

My slippers were filthy and wet, less fuzzy kitten and more stray cat, and I realized I should have brushed my teeth. Even I could smell my death-breath. I think it was the first time since I met George that I was grateful we didn't live together.

'Painkillers, please. The strongest ones,' I said, before a wave of weakness forced me to prop myself against the counter. 'I feel so bad.'

'That door was supposed to be locked,' he glared. 'We're not open.'

It wasn't Cristos, who was used to me popping in. I wondered if he'd lost his job too, until I remembered I never usually came in during the day, because I was working, like a normal person with a job.

'Please, I just need this pain to end.'

'Sorry, love. I haven't got time for this. You'll have to leave.'

He was looking at me as if I was a complete nut-job, and once I caught my reflection in the glass counter, I could see why.

Yesterday's mascara was smeared beneath my eyes, which were pink and sore from rubbing away the ache behind them.

My hair was lank and greasy with flu and my lips were cracked by a burning temperature.

'Oh no! I'm not mad, or anything,' I said, attempting a smile as I brushed my sweat-damp fringe from my bright, red face. 'I'm just very ill. Here,' I said, producing the mitt full of change, along with an extra strong mint I decided to pop in my mouth, despite having found it stuck inside my coat pocket. 'I've got money.'

'Yer, I see that,' he said, looking towards the door, wishing me on my way. 'Just get out the shop. I don't care whether you're homeless, or not.'

'I'm not homeless! I live down the road. I know Cristos who works here.'

He stared, anticipating my next move with confusion.

'He knows me,' I smiled. 'I just need something for flu. Please?'

Thankfully, even though I could tell he didn't want to turn his back on me in case I stole a paper or produced a gun, he selected a box of tablets and reluctantly counted out change. Still struggling to stand up straight, my eyes landed on the shelves. And there she was.

Like I said, Lara always turned up when I least expected her. Even though my eyes were swimming in all directions, I picked my sister out — all metallic make-up and backcombed up-do on the front cover of *Female Flair*, as I fought the urge to rest my head on the counter and quietly die.

'That's my sister!' I declared, doling out an extra £2.30 as I put the magazine on the counter.

'Yeah right, that's yer sister,' he said. 'Now get yer stuff, and get out!'

George had texted to wish me luck, and once I'd read his message I was determined not to let him down. I showered, dosed up, dressed, and got over the shocking lack of customer service, let alone compassion, in the world.

I was soon dispatched outside the publishing house, noticing a rather nice-looking cake shop, Francine's, across the road, and imagining lunch hours spent perusing artisan breads, carrying the latest Dan Brown under my arm, stamped with top secret instructions about editorial changes and late night deadlines.

Could all that really happen to me? I peered into my future and saw a grown up. Someone taken seriously, who knew serious things, and did serious work, and I realized, more than anything, I wanted this job. I needed this chance. I could *do* this, just like George said.

Soon, an attractive woman of about fifty, with short, sharp, peroxide hair and massive, dangly earrings, strode towards me, offering a manicured talon.

'Genevieve Manley. And you must be Jennifer Taylor?'

Flu heat burned beneath my blouse, the floor rose to meet me, but with the promise of getting back into bed in the near future, I had it under control in seconds.

'Yes, thank you,' I said, getting to my feet, and having a bit of a, 'woo, it's high up here', moment as I followed her long, elegant steps to the lift.

'Actually, we'll take the stairs, it's far quicker.' She smiled, loping across to an elaborate staircase, which she climbed with the speed and agility of an Olympian.

Gripping the banister, I tried to keep up, but it was exhausting, especially as the front of my shoe kept getting caught inside my trousers.

While Genevieve ascended with conveyor-belt grace, I was climbing up my own leg instead of the stairs.

'You okay, there?' Genevieve asked, already at the top.

'Fine!' I said, a little too brightly, but she was already through the door.

She apologized as her phone rang, taking the call as I took a seat.

The sun glared through her office window, threatening to cook my wincing eyes as my face began to burn, and my head began to pound. It was time for another tablet, but I'd deal with that later. For now, I was trying not to drown in my own sweat.

'So, Jennifer, you're interested in working with us...' she said, hanging up abruptly.

It took me a second before I realized she was asking me a question.

'Yes. Yes, I am.'

She stared, prompting me with a raised brow, as the sunlight continued in my direction with the intensity of an interrogation lamp.

'Oh, right. Well, *erm*, I'm interested in working with you because ... I love books in a discerning way.'

She nodded.

'And ... I have a solid grasp of the digital publishing industry...'

I think, at this stage, we both realized I was quoting directly from the job ad.

'And in five years' time,' I began, trying to remember all the impressive-sounding stuff I'd committed to memory, 'I see myself sitting there, like you, and publishing lots of really good books. Really *great* ones that people will buy, *online*, because that's the nature of the digital age we live in.'

I was quite proud of myself, especially that last bit, but by now my eyes were watering so badly, and my head aching so steadily, I could barely make out Genevieve's profile, let alone what she was saying, apart from, '*Acquisition* … *manuscript* … *popular titles*…'

I dabbed my eyes on my sleeve, until, luckily, her phone rang again, and, even though I knew it might look a little odd, I fished out my sunglasses and the remains of a tissue from my handbag.

'Thank you, Hayley. Please let her know I'll be with her shortly.'

Phone down, she was staring again.

'Are you okay there, Jennifer?'

'Oh, these?' I replied, waggling my sunglasses. 'They're … prescription, light reactor things … all the better to see you with, Mr. Wolf!'

'Let's get back on track, shall we?' Genevieve cleared her throat. 'Where were we?'

'Well, we were talking about popular titles. I know all about those,' I replied, trying to think of something to say, and, as I did, suddenly remembering Mum's advice about not slouching.

I sat up, nice and straight.

Then felt the front of my jacket give way completely.

I guessed the chiming noise was my top button, skipping merrily across Genevieve's tiled floor. She looked towards it, until her eyes returned to mine and slowly descended towards my bust, which had made a proud bid to escape.

I hunched inside my blouse, aware my black bra was clearly showing through the white cotton. I know I should have worn a white one, but like every other white bra, it was now grey and resigned to sleeping in.

'I read all the Harry Potters, and I definitely know my Twilights from my elbow,' I said, letting out a smug-but-not-nasty laugh, hoping to divert Genevieve's attention back to my new job.

Genevieve looked confused, so I elaborated.

'We all went to see the films too. You know, at the shop, because that's what customers expect. I mean, I wouldn't say if something was just crap or something, obviously,' I giggled, 'but I'm, just crazy about books and the digital age.'

The next thing I knew, Genevieve was standing to offer her hand, which I'd read was a good sign. A short interview meant they knew they'd got the right person, whereas a longer one indicated they might be trying to work out why you were there in the first place.

'We'll be in touch,' she assured me, stooping to pick the button up from the floor.

'Oh, that's not mine...'

She looked at my jacket; little more than a low-cut petticoat, hoisting my lacey-bra-ed bosom up and out, in the style of Moll Flanders working the Stock Exchange.

'I mean, that's mine, *the button*,' I stuttered, realizing I was making the whole thing worse, 'I meant, the jacket's not...'

I shook my head in a 'silly me' kind of way, and went to shake her hand, but as I was holding my soggy tissue and Genevieve had hold of the button, it wasn't quite the firm, business-like gesture I'd been planning on for days.

'Sorry, all finger's and thumbs,' I laughed, pulling the tissue from her palm. She smiled back, which, given the circumstances, was definitely another step in the 'right job' direction. I admit, it hadn't all gone according to plan, but surely even Genevieve Manly had an off-day now and again?

'I'll walk down with you, Jennifer.'

We both knew the next applicant was waiting, which was a bit awkward, but thankfully, I'd got the hang of hitching up my trousers as I walked, and the sunglasses were definitely doing the trick of soothing my eyes.

It was only as I approached the last few steps that I heard a voice I recognized:

'*Jenny?*'

I looked up.

My old boss, Angela, was standing in front of the reception desk.

I forgot to look down.

A split second of trouser-leg-meets-pointy-shoe later, and I was on my knees at Angela's feet, as if praying for my old job back.

Genevieve's office got in touch the next day to say I hadn't got it. I was a bit shocked to be honest, as Genevieve had personally helped me to my feet, which I thought was really nice of her, and she had insisted the receptionist brought me a glass of water before disappearing with Angela, who hadn't even asked if I was alright, just stood there, looking mortified on my behalf.

I tried not to take the rejection personally, but it wasn't as if Genevieve would realize she'd made a huge mistake and ask me to work for her after all, let alone give me my own office with my name on the door, the way I'd imagined when I had a particularly busy day at Brookhouse.

Why couldn't Angela — mean, smug, Angela — have gone tumbling down the stairs while I looked on, all cool and serene? Fair enough, she'd been 'demoted' to Assistant Manager, but it was at Head Office for goodness sake, and at least she still had a job. She didn't need to find a new one, and now there was a good chance she'd end up working with Genevieve — doing *my* new job!

Even worse, Lara had texted to wish me luck that morning with my 'new, publishing career', so I made a mental note never to mention job interviews to my mum again.

Nothing like that ever happened to Lara. She used to go to loads of interviews, but they called them Bookings. She'd hand over her portfolio while the photographer, or agent, or whoever, decided whether she was gorgeous enough for the job.

Can you imagine?

No questions about what she thought her strengths were, apart from looking perfect. A simple stand, smile, and strut. Lara was brilliant at all three. After a couple of years she had people asking to book her without having to parade herself round, and then she became 'Lara'. A model with only one name, literally paid to be herself. Paid for existing!

It was amazing when you thought about it. Worth having to exercise and give up chocolate for. Anything rather than working for a miserable boss and doing overtime for free. I mean, why couldn't we at least have been born identical twins?

The day went from bad to barmy. I might have failed to get a job, but I'd become a local hero. Seriously. On the way back from the interview, I noticed Cristos waving goodbye to a police car, and, despite how ill I felt, seeing him there, big grin on his face, when I'd practically been thrown out by the bloke he had working there, I decided to do something about it. I was going to complain for once.

This wasn't something that came naturally. The words, 'Thank you' and 'Sorry,' loitered permanently on the tip of my tongue. Even if you cursed my firstborn, slammed a door in my face, and stood on my foot, I'd still remember my manners.

I didn't deserve to be treated like a criminal just because I had flu.

Plus, I'd cut my knee as I fell down the stairs and there was nowhere else to go close-by to buy a box of plasters.

'Jennifer!' Cristos cried, raising his arms and rushing from behind the counter. 'I cannot thank you enough.'

Jeez, it went from one extreme to the other in here, I thought.

'You are my best customer!'

'Cristos? I haven't so much as bought a band-aid yet.'

'Yes, you are funny, and brave!'

'Well, I should probably be tucked up in bed, if that's what you mean. I can't remember the last time I felt this awful.'

'You saved me! You saved my shop!'

'Saved you? How?'

'From the robbery! This morning I saw you, from there,' he pointed towards the back door. 'He put gag in my mouth, tied hands like this,' he said, demonstrating his hands being tied behind his back. 'But then,' he smiled. 'I hear the door, see you, and get my shoe off like this,' he demonstrated again, 'push panic button with my toe while you still talk, talk, talk, to the robber! So, I thank you, so many, many, times!'

He insisted I take the plasters for free, along with a cinema-sized bag of peanut M&Ms and a box of king-size tissues, but even though I should have been on top of the world, back home, the place seemed horribly small, while the day had been long and dreary. The only trace of the outside world was my latest gas bill.

I yanked off my suit and pulled back the covers, getting ready to curl up and die, until the bleep of my mobile interrupted sniffles of self-pity. A text from George, asking how I'd got on, but I couldn't face him, not now. My dream of making him proud at dinner parties had started out as:

This is my girlfriend, Jennifer. She's in publishing…

And had now become:

This is my girlfriend, Jennifer. She's…

In debt…

Insane…

Living in a hostel…

Insufficient funds in her bank account…

…just a friend. I hardly know the girl.

I succumbed to flu and misery, spending the next 12 hours in bed, drifting in and out of fever-induced dreams which sent me falling down staircases, into the arms of my waiting mother, until Lara appeared, and I'd fall, fall, fall, back into the basement of Brookhouse Books, landing with a thud at Angela's feet, while George pointed and laughed as he took my sister in his arms.

I'd been standing by the window for the last five minutes, supposedly checking everything was packed up, but actually feeling rather sad, as I watched Luke loading the car.

'Come on, Jen. Your carriage awaits!' he shouted, his voice echoing inside the downstairs hallway.

Shutting the front door, I'd wondered exactly what was happening to my life. We were about to drive to Ingleford, better known as where my parents lived. I was home for the holidays, indefinitely, as I couldn't afford the rent on my flat, and was about to be reunited with my sister, who couldn't have picked a worse year to come home because:

a) I'd lost my job;

b) had to give up my flat (see point a); and

c) split up with my boyfriend, George (see points a and b).

Lara had called me, I thought because Mum had tipped her off about my sudden downfall, but actually because, she said, she had big news:

'I'm coming home for Christmas!'

'I know! Mum said. It'll be so good to see you,' I replied, hoping to make the last bit sound convincing, because I was actually mortified by the thought of having to catch up with her when my life had gone completely to pieces.

'Well, it's not just that,' she said, pausing for effect. 'I thought I better tell you before the dress fitting. Guess what? I'm getting married!'

I fought off déjà vu quickly enough to offer her congratulations, before she continued with helium-inflated enthusiasm.

'In New York! In January! And you're going to be my bridesmaid! Are you excited?'

Despite protests about paying for tickets (her apparently rich husband-to-be had insisted on paying for all of our flights) and my yearning to knock off a few inches as she demanded my measurements, the deed was done, and I was made to swear not to tell our parents before she 'surprised' them over Christmas with a two-week, New York vacation, which happened to include her third wedding.

I walked down to the car, strangely pleased as the rain started up right on cue, as if aware that the least it could do was commiserate with me. I didn't even care if my hair got ruined. I wanted sodden farewells in howling winds. Specifically, I wanted George to show up, windswept and desperate for me never to leave, begging me to stay with him forever.

In the movie-version secretly playing out in my head, George placed his hands on my shoulders and whispered apologies, pulling me closer. The shower grew heavier as he kissed me, and the future Christmas number one roared into action just before the credits rolled. But this wasn't the movie-version, and even if it were, someone like me wouldn't be starring in it.

I cut back to reality, heaving my last rucksack into the back of the car, and slammed the boot.

'It's the end of an era,' Luke huffed.

I turned back to the ramshackle old building I'd called home for the last three years, chest numb, heart racing, hoping to see my former boyfriend dashing around the corner; collar turned up against the cold, clutching a bouquet in one hand and a fistful of heartfelt declarations in the other.

'Yep. We've had some good times, number four and me.'

'What?' Luke exhaled, flicking his fag into the nearest grid. 'I meant *that*. *That* was officially my last cigarette. If I can get through Christmas without nicotine, New Year will be a doddle.'

'Well, I'm not making any resolutions for New Year,' I pledged, opening the passenger door, unable to resist another quick glance down the road as Luke jumped into the driver's side.

'Just off the top of my head, how about getting a job, a place to live, and finding a man who truly loves you?'

'Thanks, Luke. A girl can dream.'

'Hey, at least you've still got your sense of humour — and me,' he said, giving my knee a jiggle as he reached for the gear stick.

And then he stopped.

And I knew what was coming.

The stinger.

One of Luke's harrowing observations, always delivered, he said, "for the benefit of my emotional well-being".

Pseudo-psychology was a hobby of his, usually indulged in over drinks, past midnight, when I was willing to humour him.

'Jen?' he said, holding my gaze. 'He's not coming.'

'Who?' I managed.

'*Father Christmas*. Who d'ya think I mean? *George*.'

I pulled an incredulous face that even I could tell was completely, well, credulous, I suppose.

'George is the last person I want to see.'

'So you're not waiting for him to show up and ask you, no, sorry, *beg you*, to stay?'

'No. I'm not.'

'Of course you are! You're human, occasionally...'

'*I* finished with *him*, remember?'

I slotted my seatbelt, put my handbag on the floor, and prepared to surrender the remains of my tattered life to the mercy of Luke's driving — a homicidal dash, if our last trip to Brighton was anything to go by.

'Exactly. That's why I thought he might come running down the street with some last minute, "I love you, forgive me," speech. You know, hair wet, slightly out of breath, the way women always imagine when they've just split up with someone they were really into...'

Sometimes, there's nothing worse than a friend who knows you too well. Thanks to too many drunken confessions, and a harrowing incident involving a Brazilian wax and a back-to-front G-string, we'd gone past the point of mutual respect and were somewhere between affectionate pity and reassuring predictability.

I pressed Stop on my secret Movie Reunion scene and quickly changed channel to Forthcoming Features, which included dramatic all-over-body toning and finding the love of my life.

I was going to be okay. George wasn't coming, but I was absolutely fine.

'You're ridiculous sometimes, do you know that?' I attempted to laugh, despite the lump of emotion lodged inside my throat.

'Why do you think I took so long finishing my fag?'

'Because you're anti-social, inconsiderate, and hell-bent on developing cancer, would be my guess.'

'I said it was my last one,' he sulked, unzipping his coat. 'I can give him another five minutes if you want?'

'No, I don't want. *Thank you.*'

'You're a piece of work, lady,' he said, in a Humphrey Bogart voice.

'Well, what do you expect when it feels like you're going out of your way to upset me?'

'How? By reading your mind?'

'I wasn't expecting my *ex*-boyfriend to show up. Why are you even mentioning him?' I stared out of the windscreen, rigid with temper, and pride, and hurt, and everything else that made me feel even more sorry for myself. 'Friends are supposed to make people feel better, Luke, not bloody worse.'

'Actually, Jennifer,' I could tell he was mad if he was using my full name. 'This friend tells the truth, turns up first thing on a Saturday morning, and helps load up your stuff, before driving you all the way home to your parents' for Christmas. So, sorry if I'm a let down...'

'Exactly. Christmas with the family. And the rest of my life, if I don't find a job to cover my rent. Oh, joy. How can I ever thank you enough?'

'You are so ungrateful. Back home isn't exactly the worst place you could be.'

'How do you work that one out? All I want to do is go to bed, cry, live in my pyjamas, and not shower for a week. Instead, I've got to scrub myself up, get dressed, and keep Mum and Dad happy, posing for family photographs, stood next to Lara.'

It didn't help that while my life was a series of dead-ends and near-misses, Lara had been catapulted into the kind of existence that only happened to beautiful people with wonderful lives.

'Right, engine on. Mirror. Signal. Manoeuvre,' Luke sighed, finally putting the key into the ignition.

I turned to face him as tears caught inside my throat.

'It's just so depressing, having to go home like this...'

'And, engine off. Gear in neutral. I'm all ears.'

'George,' I shook my head, holding my breath in temper. 'He's just, such ... such a fake! He may as well still be married to his ex-wife, the way he expects me to exist on the outside of everything, tiptoeing around the edges.'

'I'm impressed. I haven't seen you this angry since someone nicked your coconut yogurt from the staff canteen,' he smirked. 'Oh, now, is that a smile I see rising from the depths of despondency?'

But I couldn't speak. Every tear I'd tried to digest had risen in a tsunami in the passenger side.

'There's a packet of tissues in the glove box,' he said. 'We could go and see him right now,' he suggested, despite the fact he didn't 'do' romance. 'It's not too late to change your mind, you know?'

I shook my head, wiping tears away, clearing my thoughts.

'There's too much to sort out.'

'You're sure?'

'Uh-hum,' I managed, wiping my nose. 'I'm fine.'

'Well, okay,' he fastened his seatbelt. 'Right, take a deep breath,' he said, starting the car again, 'because I can't remember the last time I drove this thing any real distance,' he confessed, turning on the windscreen wipers. 'I've no idea where we're going. And there's a good chance we'll never reach our destination alive. But what the hell,' he winked. 'I'm game if you are?'

And with a rev of the engine, I managed to laugh.

'Losing that job was the slap in the face we both needed,' Luke announced, as we made it onto the motorway, thankfully without a detour to A&E. 'It was about time we got away from that dump and started concentrating on our lives. Making things happen,' he said, with a look he usually reserved for pay day, 'like the detective novel I'm going to write...'

'You're writing a detective novel?'

Luke was always planning his next big step, but this one in particular had never been mentioned in broad daylight while either of us was sober. More to the point, any talk of writing was only ever mentioned by me. Never Luke. The only time Luke used the 'I'm a writer' line was while loitering around the Academic section, trying to catch the eye of any pretty students he could regale with Byronesque tales of impending literary stardom.

'It's something I've been thinking about a lot recently,' he continued, producing yet another cigarette, 'and now's the perfect time to make it happen.'

'I thought you said you were giving those things up?'

'I will, I will! As soon as I've finished writing. It's very stressful. Anyway, all the literary greats were smokers.'

'Yeah, and drug addicts. And alcoholics. And then dead.'

'This is no death!' he announced, high on life and nicotine. 'This is only the beginning! I used to adlib all my own scripts, you know, when I did my TV stuff? It was one of the reasons I took the job at Brookhouse in the first place,' he explained, engaging the in-car lighter. 'Thought it was a step closer, so now's the time to step it up. Although, let's just say *mi padre* isn't exactly pleased...'

Luke's dad was old-school Spanish. His parents owned a really nice restaurant, *La Cocina*, which Luke refused to work in, despite the fact he was an amazing cook, who could pretty much rustle anything up from scratch, quicker than I could navigate the frozen aisle of my local *supermercado*.

'I'm pathetic,' I said. 'Twenty-nine years old. Single. Going home to my parents. All I need is a cat.'

'You couldn't afford to feed one, not at the moment,' he said, rolling down the window.

'That's true,' I nodded. 'Oh Luke, what's *my* next big step? You're always thinking of different stuff to do. Can't you invent something for me?' I said, batting away a cloud of drifting ash.

Luke was always at the centre of his next adventure. Last year, there was Luke the Dog Walker, who became weekend puppy au pair to Blanche, a two-year-old Chihuahua whose owner was a twenty-three-year-old blonde with fake boobs and an impressive home gym. Things went horribly wrong when the little dog, possibly sensing the real object of Luke's affections, locked her tiny, but fully formed teeth around the tip of Luke's nose, as he stalked her tightly toned owner during a vigorous bout of cardio.

'Disfigured!' Luke had panted down the phone. 'I could have been disfigured! All for the sake of a girl with no feeling in her nipples!'

Before that, there was the Luke who could whip up a cocktail so fast, he'd considered a career as a mixologist, until his mum branded bar work as 'common', and we'd decided his real talent lay in drinking the things, rather than wasting time juicing limes and crushing ice.

'I can't go back to another job I hate,' I whined, pulling down the sun visor and pulling at my fringe in the mirror. 'I had dreams. Actual *dreams*. And now this is my life. I have to change it!'

'With new hair?'

'Oh, I don't know,' I said, snapping the mirror shut. 'New Jennifer. I need a new Jennifer. And I need to start understanding things like the "digital revolution" even though I'm only just getting used to the industrial one…'

'Can you please postpone the midlife crisis until I'm off the motorway?' Luke asked, one hand tightening around the wheel as he balanced his fag out of the window. 'I can't be this tense and single-handedly gift-wrap your self-esteem. So listen, sourpuss,' he grimaced, as he switched back into the slow lane as the rain picked up, 'if you want to write, you should. You always had some battered, little notepad on the go, even if it was only filled with those daft little "to do" lists. Love's too much of a distraction. I always write my best stuff when I'm miserable or heartbroken.'

'I'm not miserable, or … well, yes, I am a little heartbroken, but not the way you make it sound…'

'Well, *anyway*,' he drawled, one eye on the road. 'The writing stuff: this fantastic little website, yourstory.com, has all the major publishers checking in on it. You post your stuff, just the initial chapter, and the more readers who like it and want to read more, the higher up the ranks you go, and the closer to getting published,' he said, doing his best to look intriguing.

'Why don't you put something up on there? If no one else likes it, you know you've always got me to give you five stars,' he smirked.

'I suppose so,' I said, a little embarrassed by how irritated I felt at our clashing ambitions. 'But don't stop with the restaurant idea, just to prove your dad wrong.'

'Nah,' he shrugged. 'He gave up on me a long time ago, don't worry. Anyway,' he trilled, with devilment in his eye. 'It's called *The Spanish Detective*. It's very noir, but very now.'

'Sounds good,' I smiled, as a blast of wind did its worst to my home blow-dry. 'What happens?'

'I don't know yet. I've got to write the thing first!'

Even if Luke was a daydreamer, at least he was busy making plans. The only thing I knew about my future was that I'd soon be back in my childhood bedroom with Mum lighting sympathy candles, and planning a New Year Novena if my circumstances didn't change.

Now that I was strapped into the passenger side, jobless, loveless, and leaving my past behind, the road signs of reality had begun to hit me right between the eyes.

Chapter 4

Lara

I woke up in a crumby hotel room next to the airport, the light almost unbearable, as I recalled brief glimpses of myself acting like a complete idiot on yesterday's flight.

The heavyweight of embarrassment rolled over and hogged the starched, almost surgical sheets, as I glanced at the empty wine bottle on the bedside. I remembered drinking it, didn't remember buying it, couldn't tell you how I got into my room, but I'd managed to fold my clothes and take off my earrings.

Practice makes perfect, I guessed.

It was just after eleven o'clock but I was still so tired. The fact I'd started drinking for the first time in months probably hadn't helped. The stress of the wedding and getting ready to muster the levels of enthusiasm required for a successful Taylor family Christmas were finally starting to get to me.

Once, when confronted by a wall of magazines, I'd have hurried past, not wanting anyone to recognize me from the half a dozen covers I was featured across, immortalized in a series of glossy fantasies that had us all fooled, myself included, but waiting in the queue that morning, needing to hope they still remembered me, I couldn't resist scanning the titles. Just as I was going from one fresh-faced teenage sensation to the next — there I was, grinning right back at myself:

FEMALE FLAIR
Feeling hot, hot, hot?

I have to confess, I was relieved to still have a face out there in the world. Until my eyes were drawn to the subheading: *Our must-read guide to menopause.*

Menopause? The face of *menopause* at thirty-two-years-old?

That just about summed up my universe.

'What can I get you?' the man behind the counter asked, breaking my concentration. I asked for some cigarettes, still shaky from all the alcohol the day before, but aware he was double-checking me, trying to place my face, as he worked the cash register. I gave a quick glance behind me, no one about, so I lowered my voice:

'Female Flair.'

'Sorry, love?'

'If you're wondering where it is you've seen me.' I smiled, giving a slight nod to the magazine stand, confident that the menopause thing wouldn't be off-putting, not to a man of his age. 'I'm on the cover of *Female Flair* this month.'

He chewed his gum, still staring.

'That you an' all, then, is it?'

He lifted one of the red headers from off the counter, pointing to an article in the weekly *Showbiz!* round-up, not even a column long, completely missable, apart from the accompanying, quarter-page photograph of me in my sweats, which I couldn't remember having been taken:

Former model Lara isn't such a Charmer!

By Daniel Chatterton.

Former model, Lara Taylor, who once graced the covers of your favourite glossy magazines and glided down catwalks across the globe, was a real sight for sore eyes on a recent red-eye flight from New York!

Looking tired and long-past her fashionable hey-day, former beauty, Lara, 32, haggled for alcohol and argued with patient airline staff, before falling into a suspiciously deep sleep.

Maybe she's suffering from exhaustion…

It took a second before I realized.

That loser on the flight: *Daniel Chatterton.*

I'd been his sudden deadline.

And thirty-two? He hadn't even bothered to check my Wiki page, which I'd made sure had me down as a mere slip of a girl at thirty.

'Don't worry, love. Tomorra's fish'n'chip wrapper, that is.'

I gave a polite smile, dragging my suitcase behind me and almost putting on my sunglasses, before I reminded myself how I really didn't want to attract any more attention and end up in some other rag claiming I'd had my eye bags removed, or filled, or whatever it was folks were doing to fight the good fight these days.

I'd never been tabloid fodder before, apart from a few short-lived references to my divorce from Travis, which happened to coincide with breaking news of a far more interesting political affair, but those people dealt in disaster, I thought, as the taxi driver started the engine and asked me where I was off to.

The press weren't interested in anything apart from two things: death and failure. And so, while I was still alive to tell the tale, I was suddenly tabloid-worthy.

The world was a positive, supportive place … unless you passed by thirty without big plans for the next stage of your existence. I sat back, closed my eyes and let the last few months come back to haunt me.

I'd started the year feeling optimistic, but at a meeting with my agent, Bill Staniss, a red alert had started up.

'I think it's time to review where we're at, Lara.'

As soon as I'd heard that line, I was panicked.

'I think we need to discuss a new direction, a new *era*, for you, if you like.'

I stayed silent. I'd known Bill long enough not to put up a struggle once he'd already set his mind to doing something.

'*Alexis Mail Order*,' he announced, putting a heavy-looking proof book on his desk between us. 'Extremely market-focused. Commercially viable and looking for a great model to spearhead their launch campaign.'

'It's a *catalogue*, Bill.'

'That's right,' he nodded. 'And a soon-to-be home shopping network, with a considerable marketing budget and the potential to negotiate your own designer collection. So,' he raised his brow, seemingly confident, 'what d'ya think?'

'What do I think?'

I took a long drink of water, searching for the words.

'I think, *catalogue*...'

'And I think —' he met my eye, playing hard-ball agent instead of the usual Good Cop approach — 'that it's time to start building something we can work with for the next ten years.'

'You want me to start modelling catalogues? I never modelled *catalogues* my whole life. Not even when I was unknown, inexperienced and seriously overdrawn, did I ever work catalogue fashion.'

'Exactly. And now you're of a certain —' I almost dared him to say it — '*age* ... and this is a viable proposition.'

'*Viable?*'

'Yes, sweetheart. Viable.'

'How? Are you insane? Taking a job at Walmart is more viable than doing this.' I went to take another drink, but my glass was empty. I had a feeling I'd be draining a few more before the end of the day. 'What the hell's going on with this, Bill?'

He paused to refill my glass while I wished I could turn water into wine, or gin, or vodka, but I've never been the religious type. That's one of the reasons I could never settle in Los Angeles. If it wasn't religion, it was recovery, or New Age, Illuminati bullshit. Anything they could plug into their heads to avoid reality, stuck out there in the desert of lost opportunities. New York was stark reality on a daily basis. If you didn't like it, you could turn it down, but you could never tune it out for too long. The city was big and bold enough to keep you in permanent close-up. Who knows, I thought, maybe a move to L.A. would be Bill's next helpful suggestion...

'Look, Lara,' he said, shaking his head, folding his arms. 'The fact is the industry's changed. The ... *girls* ... have changed, the work's changed, and you...' he absentmindedly thumbed his nose, 'haven't.'

'I can change!' I crossed my legs with the enthusiasm of a young colt, clapping my hands together to drum up his interest, his *belief*, whatever it was he needed. 'Is that what all this is about?' I laughed, throwing my head back, reminding him of my trademark move: *Lara laughing*. 'Look, that's easy to fix. I'll start with a haircut,' I insisted, grabbing my cell from my handbag. 'I'll call Monroe right now and get him to put some sketches together, really let him get out there, dream up some wonder weave...'

'Lara,' Bill said, raising his voice. 'It's not about your style. The girls coming in now? They're half your age. They've got that certain, *youthful* —'

'Oh, I see. I'm being punished because I'm not fifteen and eating cotton wool for breakfast anymore?' I said, snapping my cell shut.

'Lara, let's not lose focus —'

'*Lose focus?* You're the one losing focus! I've been with you for how long? I thought you were a lot smarter than this, Bill. A *lot* smarter!'

'No. You need to get smarter, Lara,' he said, getting to his feet. 'You *never* listen. Why has this never occurred to you? It was hard enough after that business with Travis —'

'Don't!'

'We can't ignore it. You were away for nearly two years! Who does that? And I was still here, still representing *your illusion* of a career.'

'*Illusion?*'

'You know what I mean,' he muttered, turning to face the window. 'We've moved on. They've moved on.'

'Okay, so I took a little time away.' I swallowed, trying to find my voice. 'But so have other people. It didn't do Elle, or Yasmin, or anyone else, any harm. Hey, at least I haven't loosened up around the middle with kids.' I gave a weak smile, pressing my hand against my flat stomach. 'Surely I deserve something better than this?'

Bill sighed, sat back down.

His silence was killing me.

'Sweetheart, you've got to readjust, reacclimatize. We can't get you premium bookings any more. The momentum's just not there, honey. You already rode that wave the first time around...'

'But Bill —'

He pushed up his glasses, massaging the bridge of his nose, before he continued.

'I told you to invest. *Design* the lingerie range, the new leisure suit, whatever the hell they offer you, *take it*, but there's been no investment. And if you haven't invested in yourself, how'd you expect me to, or anyone else for that matter?'

'I've invested my whole life in you, Bill. Can't you come up with something?'

'I did,' he said, shoving the catalogue back towards me. 'This could be *great* for you. They want you. They want your name.'

'My *illusion* of a name, you mean?'

'They love the whole Anglophile thing,' he continued, ignoring my protests. 'They *asked* for you. Do you know the last time I met a client who specifically asked for you, Lara?'

'I'm sorry I'm such a drag, Bill. It must have been so much easier for you to bankroll your life while I was still bringing in more dollars than anyone else at this agency.'

'Don't you turn this on me. You're making this personal.'

I stood up, heart already at the bar, dreaming of annihilation.

'Fuck you, Bill!'

'Well, that's great, Lara. That's just sweet of you.'

'Don't expect me to sit here and be polite while you *end me*, Bill. You wouldn't be sat there, playing God behind that desk, without me.'

'Oh, so that's what you think? Well, fuck you, too, Lara. See yourself out.'

And so, that's the moment I stopped working with Bill Staniss. The best agent a girl ever had. The worst a grown woman could wish for, but, very quickly, I realized he was right. A few people had actually taken my calls, a couple even met with me for lunch, but while they were happy to reminisce about good times we had in the past, it was time to get the bill as soon as I talked about the here and now.

And, after a couple of months, the only Bill I could afford wouldn't take my calls.

Chapter 5

Jennifer

Monday was the first day of my new job. I'd accepted my new Christmas job gracefully because Dad had found it for me and because moving back home broke, with nothing but big plans and a small budget, was the life-choice of socially inadequate, middle-aged men, who spent far too much time alone in their bedrooms. *Trouserless.*

Dad worked at Home For All Seasons, an interiors and gardening centre where everyone in Ingleford bought everything. As soon as I heard the word 'little', I guessed it wasn't going to be the stuff of future mortgage repayments, but who was I to be picky?

'They need people to deliver Christmas trees! How lovely is that? He put your name on the list. It's only two weeks' work. I know it's not forever, but it's a start. He said they might have something coming up in Sheds in the New Year — fingers crossed!' Mum trilled. I didn't want to sound ungrateful, finding me a job was more than I'd managed to do, but I appreciated Mum's reassurance that it wasn't going to be forever.

Anyway, I thought, what better way to cheer myself up than by delivering the ultimate Christmas centrepiece to lots of happy customers? I pictured myself putting smiles on pensioners' faces, arriving at houses while excited children waited by windows.

'We'll have to call you Santa's Little Helper!'

'Please don't…'

'He was going to nominate your sister, too,' Mum had giggled. 'Thought it might be cute, like when the two of you ran that lemonade stall at the summer fair. Can you imagine? You order a Christmas tree and end up with a super model on your doorstep! Your father just doesn't think sometimes…'

As tempted as I was, I didn't correct the 'super' model bit, because it's not as if Lara had married a *Rolling Stone* or appeared in a Duran Duran video. To Mum she'd be 'Super' whatever she did. Unlike me. The daughter who could quite feasibly deliver coal, collect garbage, or drop off your Christmas tree without her staggering beauty rendering the whole thing farcical.

When I'd arrived for my first day, despite attempts to appeal to the good nature of my line manager, Des, I found out that delivering Christmas trees to the good people of Ingleford also involved dressing up to get customers in the festive spirit. I'd argued that anyone buying a Christmas tree was already feeling pretty festive, but Des was adamant.

He'd given the bell on the end of my over-sized hat a hearty shake and had a good chuckle at my expense. As well as the hat, I wore a red and green-striped fleece, plus a pair of Wellington boots adorned with gold bells, which tinkled with each step. To top it all off there was a name-badge which read: '*Here to H-Elf*', which stabbed me in the throat every time I yanked a tree out from the back of the van.

As usual, Lara manifested when I least expected her. Dad and I were wandering out of the kitchen, engrossed in Bakewell tarts, as excited screams came from the porch.

And there, in all her high-resolution gorgeousness, hours earlier than planned, stood my sister.

'*Guess what?*' she shrieked, as Mum wheeled in the suitcase behind her. 'I'm engaged!'

Before I could swallow my glacé cherry, her left hand was thrust in front of our mother. There, no excuse for missing it, sat a yellow stone so huge it could have been laid by Big Bird. Lara gave me a wink, acknowledging the successful conclusion of our sisterly pact to keep schtum about her engagement.

'To whom?' Mum asked, trying to sound light-hearted and laidback, which, coming from my mother, immediately translated as disapproving and concerned.

'It's okay, Mum,' she said. 'His name's Silvano. He's wonderful. Mature. Successful. And —' she grinned so wide, even I was starting to feel slightly convinced — 'he is absolutely the best man I have ever known. I love him! You'll love him too,' she promised, grabbing Mum by the elbows and jumping up and down on the spot.

All this and she hadn't even taken off her coat yet.

Welcome to the world of my sister.

'Jen?' It was as if she had only just realized I was standing there. 'What the hell are you wearing?' She turned to my parents. 'Oh my God! I take it that's that the outfit, Mum?' She sniggered, as Mum tried to bite away the smirk from her face. 'You're right, she really does look like one of those little garden gnome things!'

'Thanks, Lara. Great to see you too,' I said, exchanging a look with my father, who seemed more sympathetic to my plight.

'Oh, come on,' she beamed. 'Don't be such a sulk. You're dressed for laughs, so I laughed. Get over it,' she muttered, eyeing Mum for support.

'I'm not dressed for laughs. I'm dressed for work.'

'Yes, so I heard,' she snapped. 'So maybe you shouldn't be so touchy? Wearing a stupid outfit can't be any worse than not having a job at all. If it weren't for Mum and Dad, you'd still be unemployed and virtually homeless, wouldn't you?'

I pulled the stupid elf hat from my head, put the rest of my Bakewell tart in my mouth and braced myself for the rest of our family Christmas reunion.

Ho-Ho-Ho!

Chapter 6

Lara

I slipped off my shoes, turned on my laptop and sighed with annoyance as I propped up the pillows and settled onto my old bed. The only way my sister would understand stress was if I put it in a cake tin and baked it for lunch.

It must be so nice, being able to come back home to open arms every time things got too 'icky' for her. Dad finding her a job. Mum making her meals, delighted to have her back, I thought, tapping away, updating the diary my counsellor still insisted I keep, despite the fact I'd said it only made me feel worse most of the time.

It was good to transfer my thoughts, she said, to record my progress with regular instalments of all the incidents which had led up to the here and now. But, as I typed, all I felt was anger. Not one of them ever asked how I was or if I was okay. They assumed everything was just great, not because they knew it was, but because they knew for a fact that it wasn't. By silently agreeing not to raise the topic, everything was easier for them to deal with. Their perfect family remained perfect and anything resembling the ugly truth, anything that might complicate their life with facts, would be selfish of me to mention. Plus, let's not forget, Jennifer had already filled that space in the grand scheme of things. My sister was always in some crisis over something, so God forbid I distract them from their younger daughter.

The only saving grace was that Dad kept offering me a non-judgmental amount of alcohol, seeing as it was the holidays, so

I'd at least been able to sleep-walk through the last couple of days, topping up my glass before he could notice his diminishing supplies.

They hadn't a clue what I'd been through during the last six months, the constant pressure I'd been under. I closed my eyes, inhaled slowly and deeply, until the rest of the house became a faint murmur and, like my counsellor instructed, I continued to write, pretending I was mailing her, as I recalled the moment I knew my career — my life — was all over.

I had been in Monroe's hot seat at his salon at the time, working on what he described as a "dramatic, new episode in my overall look", which roughly translated as a new haircut. We'd settled on a graduated mid-cut accentuated by flaxen highlights.

As I waited for my arrival coffee, my agent's office got in touch with my accountant, who unfortunately got back in touch with me. We were in crisis, he said, which basically meant I had nothing coming in to saddle up the everything galloping out faster than you could count it. Phone call over. I suddenly had the urge to bolt. From there. From then. From everything.

I had friends who were able to live as if each day were a new adventure in shopping, entertaining and travelling. These were the same girls I'd lived with, working our way up the modelling ranks, but now I was out of the loop. Despite earning a fair start at life at the beginning of their careers through various, well-paid modelling assignments, what these women all had in common now was someone looking out for them. A husband. A trust fund. A generous well-wisher. All I had to bolster my bank account was my last pay cheque, a little excess from a hair dye commercial way back in February.

Money had always been like a cruel school friend to me. One minute, off we went, hitting all the best places, doing all the very enjoyable things, buying us a whole lot of nice. The next, she was gone, mocking me to mutual acquaintances, telling me we couldn't be friends, for *obvious* reasons.

'I'm sorry, I've an appointment,' I'd told Monroe that afternoon, snapping my cell shut after my accountant declared I'd reached crisis point and clawing at my cutting gown.

I knew feigning something of far higher importance was key. Monroe swore he was a bastion of confidentiality, although every time I met him I could have built a fortune blackmailing the faces he named as adulterers, criminals, sexual deviants and the occasional, highly-sensitive case of alopecia. And that was among his own staff, let alone his high-profile clients.

'Yes, you do — with me, babe,' he said, hands on emaciated hips, a glimpse of the Downtown boy he was. 'I can't promise when my next slot's available.'

The truth was, despite Bill suggesting I needed to change things, I was in no financial state to maintain a Monroe creation. My accountant had just confirmed my money tree had barely grown roots, so I knew I really couldn't afford to get mine done every six weeks.

'Well, forget the fancy stuff. Cut the damn thing,' I blustered, wondering why I'd decided a new haircut was ever going to fix things in the first place. '*Short*. As short as I can handle. And you'll have to make it quick. I'm running really late here.'

'Honey, this is an investment. We can't rush these things. How will you give that trademark grin without the trademark hair toss?'

But, as Bill had already pointed out, my trademark grin was no longer a trademark. That look had been laughed right off the front covers by a new generation of girls whose eyebrows weighed more than they did, hair scraped back, their expressions pained.

'Well, darling,' I managed, giving my watch a quick glance as if I really did need to be someplace else, 'this pooch needs to learn herself some new tricks. Forget it. I'll book in next month.'

'Are you crazy?'

I threw off my gown, grabbed my handbag and walked out amid Monroe's heckling. Haircuts by people who referred to themselves as Hair Architects were now strictly off my list of priorities in life.

I could still remember that terrifying walk back to my apartment, lost in a daze of unpaid demands and a steady fog of fear and self-pity. And then, when I least needed it, only moments from my place on a huge billboard, in a classic white shirt, blue jeans-combo, right where no one could miss her, came the final straw:

Amber Rhodes IS Alexis.
Alexis Instant Order IS You!

It had been less than three months since I'd last seen Bill and now Amber Rhodes had taken my Alexis job? Amber, who had been my idol when I started out and didn't floss her teeth on anything less than a $100 bill!

Her all-seeing, photoshopped gaze peered down at me, following me across the street, singling me out as I strode along the avenue, until I'd finally shut my front door, dragged off my coat, sickened by the thought of losing what little I had left.

I slumped onto the sofa, light-headed with worry, trying to convince myself that maybe I needed time out to readjust, like Bill said. I lay back against the cushions, every cell in my body seeming to ricochet in shock.

Right then, I'd been staring into the past, believing it was all I had left to my name. Lara Taylor's shadow didn't stretch as far as my future. The shooting star of success had long since exploded. My beautiful dream had become stark reality and I was so tired of it all. If I'd been smart, like Bill said, I'd have listened to him and saved a nest egg or had some investments to play with, but Travis had put an end to those kinds of plans. I'd invested everything in what I assumed was my life with him, only to have him set his people on me like coyotes.

Apparently our ranch had been *my gift* to him, along with the recording studio complex. All that and the cowboy boot-wearing bastard even asked for the ring back. I had sat forward, suddenly alert, on the edge of the settee as if it were a cliff-face, with the silence closing in on me. Time was tick … tick … ticking. And all I could do was listen to the sound of each calculated breath, until the unease became the feeling that *they* or *life* or *something* was listening, watching, waiting, to fold in on me. Waiting for me to fail.

So, I was very sorry if Jennifer had lost her job or cried a few tears over some guy she'd been dating for barely a year, but I'd trade her problems with mine in a heartbeat.

The sound of laughter rising up from the kitchen broke through my thoughts. I pressed 'Save', switched off my computer and for the first time since I arrived in England was relieved to be here, on the other side of it all.

This year had been the worst of my life, but once I married Silvano, all that would change.

Chapter 7

Jennifer

As the days wore on, I'd felt more depressed by the thought of my Christmas job ending than having to show up to work dressed as a circus attraction.

Lara was right. I was in no position to be turning my nose up at delivering Christmas trees. And, to be honest, I probably deserved it, because I hadn't exactly pushed myself on the ambition front when I'd had a job that didn't require dressing up for laughs. The last three years at the bookshop had flown by, not because I was dedicated to hardcore career advancement, but because I'd got used to not doing anything else except showing up every morning.

My only consolation had been George. My Monday-to-Friday Man.

During the weekends he had an ex-wife, an eight-year-old daughter and a five-year-old son, which meant Susanna and Charlie spent the weekend with their dad while I patiently waited for our Monday night reunion.

George was older, by twelve years to be exact, and wiser than anyone I'd gone out with before; he did cryptic crosswords for fun and understood stuff about the global economy that made me want to stick my fingers in my ears, rock back-and-forth and eat cubed fudge. And he was a vet, which meant he wasn't just lovely to me, but kind to small animals as well.

Despite my boring existence, I had a man worth breaking a Galaxy Caramel in half for, a man so well balanced that when I first told him Lara Taylor, the top model, was my sister, he didn't even flinch.

'So, you're the brains of the family, then?'

I knew he sensed my weakness.

'Lara's not stupid. She's pretty smart to be honest. Don't you think she's gorgeous?' I demanded, almost ripping the magazine in half, turning over to the next page, featuring a shot of my sister applying glossy lipstick across her slightly parted mouth, a knowing look playing across her smoky eyes.

'She's beautiful,' he nodded. 'In that very tall, very thin, model way. But you're not a model,' he pointed out, eyes smiling.

By the way, his eyes did actually smile, with crinkles at the corner that made me want to curl up at his feet.

'No,' I agreed. 'I'm not.'

'What are you getting at here?' he asked, taking a sip of wine. 'Is this a test? I'm going to see the model sister and think less of you?'

That was exactly what it was, which is why I'd barely mentioned Lara for the first three months of our relationship.

'Of course not,' I said, as I took an unfortunately noisy slurp of wine. I smiled and sat back in my seat.

He was perfect, and he loved me.

He told me so himself.

And not just in bed, or when I was wearing make-up. So why had everything gone so wrong between us? I still didn't fully understand it and I caught myself thinking about it every time I was alone, which wasn't very often now I was living back home, but perhaps that was a good thing.

Unlike the boyfriends in my past, George always believed in me. He was the first person I called when they made me redundant, because I knew the sound of his voice would make me feel better in seconds.

'Jennifer?' he'd said. 'You'll find another job before you know it. And next time round, they'll see how great you are, and hey, look on the bright side,' he added, 'you might even like the new job and not dread going to bed on Sunday night the same way my kids dread going to school on Monday morning.'

George was determined to find my dream job, but more worryingly, he seemed to think I was far more capable and qualified than I actually was. No average, run-of-the-mill job advert was good enough for his girlfriend. And that was frightening, because what if he actually thought he was dating a grown-up woman who was ready to take on the world?

I stood in a daze of recollection, wondering what my delicious George was doing right now.

I finished drying the dishes as Lara waltzed into the kitchen. She grabbed a satsuma from Mum's fruit bowl and slid onto a chair at the breakfast bar. Now, as I've said, despite the occasional text, Lara took no notice of my existence, which is why I was so surprised when she asked me what happened with work.

'Oh, it's all digital, online, downloading stuff, nowadays,' I explained.

'So,' Lara said, looking uncharacteristically thoughtful, 'it was only a matter of time before the store closed, then?'

'I suppose so.'

'You've got to have a Plan B, sis...'

My heart thumped in annoyance. That was easy for her to say. She only had to smile while someone took her picture.

'So, what's next?' she asked, looking bored as she absentmindedly checked her phone. 'You can't deliver Christmas trees for the rest of your life.'

'Really?' I asked, running out of patience with my sister, who knew nothing about being fired or being poor. 'Well, you could have broken it to me more gently. I was planning a move to Lapland.'

'Going to Lapland would be a lot more ambitious than traipsing back home to your parents every time things don't work out,' she drawled. 'Are you ever going to stand on your own two feet?'

'Are you?' I asked, which even for me, was a lame retort. Lara glared and left the kitchen, leaving me to ponder whether I wouldn't be better off in Lapland after all.

I thought I'd spend my Sunday off with Mum, head to the village to find a present for Dad that wasn't woollen or car-related, but before I could suggest it, Lara bounded downstairs with other ideas.

'Surprise!' she said, and for a moment I thought she was going to shock-bomb our breakfast with her wedding announcement, but instead, she gushed, 'We better get a move on, Mum. We're going for a treatment day. At a spa!'

'What *spa*?' Mum asked, busy at the kitchen sink. She said the word spa the same way some people would say ovarian cyst. 'I don't want to be shuffling around in paper knickers all day, Lara. I've a million things to do.'

'That's the point,' Lara said, souring slightly. 'I thought it might be a nice break.'

'I've got a head full of rollers,' Mum said, drying her hands on an unflattering tea-towel rendition of Wills and Kate that looked as if it had been sketched by baby Prince George, 'and your sister's not even finished her porridge yet.'

'It's only for the two of us,' Lara said. 'Sorry, I didn't think you'd be interested, Jen.'

And you didn't want me there, I thought, but secretly relieved I wasn't invited. 'Don't worry, I've got stuff to do today, anyway.'

This year, I'd convinced myself that instead of expensive presents 'thoughtful' presents were the way to go. Losing your job was one thing, losing it a month before Christmas was particularly harsh for someone who didn't plan her gift buying months ahead, unlike my mother. I'd managed to find a gorgeous-looking hardback book with a brown-paper backed cover and the words: *Our Story: Sisters* for Lara. I could compile it using old photographs and all the things I remembered about her. It was sentimental, something my sister could treasure forever.

I had found Mum the perfect Christmas gift. An ornate, teal vase, depicting a flight of golden geese. Sounds awful, I know, but Mum was obsessed with colour schemes, and teal had been her colour of choice for the last few years.

Unfortunately the lounge had recently had a makeover, from top-to-floor teal to fuchsia. Mum had even colour-coded the Christmas tree this year, decorating it in every pink festive and not-so-festive adornment she could find, including butterflies, hearts and flowers, until it looked less like a Christmas tree and more like a statement of Gay Pride.

'What happened to the blue?'

'The blue? Old news,' Mum said, waving away her former preference. 'That's out of date now.'

'I liked it.'

Obviously, I didn't. What I liked was the blue vase Luke had helped me order for her for Christmas, delivered to his permanent address rather than my former one, which reminded me, I thought, making a grab for my mobile, I'd forgotten to text him to arrange to bring it over.

Determined to get something right, I still had Lara's present to make.

Mum directed me to the bureau, crammed full of photo albums, as promised. I'd seen them all before, but I was filled with glad tidings.

'Look at the pair of you!' Mum said, leafing through the photos. 'Doesn't Lara look a dream? Look at this one!'

Lara and me at the zoo. I was about four, which would make Lara about seven. She was looking chic in bib and braces, smiling sweetly. No one realized I'd broken three toes, skedaddling down to the picnic area, although, with my face distorted by tears and ponytail yanked out on the journey downhill, there were clear indications of distress right under their noses.

Looking back, no matter how dodgy Dad's efforts with the camera, or how bad Mum's fashion sense, Lara single-handedly explained the term photogenic; as if she had had her makeup and lighting done since birth — and standing next to me had definitely helped.

'Remember your favourite outfit?' Mum asked, passing a shot of me in my lemon-print short set. Lara standing next to me in denim cut-offs, her endless legs already destined for catwalks and limousines. Me, next to her, knock-kneed, with a pelt of dark hair running from shoe-to-calf like a pair of Dad's socks.

'Your sister was so fair. I think you got those legs from Granny Taylor,' she muttered, opening the bureau door and pulling out a box brimming with memorabilia. 'Look at these! Incredible, really…' She smiled, leafing through a scrapbook of magazines, dating back from Lara's very first front cover. 'And her Captain's badge!' she grinned, rubbing her thumb across the shiny, red pin, which was Lara's prize possession, always clipped to her school blazer. 'We were so proud. I can still remember that long, golden plait. And fearless, your dad used to say, absolutely fearless on the sports field. Oh,' she said, squinting, the way she did when she found something appalling. 'This one's you. After your haircut.'

We both knew which haircut she meant. I'd not long started high school and endured a full year of emotional scarring after a rogue toffee somehow made it onto my pillow. Despite Mum's concerted efforts to melt, ply, and pray for the toffee to loosen, my hair had to be cut into a style known as 'Man Head' throughout school.

Meanwhile, Lara was rocking a Rachel-do, as nicely as Jennifer Aniston.

'Mum! We're going to be late!'

'Okay, two ticks! I'm with you!'

Mum pulled a face and lowered her voice.

'*Wiltshire Hall*. Miles away in Haversham. Used to be a hotel, years ago. Newly renovated,' she said, with a customary wave away at nothing. 'Goodness knows what time this football your father's watching is supposed to finish,' she said, pulling on a scarf.

'Mum, we've got to go!'

'There might be some more albums in your sister's old wardrobe, but don't go in there until we're back, for goodness sake,' she said, with a spritz of hairspray.

'I won't. I'm not twelve any more,' I laughed. 'I just really need to make a start on her present. You know how hard it is, finding things for Lara.'

They shouted farewells before the car pulled away and, mainly because of her prevailing insistence that I keep out and because I was probably just as childish as my mum suspected, I wandered into my sister's room, looking for inspiration.

The room was a mess already. Discarded underwear on the floor, makeup-blotted tissues strewn across the bedside table. The air was stale with what looked like the remains of a whole packet of fags, stubbed out on Mum's best china, and beneath the saucer was the glossy, red laptop I'd seen my sister typing away into every chance she got. I was curious, I admit, especially as she quickly closed it every time one of us got near.

Just as I was about to give in and switch the thing on my mobile sounded up, the sudden shock of it reverberating along my arm, sending discarded cigarette butts and ash all over her bed.

Quickly surveying the damage, I pulled the phone from my back pocket.

Luke.

'I got your text and yes, I've got the vase. It's as hideous as it looks — your mum's going to love it. I'll be down a.s.a.p, but more importantly, I'm up! I'm on!'

'Up and on what?' I asked, wiping ash from the back of my hand.

'My first installment. Posted! Go to yourstory.com/SpanishDetective.'

'Right now?' I asked, opening the window.

'Yes, right now!' Luke said. 'Hello? Don't you recognise the voice of sheer excitement when you hear it?'

'But Dad's PC takes about an hour to get going,' I sighed, all the while convincing myself that the easiest thing to do all round would be to switch on the little device that was right within sneezing distance, but first, I'd have to strip my sister's bed and have it washed and dried before she got back.

'Well, do it!' Luke chorused. 'I want your feedback. Get straight back to me!'

I navigated the washing machine and gave Lara's room a quick whiz with the vacuum, all the while drifting back to the sight of her computer, lying there, waiting to be switched on.

No! I should respect my sister's privacy, the same way I'd want her to respect mine if I left something personal and private lying around. But, if she had left it lying around, maybe it wasn't all that private in the first place?

Stop it. I scolded myself, but before I knew it, I was switching it on — *for Luke*, I'd convinced myself. It'd probably be password protected anyway, I thought, if the way Lara was so funny about anyone so much as sitting next to her while she was using it was anything to go by. But the machine started up, not a password request, not a murmur, and as it did, my eye was instantly drawn to a document on the right of the screen: DIARY.

I hesitated then went straight to the internet icon before I gave into temptation and seconds later, found Luke's work:

The Spanish Detective by Lucian De Cosa

He sat alone, as he preferred. The bar was dark, plagued by shadows, as he was. He was popular, charismatic, undeniably handsome, but a loner he was, nevertheless.

The case he was working on was the hardest of his career. All over the country, high-profile men were being killed in their beds. Poisoned by an untraceable substance, a single rose on the bedside, petals strewn upon the covers. Meanwhile, their bank accounts showed withdrawals of thousands in the weeks leading up to their demise.

He was deep in thought, toying with a matchstick, as the barmaid looked his way.

Smoking was a habit he had returned to in the middle of the case. He was a young, agile detective with an old school heart. Call him old fashioned, he wasn't concerned with convention. He was drawn to danger, and danger was strangely drawn to him.

The barmaid approached, her breasts threatening to spill over the top of her corset. He almost pitied her.

"Señor?" she enquired, pupils dilating, wearing a lipsticked smile of desperation.

He didn't meet her eye, had no time for cheap infatuation. He was a busy man, a clever man, a renegade.

"Rioja," he said, lifting his square, determined jaw in the direction of the dusty bottles, which lined the bar. "One glass. I prefer to drink alone."

"Alone?" she replied, her voice betraying longing. "A man such as yourself must never drink alone for too long, kind sir…" she giggled, flicking a thick mane of curled hair across her shoulder.

"Ah, but you are wrong," he assured her. "I am alone at all times. Even in company."

"Maybe," she suggested, placing the glass in front of him, her breasts jiggling like castanets, "you have yet to find the right kind of company, for a man like you…"

He knew she meant she wanted to bed him. He'd bedded hundreds of women all over Spain. He was, after all, a Spanish detective.

It was terrible. Too terrible for a friend ever to comment on, and that was just the opening scene. Maybe it was because I was so disappointed with Luke's story, appetite piqued for a genuine page-turner, that moments later, with her duvet transferred to the tumble dryer, I was reading my sister's words, scrolling through her diary, discovering the thoughts within her perfectly styled head:

The only way my sister would understand stress was if I put it in a cake tin and baked it for lunch. It must be so nice, coming back home to open arms every time things get too 'icky' for her. Dad finding her a job. Mum making her meals, delighted to have her back. Actually wish I was more like Jen. They make everything so easy for her, never give her a hard time. She's always the shining example, and I'm the problem.

Was she kidding? I couldn't even step foot in a shop, let alone back at home, without being reminded how Lara was the beautiful one; the one with men at her feet whose only problem was jet lag. I scrolled down:

Mum dropping her usual remarks today. Jennifer's put on weight. Heard Mum telling her it was nicer than being 'all skin and bone'. I'm not skinny, not any more, just not covered in fat like them. Mum's always on a diet. That says it all.

So, I was covered in fat, was I? I thought, pushing my finger against my, I admit, slightly protruding tummy. The cow. No wonder she had given me the choc-a-day Advent calendar Dad bought for her.

I remember the time Mum slapped my face because she found me making myself sick after dinner, like she didn't know exactly what I'd been doing for months! That was her attempt at motherly love! Then off she went, serving Jen second helpings.

I sat back, some things slowly making sense. I remembered how funny Lara always was about the bathroom. She'd leave you waiting for ages, no matter how desperate you were to pee, but I never knew she did that. *Bulimic.* I looked away from the screen for a second, wondering where I was when all of this was happening. I couldn't imagine Mum slapping anyone. Unless Lara was exaggerating? That wouldn't surprise me.

Nothing changes. Dreading telling them about the wedding. When Jen gets married, it'll be different. They'll be thrilled. They love having her home. Feel like they're wondering why I'm here. Starting to think the same myself.

I was the one they loved having home? I don't think so. Even after she left, it was all about her. I didn't even bother saying when I got my first period because they were always worrying about Lara, Mum crying, or going on about how stunning she looked in her latest photos. Mum and Dad adored her, always had. She was deluded. It was like we'd grown up in different houses. Was she mixing Mum and Dad up with parents from a past life? They were all smiles the minute they saw her. I got none of that, I thought, speeding through another teeth-clenching instalment of my sister's monologue, written a few months earlier:

Mum and Dad only want to know about work. Nothing to tell, so make up all my big opportunities, my charmed existence. One day I'll tell them the truth about how they left me to fend for myself with strangers who wanted to get me high, get me naked.

The more I read, the more famous names jump out from Lara's words, and the more I learn about the way she was treated. Standing near-naked while people pawed and criticized, or ogled her, as if she wasn't there. Even when she was on some glamorous shoot, they would style her hair in a buzz of conversation above her head, work on her face for hours, until she forgot who she was underneath the makeup and posed in front of the camera. A photographer spiked her drink. Some creep on a boat treated the models like prostitutes. The girls said you weren't allowed to say no to him.

The more I read, the more she blamed our parents, as if they had sent her away and left her alone in the dark.

I'd switched Lara's computer off as soon as Dad had got back from the match. I was riddled with guilt as I busied myself with her Christmas present scrapbook, with words I wished I'd never read whirling around inside my head.

I'd set up camp in the middle of the landing, cross-legged in a warm pool of winter sunlight, but rather than the sentimental labour of love I'd imagined, while I filled *Our Story: Sisters* with all the best old photographs I could find, I couldn't muster any meaningful captions to accompany them, not as I realized I'd never really known her at all. I'd pictured handing her a book full of wonderful memories, but we really didn't have any, not as far as she was concerned. What was I supposed to say?

Here you are — just before Mum and Dad sent you away!

Teen Lara. Unhappy and skeletal!

On the last page, I stuck her first postcard from New York, the one that said she loved and missed us. The one I remembered Mum kissing, over and over again, the morning it arrived.

Poor Mum. She wanted to believe Lara was the most beautiful, happy girl in existence, every hope and dream for her elder daughter stored away for posterity in her old memory box, filled with Lara's many achievements, and the odd decent school report from me.

Why would Lara want to twist our family into something ugly and unloving? If anything, Mum and Dad were far too interested in the many disappointments of my life, too eager to offer opinions or hindsight, but Lara was the one who had escaped having to explain herself. She was their greatest success story, their biggest surprise, and proudest achievement.

'Jen?' Dad called. 'I'm putting the rest of your worldly goods in the garage before your mother gets back, okay?'

'Thanks, Dad,' I shouted. 'I'll be down in a sec. I'll give you a hand.'

Mum had been dropping major hints. She couldn't live with boxes stacked up by the mahogany hat-stand a moment longer. Not that I had much stuff stacked up, I thought. Packing had been depressingly easy. My life quickly reduced to a student-sized collection of clothes, old CDs, and treasured books.

It was quite shocking. Even the bed wasn't mine. Where was the buy-it-now, pay-for-it-in-twenty-years-time settee? The flat-pack, self-assemble coffee table? The matching bedroom lighting?

All I had in the world was either a hand-me-down from Mum or something that wouldn't break a £25 monthly household budget. Which was my excuse for having mismatched bedding and plastic kitchenware. No wonder George always insisted we go to his place. My place wasn't a home. It had been a base, offering the basic necessities of a roof, four walls, and semi-functioning plumbing.

'Don't worry, love,' Dad said, placing a protective arm around my shoulder. 'You'll be back on your feet in no time.'

I made a decision there and then, surveying the huddle of boxes and bags — I had to build a life for myself. A life which included some attempt at interior design, and the grown-up wage to fund an improved, more sophisticated lifestyle. The only problem was my plans never went according to plan.

Chapter 8

Lara

I officially had a love/hate relationship with being back home. On the one hand, being in Ingleford put everything in perspective. I was going through a temporary glitch, but some things I could always count on; like the sound of the tumble-dryer in the evening; Dad's first coffee of the day; and the need to take off my shoes as soon as I entered the porch, where Mum stood by with thermal socks, offering an arm for me to lean on, as if direct foot-to-carpet contact might cause irreparable damage.

My parents loved me being back in England, but it was frustrating, especially with the wedding being so close. I hadn't been keen on letting my folks in on the news until I saw them face-to-face. I couldn't have stood the deafening silence if I'd told them over the phone. The here-we-go-again treatment. Not for the third time.

I woke every morning, exhausted by the thought of Operation Home for the Holidays, when I became a picture of happiness, but there was only so long a girl could wear a grin before you had to change into something a little more comfortable.

Mum telepathically demanded her Christmas production was award winning, with all cast members taking a hearty bow as the curtain closed. Dad remained as oblivious as ever. The only thing he'd ever been allowed to control in his life was the TV remote. The rest of the time he had Mum to dictate what to wear, what to eat, when it was time to trim his toenails.

Wedded bliss…

Maybe that's why I felt so tense about Silvano.

We'd decided to spend Christmas apart, especially as his mother wouldn't hear of him being anyplace else. She insisted Christmas was a family time, making sure to underline my existence outside the bloodline, with a sharp look in my direction every time the subject was broached.

He was so in love with the idea of me being here, in cute, little England, for the holidays, and I guess I could see his point, but as quaint as Ingleford was, the novelty only lasted as long as the artificial flurries cascading inside Mum's snow globe. Any longer, and you felt trapped inside one, desperate to escape.

I'd spoken with Silv a couple of times, mainly by text message because I didn't want my family overhearing our wedding plans until they knew they were part of them. Not that I was the one making any plans.

'Mother's got everything taken care of. All you need to do is book in for the final dress fitting. It's going to be wonderful. That woman could organize a function in her sleep, and still wake up fresh as a daisy,' Silvano tried to reassure me.

But I wasn't reassured, not with Dolores at the helm. What exactly had she organized? A swarm of killer bees in the bridal bouquet? Arsenic on tap for the bridal toast?

At first I'd argued it was way too soon. How would we organize our wedding at such short notice? But he'd grabbed hold of my hand, told me he couldn't think of a better time to begin a new life than at the start of a new year, and insisted we hold it at the hotel, which was soon to become my new home.

Silvano being Silvano, he'd already allocated rooms for my family, booked and paid for their flights. December 28th we were all going to fly out, but only after I'd worked out how to tell them about the whole wedding thing in the first place.

'Mind this bend coming up, Lara,' Mum said, holding onto the side of her seat as if she was riding a toboggan. 'I wish you'd let me drive.'

'No, thanks. We're due to arrive before Christmas, not after.'

I turned over the radio as Mum began complaining about sports commentary, glanced down at my hand, and managed a quick smile. This time, I was making the right choice, with the right man, at the right time, I reminded myself.

Thirty-two-years-old and divorced twice. That wasn't going to make anyone feel great, but those other times, it had always been about them. This time, for the first time, it was about doing the best thing for me. I smiled, starting to relax. I'd missed driving, especially down these winding roads, overset by trees and hemmed in by woodland. It was Christmas-card perfect, and fantastic to be behind the wheel, rather than running down cabs, or wrapping up to walk the avenues.

'What time will we head back, then?'

'We haven't even arrived yet, Mum. You might even enjoy yourself.'

I noticed the quick rise of her brow, the polite smile she gave when something wasn't to her liking, simply because it wasn't her decision.

'I left your sister some soup and rolls. You know what she's like with cooking.'

Typical. Jennifer played the game so well that she didn't realize it was a game at all. How's that for subservient? *The dream daughter.* The one who still needed mothering, never grew up, and lived all alone in the big, bad, world.

'She moved out a long time ago, Mum. I'm sure she knows how to eat.'

'Well, I wish we could say the same thing about you…'

I gave her a quick glance, but like the expert she was in throwing grenades and bypassing the explosion, she kept her eye on the road.

Unlike Jen, I'd been a long, bony child, all knees and elbows. Dad said I was like a pony, with my long, blonde hair and gangly limbs, but I'd notice Mum frowning sometimes, usually when I was stood next to my sister. I always hovered over Jen, growing out of our matching outfits far too soon for Mum's liking. She said I must have got it from my dad's side of the family. That Granny Taylor was as tall as a house and as thin as a stick. I'd pull down cuffs and hemlines, shrinking inside my clothes to make them last before Mum noticed, but by the time I was about fourteen, I started to jut out of everything. I couldn't stay within the lines my mother had long ago drawn for how her daughter should look. That was Jennifer's job. I was the mess that couldn't be erased, no matter how hard both of us tried.

Growing up, I kept my thoughts inside my head, until I wanted to scream them out at everyone around me. But all that did was to remind me how no one else was listening, and that thought left me exhausted, and hating myself even more.

I don't know why I chose food. Maybe because mealtimes were so regimented in our house. The dinner table was another stage for the big, family performance. I was perpetually starving, but feeling weak somehow made me feel stronger. It was easy to skip breakfast and lunch, but mealtimes at home were a spectator sport, everyone sitting around congratulating Mum on her culinary prowess. I chewed and chewed tiny mouthfuls, learning how to get unwanted morsels into bits of paper secreted beneath sleeves and under waistbands without anyone noticing. I'd pick arguments or stress out over some imaginary school project, just to get sent to my room, anything to avoid finishing a meal.

I knew what eating disorders were. Loads of magazines had articles about anorexia or bulimia, but I never felt as if they were talking about me. It was my life, as normal and regular as brushing my teeth, and I had no desire to join the rest of the family or the kids in the school canteen at the universal trough.

My empty body emptied my mind, and I loved feeling light and clean as much as I loved watching Jennifer and my mother eating, knowing I was avoiding all the calories they were stuffing into their bodies. I'd started to feel great about my figure. My thighs were thinner, stomach flatter. I was tall, and long, and my own person, not the genetic mutation I used to see. It soon became a point of conversation, and I secretly enjoyed the concern. Mum worried that I was looking too skinny, but instead of wishing I had Jen's curves the way I used to, I started to enjoy looking different from the other women in my family.

Once the modelling really took off, food was the first and last thing on my mind. All the other girls were the same, newborns on the scene, no longer able to digest solids or sleep alone at night. Right then, life was far too fast to digest.

'Used to be a hotel, restaurant thing, this place,' Mum piped up as we turned into the gravel entrance of Wiltshire Hall.

'Did you ever come here, then?'

'Not really.'

Mum's disapproval was palpable, but that was to be expected.

'It's a beautiful-looking place,' I said, surveying the grounds. 'The pictures don't do it justice. Apparently the same family have owned it for generations.'

'Hopi Ear Candling?'

Mum scrutinized every treatment, scrunching up her features as if this wasn't a treat, but some sort of ordeal I was putting her through. 'What time did you say lunch was? I'm so hungry.'

'1.30 p.m. Mum. It says so right here, in the brochure.'

I was determined not to take the bait. I'd worked with some of the most notoriously difficult people in the industry, but their ability to rile me paled in significance to spending time alone with my mother.

I kept remembering Silvano's face when he had insisted on picking up the tab for today, telling me how important it was to spend quality time with my parents, especially when I saw them so rarely.

'It's relaxing, Mum. Clears the sinus, cleanses the ears, helps with hearing.'

'With an actual *candle*?'

'Yes. You know, a tapered one, to fit.'

'They stick a *candle* inside your ear?'

'No, they just light one in church and pray for your health every Sunday ... yes, Mum. They balance a special candle in your ear.'

'There's no need for that attitude, Lara. Hmm,' she said, unimpressed squint resolutely in place. 'I don't see how filling my ears with wax is supposed to help with my hearing. I thought the idea was to remove it...'

'No, Mum, they —'

'Roll on lunch time, that's all I can say, oh...' she said, working her way down the menu.

'What's up?'

'Organic this, wheat-free that. Can I not just have something normal? Two pieces of white bread and a nice bit of ham will do me just fine.'

'It's not fancy, it's healthier, that's all. Bread's a no go, especially white bread. I've told you that.'

'Well, it depends what you use it for, perfectly fine for eating, in my opinion, not that my opinion counts for much these days. Never done me and your dad any harm, white bread.'

What was the point? I cleared my throat, moved on. 'What about the Swedish massage?' I suggested, tracing a finger down the treatment brochure.

'Swedish? You know, I might just give that a whirl,' she said, leaning forward with a girlish smile. 'I used to love ABBA.'

'I don't think ABBA have got anything to do with it, Mum.'

'I know, I know. I was kidding. Do they not have a sense of humour over there in New York? Pity they don't sell that in their brochure. Organic sense of humour,' she chuckled. 'What are you going to opt for, then?'

I already knew exactly what I wanted. I'd seen it online when I was planning our visit.

'I've arranged to go horse-riding.'

'Horse-riding? Right now? I thought we were here to relax?'

'It is relaxing. I'll be back by the time you've had your ABBA massage.'

'Well, don't go galloping too far. They're serving lunch at 1.30 p.m. remember?'

'Enjoy your massage,' I said, picking up my things, and leaving her to relax and at least try to enjoy herself.

'*Massage*,' she muttered, 'I don't need a massage. Quick Ploughman's is all I want…'

To be honest, I wasn't feeling that enthusiastic about the horse-riding myself. The only thing I ever needed when I was this stressed out was a run. Preferably, in the opposite direction from my mother. In fact, jogging had been exactly how my relationship had started with Silvano.

I didn't recognize him at first. I thought he was some weirdo stalker.

'Lara? *Lara Taylor?* Is that you?'

I was stood on the sidewalk, getting my breath back. Technically, it was a fast walk rather than a run, but I'd done it. I'd finally got out of my place, put on my sneakers, and circled the block, three times.

It was a perfect morning in New York. My first perfect morning of the year, since that phone call from my accountant, and the lack of any contact from Bill after I'd walked out on him.

I wiped my mouth, screwing the top back on my bottle of water.

'Sylvester?'

'Silvano!' he said, moving in closer to place kisses either side of my cheeks. 'You look...' He examined my face, searching for the words. 'What happened to your hair?'

'I cut it.'

Technically, I'd hacked off lock after lock, watching the hair fly past my shoulders as if caught in yesterday's breeze. I'd watched in the mirror, half a bottle of vodka down, trying to see myself again, trying to find the person I could actually feel, not the one in disguise.

'Anyway,' I said, as pleasantly as possible. 'Nice to see you again, Silvano.'

I turned away. He grabbed my elbow.

'I'm sorry if I offended you,' he said, slowly removing his hand. 'It's just, well, I wasn't sure if it was you,' he explained, a slight frown drifting across his features. 'And you know how I feel about leisure-wear,' he smiled, his eyes a night-sky of mischief.

It took me a second to realize what he meant. He was wearing a grey blazer, chestnut leather boots. Immaculate. I was in breathable leggings and an oversized Calvin Klein t-shirt.

'How are you, darling?' he asked, scrutinizing me with each word. 'Talk to me.'

And for some reason, I did.

Off to the nearest coffee shop we went. I swore I'd eaten, persuaded him I was fine with a cup of mint tea, until the chatter and movement around me quickly dissolved into the background.

Sitting with him, I felt safe, comfortable even, for the first time in a long time.

I'd met Silvano on-and-off when I was a kid and he was a booker for my first agent, Gerry Roxburt, a complete sleazebag. Since then, Silvano had changed profession at least a thousand times, becoming part of the tapestry of the New York socialite circle.

His family owned The Empress Hotel, he told me, but unlike fellow members of the elite Old Money Club, I'd heard he was a good guy, not prone to demands, outbursts, or meltdowns. Rumour had it, he left that side of things to his mother, but that was all I knew. And I still hadn't worked out why he was the faintest bit interested in me, or why I'd even agreed to go for coffee with him in the first place.

He took my hand and asked, 'How can I help you, sweetheart?'

'Help me?' I slowly pulled away, completely freaked out. 'Why would I want you to help me?'

'Lara, do you remember when we first met?'

'It was a long time ago now.'

I really didn't remember at all. That whole period of my life was a high-speed merry-go-round, distorted by sound and colour, only punctuated by black and white interludes I'd rather forget.

'Well, I do. You locked yourself in the bathroom. They all tried, but I was the only one who finally got you out of there.'

I sat back in my seat, searching, but still I couldn't recall the moment.

'You were home sick, you said. Tired.' He dabbed at his mouth with a napkin. He had a great face. Full of flint and fire. 'I got you a bowl of strawberries. We ate them together, on the bathroom floor.' He raised his eyebrows in mock-disgust. 'You sang to me. It was very sweet,' he finished, placing his hand on mine. 'And that's how I remember you.' His dark eyes melted into warm chocolate. 'So what happened?'

I realized I was crying, but my chest was empty, devoid of anything apart from the drill of my own heartbeat.

'I'm still homesick, I guess.'

'Then, we'll send you home.'

'I don't have one. Nowhere I recognize, anyway.'

He looked at me questioningly.

'I mean, I don't really know where that is any more.'

'We'll find it,' he said, taking my hand again.

Silvano took me for dinner that first night. And the next. Only postponing our dates to dine with his mother, who was in poor health and doted on him. I told him everything, relishing his company. Finally, I got down to my last words with Bill.

'I'll contact him,' Silvano promised.

'You will?'

'Let's settle everything outstanding, but before that, I'm sorry darling, but we must get you to a hair salon. Short and chic, I love, but short and...' He pulled a face, tilting his head from side-to-side. 'Not so much.'

I actually laughed, secure in a warm wave of reassurance.

'Then, there's the small matter of your eating habits, and your *other* habits, my dear,' he said, placing his hand on mine. 'Don't think I haven't noticed all these meals you claim to have had before we meet, or otherwise, you're gnawing at salad leaves, sipping on wine. It's no good.'

I nodded. I was so fed up of carrying the weight of so many secrets, it was a relief to let the pretence drop.

'You're not the first girl I've met with a noticeably weak bladder, either.'

I frowned.

'Those frequent trips to the bathroom? You don't need to do any of that.'

My eyes filled with tears, and I couldn't look at him as he spoke.

'I know what you've been through,' he whispered, 'but you're not just some model, not anymore.'

When November arrived, bringing my birthday with it, Silvano organized a private room in The Empress, with Henrik, the maitre d', on standby, just for us.

Henrik led the Happy Birthday chorus, and I blew out the candle on a slice of cake Silvano insisted we share, making a wish that he would always be my closest friend — and that one day I would be able to repay him, in full.

'Lara, I've been thinking,' he said, folding his arms and relaxing into his seat, as Henrik took leave. 'That apartment of yours…'

Silvano hated my place. I knew he would. I'd put off taking him home for as long as I could. After Travis, I'd rented the first thing I found, and couldn't afford to upgrade to a new place straight away, which was probably a good thing seeing as I was already hanging off a financial precipice, by my no longer professionally manicured nails. To me, it wasn't exactly polished, nowhere near the hotel standards of luxury Silvano expected, but the place had character. The windows were air-tight, it had a deep tub I loved to soak in, and I'd picked up some great-looking stuff along the way, like my Kem Weber chair and the Patrick Nagel that hung over my bed.

But I knew Silvano, with his love of the finer things, would be far from impressed by my collective bric-a-brac.

'I don't think I like you living there.'

'Well, I won't be there forever, and actually, I like my place.'

'As much as you'd like living at The Empress?'

'Silvano, I can't move into your place. It wouldn't be right.'

I was trying to choose my words carefully, wary of hurting his feelings, but not enough to give up my place, my independence.

'Well, when you put it like that,' he nodded. 'But, it's not exactly moving in, now is it? I'd love for you to take a room. While you're between residences.'

'But I'm not between residences…'

'Okay, well then, let's look at this another way. Wouldn't it make sense for you to stay at the hotel, save some money rather than spending it on rent?'

'And how would I pay for a room at the hotel?'

'I don't need you to pay for the room.'

'So you'll lose business, and I'll still owe you money? Silvano—'

'Okay, okay!' he put his hands up in surrender. 'I hope I'm at least allowed to give you a gift?'

He lifted a big, rectangular box onto the table between us.

'Really,' I smiled, stroking his hand. 'You've done so much for me already. I don't need presents.'

'Lara,' he said. 'It's a little something for your birthday.'

'Silvano, you're my best friend, you know that.'

He nodded.

'So please let me tell you, you've done more than enough. You make me feel as if I'm taking advantage, which, I suppose, I am —'

'Lara, if you carry on, I'm liable to fall straight to sleep. I'm older than you, so please open the God damn box before it's time for my nightcap.'

I'd lifted the lid, revealing lemon tissue paper and beneath it, silk ribbons, bow after bow, but as I rummaged underneath the layers, there was nothing to be found.

'Look at little closer,' Silvano instructed, and my eyes nestled on something in the corner, tied with the biggest of all the bows.

It was a ring.

A yellow diamond almost the size of a sugar cube.

Silvano remained stoic. Attached, was a gift tag:

So you'll always have sunshine at hand.
Please be my wife?
Silvano — with love always X.

'He's gorgeous.' I smiled, brushing my hand across the warm muscle of Samson, my horse for the next 40 minutes.

The grounds at The Wiltshire were stunning. A vast quilt of greenery which rolled as far as my eye could see, promising to wrap me up, and take me away as far as my horse could carry me.

'I take it you've ridden before?'

'Yes. A long time ago now. I had a horse, George Michael.'

'*George Michael?* That was your horse's name?'

The manager of the hotel, Tom, fixed his attention on me, chewing away amusement as he met my eye.

I looked away, trying not to take in too much detail, but I couldn't help notice his pale skin, not a trace of shaving shadow; the thickness of his choppy, dark blond hair, as he meticulously smoothed and tightened the girth.

'You're not serious?' he laughed.

'Afraid so. Always liked his music.'

Luckily, I'd caught myself before I explained how funny I'd thought it was to be the only woman who could say she had been riding George Michael all morning.

'My husband wasn't too impressed either. *Ex-husband,* actually,' I clarified.

What was I doing?

Silv was miles away, and here I was riding horses, chatting to Tom, and thinking back to life with Travis. Not that it was a life. Sheer stupidity. It wasn't even fun to look back on. No way to put it all down to the craziness of youth.

I'd become a pathetic, downtrodden creature as soon as we married. It was a mistake that never should have gotten that far, and Bill had tried to tell me. When I looked back, dating Travis was when I was at my most beautiful, part of an elite group of top models who only had to show up to please our clients. I could nail a front cover on three hours' sleep, and took for granted that I would never change, that my skin would never lose its glow, my eyes bear the creases of laughter and tears. My body was taut, and the only spare inches I had, settled in all the right places. The one thing I could still enjoy was the look on Travis's face the first time I stepped out of my clothes. And the sex? As much as I hate to admit it, was the best I'd had. He was Golden, that was my name for him. Hair the colour of wheat, bronzed skin. A real country boy.

Thinking back on that particular moment, I couldn't tell myself Travis had never been in love with me. That hurt way too much. Truthfully, at first, he'd loved having me around. I was as cherished as one of his prized guitars, or the place we called home after I invested in the sprawling ranch he'd set his heart on. But just as suddenly as we'd connected, the novelty wore off, and I found myself living with a child who got his kicks putting me down and spending my cash as if it were compensation.

You mightn't believe it, but in my former life, I was always the one picking up the tab. Silvano said poor people always started out as generous, and, let's face it, I was becoming a natural at building debts rather than nest eggs.

Up until then, I guess, my finances were pretty steady. I was never a huge spender. The things I loved, I was given most of the time — clothes, shoes, jewellery, all that stuff that gives you the quick fix. I didn't even own a home before Travis, but I did manage to pay off Mum and Dad's mortgage. That was probably the grandest gesture I made to the family, I thought, taking a lungful of fresh, English air, as I remembered that now I finally had a man in my life who knew all about grand gestures, and wanted nothing in return except my love.

Silvano had slowly resuscitated me, starting with tiny sparks of happiness which soon became a consuming, undeniable flame. His gravelled voice reminded me of coal-burning fires. His dark eyes flickered with a thousand reassurances. I had nothing to offer him except my problems, but even that didn't deter him, and after several long chats, just the two of us, I was seeing a counsellor he recommended. A counsellor I trusted, and who was helping me to change my life, along with Silvano. She agreed he was helping me feel stronger, but was far more interested in trying to prise answers about my childhood, showing me the light at a long tunnel of troubled adolescence.

Samson and I reached a steady trot as I thought back to my engagement, looking over at the hotel, and noticing Tom watching us from the deck.

He waved.

Time to turn back.

Wiltshire Hall was unbelievably impressive so far. Ingleford village was cute, but this place, within driving distance, felt like another time zone, and I'd forgotten how much I loved riding, enjoyed the sense of freedom. It was so long since I'd felt free from time, worry, and everything. No matter what I did, it was never a feeling I could give to myself, always something I was gifted by other people.

'You looked like you enjoyed that?'

'It was wonderful. Thank you,' I said, dusting myself down.

'Well, come over whenever you want. Quick call in the morning, he's all yours...'

'I'd like that,' I blushed slightly, aware of Tom's appreciative gaze.

'And, I'd be delighted to, maybe, accompany you? If you don't mind the company?' he smiled. 'Gives me an excuse to saddle up, get away from business for a while.'

Tom explained he lived here while his mother had retired to France. He had taken over the running of the hotel shortly after the death of his father.

Listening to him, sometimes I felt like I'd never be happy.

I really was just like my mother.

'You look great,' I said, greeting Mum with a smile as she sat in the conservatory, skin glowing. 'Did you enjoy the massage?'

'Goodness, no. Awful girl,' she huffed, taking her glass from the wicker table. 'Sullen thing, she was. Heavy set. Grappled over my back like she was kneading dough, but the seaweed and rosemary facial was nice, and this gorgeous elderberry drink. Divine!'

'Mum, this is Tom. *The general manager*,' I said, overemphasising the fact so she could at least try to make some last-minute, positive endorsement. 'He arranged my horse-riding.'

Tom had insisted on saying hello to my mum. Not that I was encouraging him to be so attentive. He made me nervous, and he knew it.

'Pleased to meet you,' he said, extending a hand. 'Tom Reeves. I'm sorry you didn't enjoy your massage.'

'That's a private … it's a *joke*, isn't it, Lara?' she said, shaking her head in thought, smile wavering as she put on her glasses. 'It was superb, really. *Tom Reeves?* So, this is your hotel?'

'My father was the owner. He passed away a couple of years ago.'

'I'm very sorry to hear that,' Mum muttered, peering at him over the top of her specs.

'Thank you,' Tom said, 'luckily, my mother trusts my judgment.'

I gave Mum a pointed look.

'It's fantastic,' I said, 'I love the whole feeling of this place. It feels *so homely*, but, just gorgeous,' I said, with another look in Mum's direction.

'I try to make my dad proud,' Tom said, his expression growing serious at the thought. 'I only hope he'd approve of the changes I've made.'

'I'm sure he would,' I said. 'It's exceptional here, really, Tom.'

'Oh that's…' He raised his arms, searching for the words. 'It always makes my day when our guests are happy.'

'How could anyone not be?'

Apart from my mother, of course, I thought, although that was to be expected.

'You know,' Tom said, wearing a slight frown. 'I hope you don't mind me asking, but is there somewhere I recognize you from?'

'I doubt it,' Mum cut in. 'She lives in America. New York. The Big Apple,' she explained, getting to her feet and standing between Tom and me, as she suddenly informed him: 'Her fiancé owns a hotel.'

'He doesn't own it, Mum.'

I don't know why I said that. I suppose my mother stage-managing my conversation had something to do with it. And how interesting that she decided to bring Silvano up now, when she and Dad had hardly mentioned a word about my engagement or asked a question about my husband-to-be since I arrived. Even Jennifer, who I thought would want to know every detail, hadn't shown the least bit of interest. It was old news now, me getting married.

'Oh, wow,' Tom said. 'You should have said. Here's me droning on about The Wiltshire…'

'Oh, no, I don't mind at all…'

Mum's glare bruised the side of my face.

'Anyway, lovely to meet you both,' Tom said, shaking our hands. 'Enjoy the rest of your day, and please, if there's anything you need, or, like I said, if you ever fancy a return visit...' He trailed off, making an uncomfortable exit.

'What did you say that for?'

'What?' Mum asked, taking a seat. 'Well, he does, doesn't he? *Silvano*,' she exhaled. 'Your fiancé, remember?'

'What's that supposed to mean?'

'That you're engaged. Off the market. Spoken for.'

'Yes, Mother. I'm aware of that.'

'Well, make sure *Tom Reeves* is aware of that, too.'

'I'm wearing an engagement ring. And I'm sure you told him more than enough about my romantic status for him to take the hint.'

'I only said Silvano has a hotel.'

'Mum, I'm allowed to speak to other men, whether my fiancé has a hotel or not. I thought it was really nice of Tom to come over and introduce himself.'

'Yes, well, that's how it starts. First, they introduce themselves, and then they... oh that elderberry,' she managed, backing up into her seat. 'I don't think it agrees with me,' she said, growing pale.

'It took two glasses to work that one out?' I said. 'It's alcoholic. You know you can never handle your drink.'

'Would you please lower your voice. If memory serves, I'm still your mother. It was probably that massage. She's messed about with my lower intestine.'

Just like that she could do it. Raise my stress-levels to triple figures.

I looked across to the foyer.

Tom was on his mobile. Staring at me.

Mum hadn't mentioned much about spending the day at the spa once we got home, just bitched about the expense of lunch, even though I'd been more than happy to treat us. After Dad served a small bowl of lamb hotpot, she went to bed early, still complaining about the overpriced massage that was playing havoc with her digestion.

I'd woken late the next day and missed my morning call with Silvano, waiting until 5 p.m. my time to catch him at lunch, but no luck. The afternoon passed at the usual Ingleford pace. I'd decided against nipping into the village, because it wasn't worth the risk of bumping into some of the neighbours, not after I'd overheard Mum chatting to Evelyn Parry, who specialized in spreading tittle-tattle, and had been told all about my 'huge engagement ring', and how I was marrying a 'very wealthy hotelier', and 'yes, I was still very busy, and hadn't she seen me on that magazine cover, or noticed my face on the hair colour display in the pharmacy?' so instead, I put on my sweats, stretched out the aches from the horse ride the day before with some basic yoga moves — and thought of Tom.

The thing that threw me was how he'd felt so familiar, in a way I'd known with very few people before. Sure, occasionally, you meet someone and you just 'click', hit it off, whatever you want to call it, but this had been different. The closest I'd got before was with Bill Staniss.

From the moment I met Bill, I knew I could trust him, knew his words weren't littered with the false promises I'd learned were the second language of most people in the industry, that instead, he was going to be with me for the long-haul, or at least until a decade later, once our paths seemed equally destined to hit a fork in the road.

Tom was the same. There had been a kind of recognition, which I couldn't help but think, or maybe it was simply hope, was mutual. It wasn't just the way he looked, with his slim, muscular build; the thick widow's peak of hair hinting at the tow-haired young boy who'd gone before, but, something inherent, in his walk, his hands, his gaze, hinting at a strength and confidence which I'd once possessed myself. I knew I had to see him again. It was inevitable, but I was afraid, confused … happy, until my sister got home, and snapped me back into the usual routine of her self-created drama.

I'd noticed her staring at our mother, and knew exactly what was coming next.

'Mum? Are you okay?'

'Doesn't she look great?' I prompted, determined not to let Jennifer makes things worse than they already were. Mum had come home an hour early from her shift at the Post Office, complaining of migraine, and asking if it might have been because of that face treatment thing.

'Mum? You look … *weird.*'

'That's probably because you're so used to seeing her looking stressed out the whole time. Especially when you're around…' I couldn't help but add, noticing the simpering expression on my sister's face.

I'd forgotten how much Jennifer thrived on making something out of nothing. It was exactly the same during the dreaded family meal times. We'd sit around the table, Mum uncomfortably eyeing my plate as Jennifer bored us all to tears with job search plans and various poor-little-me stories, while Dad acted as the positive distraction. The joke-teller. The hearty-eater.

'Are you kidding me? She looks like she did after she crashed into that man outside the pharmacy. Not that you'll remember how shaken up she was,' Jennifer yapped, pulling out a seat from the table. 'Mum? Do you need a cup of tea? Here, sit down.'

'*He* crashed into *me*,' Mum said, waving her away. 'I'm fine, Jennifer. Honestly.'

'She's not *ill*, Jen. She's had a liquid facelift, that's all.'

'*A what?*'

'An early Christmas present. A little touch of Botox at the spa yesterday,' I explained. 'She looks fresher.'

'No, she doesn't! She looks as if she's just laid an egg!'

'Thanks, Jennifer,' Mum said, trying, but failing, to look alarmed. 'I am here you know? No wonder I've got a headache.'

'I'm not surprised she's got a headache,' Jen glared at me, 'when her eyebrows are pinned halfway up her forehead.'

'For God's sake, why do you have to be so negative all the time?'

'Negative? Why do you think that? Because you can see my *facial muscles* expressing emotion, like frowning?'

'Maybe you should work on some other emotions, like shutting the hell up.'

'I don't think "shutting up" qualifies as an emotion,' Jen said, with a sneer I hadn't heard since, well, probably the last time I saw my sister. 'And only you would think having our mother's face injected with tranquilizer, or whatever it is, qualifies as a Christmas present.'

'It'll wear off in a few weeks. Stop overreacting...'

'Oh, yes, because I'm the one who *exaggerates* everything, aren't I?' she asked, glaring at me before turning back to Mum. 'Do you need some painkillers?'

'Yes, please,' Mum nodded, colour draining from her cheeks. 'It's been a long day.'

'Laura,' Jen said, as she filled the kettle, 'can you grab Mum a couple of headache tablets from the drawer, please?'

'My name's *Lara*.'

'Well, it was "Laura" for the *eighteen years* we grew up together. Forgive me if I slip up occasionally on the odd times I actually see you...'

'Girls!' Mum called, gripping her forehead.

All heads turned as the doorbell struck up.

'Thank goodness for that,' Mum said. 'Will that be him?'

'Who?' I asked, out of the loop, as usual.

'Barry Hogg. He's still taking you out tonight, Jen, isn't he?'

'Barry Hogg?' I couldn't help but perk up. 'You're going out with *Barry Hogg*?'

'No. I'm not "going out" with him. We're going for a drink, that's all. A Christmas

drink, because today was our last day at work. Okay?'

'Just the two of you?'

'We *work* together.'

'Aren't you inviting Dad, then? He works there too.'

'Inviting me where?' Dad asked, appearing in the kitchen as the doorbell sounded again. 'I take it I'm getting the door then?'

'Girls!' Mum shouted, louder this time, and just like years ago, we froze. 'Quiet!' She said, placing her hand on her temple. 'Laura, *Lara*, leave your sister alone! She could do a lot worse than meeting a nice chap like Barry.'

Jennifer stared at my mother in horror, while I struggled to lock in my laughter.

'Now,' Mum continued, straightening her blouse. 'Jennifer, go and get changed.'

'I am changed,' she said, glancing down at her jeans, and what I thought was quite a nice top, judging by Jennifer's usual standards.

'Is that what you wear on a date these days? And you wonder why you can't meet a nice man…'

'She hasn't,' I snorted. 'She's going out with Barry Hogg…'

'For Goodness sake!' Mum shrieked, growing impatient as she grabbed herself the painkillers I'd forgotten about. 'The two of you would wear out tarmac. Go and see Barry,' she told Jen. 'Your poor father's probably bored senseless already.'

I had to bite my lip at the thought of my sister spending the evening in a Barry Hogg-induced coma.

'Barry,' I could hear Jen trying to keep the disappointment from her voice. 'Hi.'

I followed her into the hallway. There he was. Blazer and tie. Bunch of flowers.

'I were just tellin' Mr. Taylor. I'm here to take you out.'

'Thought we said we'd meet at the pub?' she said, clearly mortified.

'I wanted to give you these. They're wildflowers.'

He stuck the bouquet under her nose like smelling salts.

'Thanks. They're … lovely,' Jen said, taking what looked like a bunch of nettles and handing them over to Mum. 'Right then, let's go…'

'Hi Barry! Don't you look smart? How's the slaughter shop?' I grinned.

''Fraid you'd have ter ask Mr. Hogg senior. I've been employed at Home For All Seasons. Hoping to concentrate on landscapin' work in the near future.'

'Nice to see you, Barry. Good luck!' Mum said, and as she closed the door, I nearly collapsed, I was laughing so hard.

Chapter 9

Jennifer

I'd only agreed to go for a drink because I'd felt sorry for Barry. He seemed lonely, inoffensive, harmless. And it's the 'harmless' part that should have warned me. Anyone described as harmless is usually far from it. They've earned that title by causing offense wherever they roam. Same goes for people who 'mean well'. They're the ones who put their size twenty-fives in it so many times, that after a while, you can't help but think no one's that accident-prone.

I was trying to be polite as we chatted, but after a few minutes it became clear, not only did Barry think we were on a date, but that he was doing me a great favour in asking me out in the first place. That's right, *me*, who up until recently had herself a handsome, charming boyfriend, who didn't flinch at the sight of me without my clothes on.

Now, here I sat with Barry. Rude, boring, patronizing Barry, whose face, with the ruddy jowls, drooping earlobes, and over-hanging forehead, looked like it needed circumcising. And, yes, I did feel justified in resorting to childish name-calling. I'd been duped into pitying someone who I should have realized was lonely for a very good reason — and, to add to his charismatic ways, it turned out was an ardent nose picker, too.

'Your sister's engaged, then?' he asked, working away, with the tip of his thumb edged inside his nostril. 'How old are you? You'll not want to be leaving things too late if you've plans to get in the family way.'

If this was his attempt at light conversation, I was glad we'd barely exchanged a word for the first few days of delivering trees.

'Your mum says you've parted ways with your fella,' he told me after I insisted on buying the drinks, and he let me. Mum would be proud. She brought me up to pay my own way for fear that oddbods like Barry might buy me a drink and mistake it as the go-ahead for aggravated sex in the car park. 'Says you've moved back. For good.'

He thumbed his nostril again, having a good dig disguised as an absentminded itch. I almost passed him the salt and a napkin.

'Did she? Well, you know what mothers can be like, hoping the kids are back for good.'

'Didn't give us that impression,' he frowned. 'Seemed concerned about you floatin' about back home,' he said. 'Think she'd be happy to see you settle down.'

Was he suggesting with *him*? I was fuming. What was Mum *thinking*? When did all these detailed conversations about my personal life take place? At that moment, I couldn't believe how much I missed George. The man I should be spending Christmas Eve with. The man who made me feel lovely, and listened, and would probably feel even worse than I did if he could see me, sat there with Barry Hogg.

Stone-cold sadness crept over me as I thought about my sister laughing at the state of my love life, and our mum thinking this was the best I could do. When I first came home, George had sent a message asking if I was okay. He said he felt bad about what happened, that he hadn't realized things were so tough for me financially. (I loved the way he had used the word *financially* because it sounded so grown up, so like George). I'd told him it wasn't his fault. He'd said he knew that, but I'd made him feel as if it was his fault, and then I stopped texting him because I thought that was a really irritating thing to say.

And, yes, he texted first — not me, because Luke always said getting in touch with a man first was a huge no-no — but it seemed like a stupid rule when I only wasted time wishing he'd text me, and imagining how I'd reply to him. I took a quick look at my mobile while Barry glanced up at football scores on the pub TV, chewing his thumb and calmly spitting out a piece of nail.

No messages. No missed calls.

Right now, George had become a mirage in the vast desert of Barry Hogg. I'd have given anything to be together, knowing within hours we'd be stumbling upstairs and rolling around in various states of delight and exhaustion until the sun came up. I had to resist the urge to run outside, call George, and beg him to get me out of there.

'This seat taken?'

I snapped out of my reverie. I don't think I've ever been so pleased to see anyone in my life. Even if he did look ridiculous, wearing a battered fedora.

'Luke?'

I could have leapt into his arms and kissed him. Instead, I asked, 'What are you doing here?'

'Dragged myself away from waiting for you to return my call yesterday. And I've left your mum's Christmas present in your bedroom. Are you pleased to see me?' he asked, eyeing Barry cautiously, 'or am I interrupting something?'

'No, you're not. And, yes, I am!'

Technically, Luke had saved Barry Hogg's life. Although he might just have taken a few years off mine, I realized, spying my sister making her way towards us from the bar.

'Lara's here?'

'What was I supposed to do?' he asked. 'I couldn't just flounce out and leave her sat there. Plus, your mum kept suggesting Lara might like to come with me. Has your mum had botox, by the way?'

'Early Christmas present from Lara…'

'Oh perfect,' Luke grinned. 'I'd forgotten how fabulously Stepford Wives the whole thing gets. I'm Luke, in case you were wondering,' he said, giving Barry a wave.

'Right,' Barry nodded, clearly unsettled by the strange man in the strange hat. 'I'll juss go an' 'elp yer sister with them drinks…'

'What the hell are you wearing?' I asked, leaning away to fully appraise his dubious headwear. 'It looks like something you found after penny-for-the-guy-night.'

'You mean Bonfire Night, and it helps me to write.'

'Hey guys!' Lara placed a tray of shot glasses on the table. 'We're gate-crashing, I know,' she said in this baby-staccato voice, pulling her mouth down into a fake grimace. 'Will you forgive me, Baz?'

Not me. She didn't ask if I forgave her. She was playing to her strengths as usual, wooing the men-folk with the long-lost-leggy-model routine.

And that stupid voice! And that dumb expression!

'L-l-l-lovely,' Barry spluttered. 'Lovely to see you, Lara. Lovely as ever. Let me pay fer them drinks.'

'Oh Barry, you're such a gentleman, but it's fine.'

'No, no. I insist. Stood at the bar's no place fer a lady.'

He produced a twenty-pound note, which she accepted with a flirtatious smile. All I'd got was the nose picking. Not so much as the offer of a beer mat for *my* drink. Not that I wanted to be the object of Barry's affections. I'd forgiven him for being terminally dull, turned a blind eye to his nostril excavation, but he could sod off if he thought I was going to ignore his rudeness.

'Here we go, folks! Two-for-one!' Lara squealed. 'Let's do this thing!'

'What is it?' I asked, peering into the purple concoction before taking a sniff.

'First the tequila.' Lara said, wiggling the glass, 'then, blueberry vodka.'

'No thanks.'

'What's up? On a diet, Jen?' she asked, rolling her eyes.

'I'm not about to get bombed while I'm staying with our parents, that's all.'

'We're only having a couple of drinks.'

'C'mon Jen,' Luke said, giving me a nudge as he picked up his glass. 'It's Christmas.'

'*Is it?*'

'Oh, don't be like that! It's what Jesus would have wanted,' Luke smirked, as Barry raised his glass and interrupted with a toast: 'That hand fer milkin', and this one fer drinkin'.'

'Barry! You are a riot!' Lara laughed, knocking back her shot in record time.

The tequila tasted awful. The blueberry vodka smelt like nail polish remover, but with the bad taste I already had in mouth, I decided the night couldn't get much worse.

I was wrong.

Chapter 10

Lara

I sat through my sister and Luke doing the whole festive shtick, performing their rendition of *Fairytale of New York*.

It was enough to turn a girl to drink, so it was a good job I'd started hours earlier. It was so weird being here, back in The Hayside, which used to be only pub for miles that would serve sixteen-year-old girls providing their jeans were tight enough.

My sister was so annoying, doing the usual, 'I'm so petite and silly' routine, pretending she didn't realize she was acting cute and adorable. She was the perfect sidekick for Luke, now that he'd gone a bit soft around the edges and ended up working in retail. A few years before, he'd had a pretty promising career on a hip TV show. That's how those two had met each other, after he interviewed me, not that I got credit for introducing them. Not now that Luke was Jennifer's best friend, with my mother nursing barely hidden hopes they'd end up together.

They stepped off the makeshift stage, just a step up from the pub floor, as a few drunken well-wishers clapped and wolf-whistled.

'I can't believe you made me do that,' Jennifer said, giving Luke a nudge.

She could believe it, of course. This was all part of Jennifer's unassuming act.

'C'mon, Bazzo,' I said, ignoring my sister's triumphant grin. 'What are we gonna sing? Let's show 'em how to work a crowd!'

'Oh no, Lara. I'm not cut-out for stages,' he said, taking a mouthful of beer. 'But I'm sure everyone in 'ere would give their drinking arm to watch you up on stage.'

'Barry! You're such a charmer!' I smiled, giving him a wink.

Okay, so I was flirting a little, but only because Jennifer was obviously jealous that Barry 'The Slob' Hogg, was more interested in me than he was in her.

No wonder the last one dumped her, I thought, emptying my glass. She hadn't changed. Always so needy. A lap-dog, desperate to be under someone's watchful eye at all times.

'Looks like I'm going to have to go it all alone then. Unless you want to help a girl out, Luke?'

You should have seen the look on Jennifer's face, pretending to be engrossed in some middle-aged man's version of *Unchained Melody*, while, I assume it was his wife, sat in front of him, dabbing away tears and swaying over her glass of rosé.

Jen was probably wishing some loser would serenade her like that one day.

'I think Luke's already given me his all,' she said, resting her head on his shoulder.

I could have sworn she'd convinced herself Luke was a stand-in for an actual man in her life.

'I was pretty damn good,' he said, with a sarcastic raise of his eyebrow, 'but yes, sorry, I'm done for the night.'

'Really?' I purred, placing my hand on Luke's shoulder. 'I thought you had way more stamina than that, Lukey... I know exactly what I want to sing,' I announced, finishing my vodka with a slam. 'Next round's yours, Jen!' I reminded her, skipping over to the karaoke man.

'Laura Taylor?'

I gave a vacant smile, no idea who the guy was.

'Sam Knowles. Ingleford Secondary? Before you were famous,' he croaked.

I could vaguely make out the boy he once was, but if the 15-year-old me could have seen the man he'd become, she would never have given him a second glance.

'Sam! Yes, I remember. Such a long time ago. How are you?'

'Good, yeah. Wife's over there. Remember Wendy?'

This was like a bad dream starring all of those septic losers I'd long forgotten since senior school.

I glanced across the crowd. Wendy was looking my way. Her face brought it all back. The gossip. The laughter. Nearly twenty years had passed, I was a grown woman now, I reminded myself, but the 15-year-old me made a guest appearance — and she hated Wendy's guts.

'Yes, I remember her. You two got married? How about that? Anyway, am I okay to…'

'Oh, the karaoke. Yeah, sure.'

I mightn't have been remotely interested in him, but I was pretty sure Wendy was still keeping a close eye on us.

'Thanks, Sam,' I said, giving out my best mega-watt grin, purely for his wife's benefit.

'Laura?'

'It's Lara.'

'Course, yeah,' he nodded. 'Couldn't have a piccie with you, could I?'

He was already armed with his mobile, face full of apology and optimism. This, from the same boy who treated me like dirt and humiliated me, along with his lovely wife, for all those years while I was growing up in the damn village.

I moved to his side as he held the mobile in front of our faces, matching his grin with a rueful smirk, but just before he captured us, sliding his hand, uninvited, around my waist, I quickly extended my middle finger, holding it above his head.

'Cheers, Lara. Appreciate it, like. You'll have ter say hiya to our Wend.'

'Sure. Will do, Sam.'

I strode to the middle of the stage, all eyes on me, and as the first bars of the Christina Aguilera classic sounded up, my sister actually hid her face in her hands.

I took the microphone.

'This one's for you, Barry!' I shouted, one arm, defiant, punching the air.

Chapter 11

Jennifer

'Lara's bloody heavy considering she's a bag o' bones,' Luke said, stretching the tension from his arms as he followed me into the lounge. 'I can't believe we got her upstairs.'

Lara was out cold. Thankfully, the head lolling had finally given way to shut down mode before she became even harder to handle.

'I thought that guy's wife was going to kill her...'

'I was more worried for the wife, to be honest. Did you see how scared she looked when Lara started bringing up their school days?' He smiled, taking a seat. 'Always a wild one, your sister. Breaking hearts, bending rules...'

'Except she's thirty-two and engaged. *Again*. When she tried to get on the bar?' I closed my eyes in horror at the memory, 'It's weird, you know,' I said, remembering the stuff I'd read in her diary the day before. 'I seem to annoy her on sight. I mean, we were teenagers the last time we spent any time together, but whatever it is she thinks I did to her, she knows how to hold a grudge...'

'Doesn't every teenager?'

'Not everyone leaves home to that kind of life, though. *Modelling*. They're usually much more predictable, much more like me. Dead-end job, pointless relationship, pointless everything...'

'We really don't do this enough,' Luke smirked. 'I love our chats.'

'Sorry,' I whined. 'I just feel like I hardly know her,' I debated whether to tell him, then confessed: 'I saw some stuff on her laptop; a diary, and —'

'You read her diary?'

'Is it that bad?' I winced.

'That bad? You know it is. Would you like her reading yours?'

'I haven't got a diary. I'd have nothing to put in it.'

'That's not the point.'

'Okay, well, obviously not, but only because I'd be embarrassed by how dull my life is...' I admitted, busy grabbing glasses and surveying bottles in Mum and Dad's mini bar, which usually opened for business during public holidays or times of personal crisis.

'So, what's in it?' Luke asked, settling into his seat, becoming more interested. 'Any scandal I should know about?'

'Well, I stopped once I got to the list she'd made of all the blokes she's slept with, but she's seeing a counsellor, for a start. That's who told her to keep a diary in the first place, so they can review it during her sessions.'

'So, she's in therapy, along with everyone else in America. *Big deal.* Is that it?'

'There's things in there... I don't know,' I shrugged. 'I always thought she had this glamorous life. She just sounds lonely, and messed up, I suppose.'

'Aren't we all?'

'You wouldn't say that if you'd read some of the stuff she's had to deal with on her own. None of us really knows how she lives, not until she ends up married or divorced. She just seems to hate us all; me, Mum and Dad.'

'Oh, stop worrying. Everyone goes over-the-top when they write diaries, half of that will just be her feeling sorry for herself. My diary's like a Greek tragedy, not that I'd appreciate you leafing through it. You'd feel a right prat if she caught you. I mean it. Back off.'

'I know. I know...'

'Well then. What's with you, anyway?' he asked, taking off his hat.

'Nothing much. I miss George. I nearly text —'

'I told you, if I'm really interested in someone, nothing stops me from texting. So has he?'

'Nope.'

'So, that means he's a bastard. And why would you text a bastard? Would your life be complete if only you had your very own bastard?'

'Definitely, not,' I grinned.

'So, as a former bastard, I say there'll be no texting one, agreed?'

'Former?'

'I haven't had the chance recently. Too busy with my writing, which you still haven't commented on...'

'When are you going to meet someone, Luke?' I asked, changing the subject.

'When Beyoncé gets a divorce. Or your mother. You know she adores me.'

She did. Luke flirted outrageously with her.

'Jen? You were thinking about him then, weren't you? About George?'

'No,' I said, drawing back my thoughts. 'It just feels like a big, backward step, that's all, being back home with my parents.'

'Well, I did say you could have stayed at mine. We'd have had a hoot!'

'We'd have ended up arguing over buying milk or putting bins out,' I said, adding a dash of Tia Maria and handing him his drink. 'And besides, it's your parents' place. They might have had something to say about you taking in lodgers.'

'Probably, especially as neither of us are currently employed,' he smirked. 'But at least you would have read my story by now. You still haven't read it, have you?'

'No,' I lied. 'Sorry, I've been so busy.'

'Charming,' he said, as he plonked the fedora back on his head, taking a sip. 'Oh, nice,' he said, licking his lips and peering at his glass. 'Very Ingleford at Christmas. Now all we need's some shortbread and the onset of early menopause. Right, while we're both drunk, so I'll get an honest opinion, you're reading my work. C'mon, let's get cracking.'

'We can't. Dad's computer's in the back room. We'll wake everyone up, and it's,' I gave a quick glance at my watch, 'nearly one o'clock. I'm shattered.'

'Are you kidding me?' Luke asked, sipping his drink, piercing me with a look. 'I've driven to your parents' place, delivering your mum's vase in time for Christmas. I've put up with Barry Hogg; bought you drinks; helped carry Lara to bed; and now it's technically Christmas Eve morning, and you can't even be bothered giving me an *opinion?*'

'Oh, give me your phone then. I'll look on your mobile,' I said, reaching out a hand.

'You can't read it on my mobile. I cracked the screen, peeing while texting.'

'*Nice.* Well, if you're going to be such a child, I'll have to go upstairs and get Lara's laptop thing, which will probably wake her up,' I said, hoping he'd agree it wasn't worth it.

'Off you pop then. It'll take two seconds, unlike my 45-minute drive and overnight stay in Ingleford, just to make you happy…'

I reached halfway upstairs, before I noticed light beneath my parents' door.

'Oh David! Be my king! Be my king!'

'That's right. I'm your king, Marian…'

No. Please. Don't let my parents be having sex.

'King … of your… universe…'

I froze, not knowing what to do, other than pulling my ears from my head and stamping on them, before I remembered how to walk, and did my best to ignore the medieval-themed love-making across the landing. I made my way past the creak of Lara's door, grabbing the computer while she snored beneath the covers.

Mission accomplished, I headed back into the lounge, trying not to think about the weird fancy dress sex my parents were having, and hoping Luke hadn't heard it.

'What is with that hat?' I asked him, shoving the laptop into his hand before climbing onto the couch, tucking my feet beneath me for warmth, because Dad was adamant the central heating was switched off every night at 10 p.m. 'There's not enough room in this place for you *and* that stupid thing.'

He took it back off with a huff, running his hands through his hair before he switched on the laptop.

'It's what my detective wears. Gets me in the mood.'

'And gives you an excuse to tell everyone you're a writer…'

'Hey, if that's what it takes to get me laid these days. I hate being single at Christmas…'

'I know I'm not allowed to say it, but I do miss George so much,' I sighed, pulling a cushion behind me. 'I sat there tonight, staring at Barry, and it hit me: I had the perfect man.'

'He wasn't that great.'

'I thought you liked George?'

'I liked the idea of him,' he said. 'What you told me about him.'

'What I *told you* about him? I wasn't making it up.'

'When I met him, he seemed, a bit, I don't know, shifty…'

'Shifty? You met him, for like, what, three minutes?'

'Exactly. He didn't want to meet your friends. Hid you away from his kids…'

'Bloody hell, Luke. Don't hold back,' I said, taking a drink.

'You told me yourself, he acted as if he was still married to the ex-wife.'

'I was upset when I said that.'

'Well, maybe you were right…'

'*What?* You're admitting I might be right about something as random as that?'

'I'm just saying, it was all a bit odd, that's all.'

'You know something, don't you?'

His silence was enough to confirm my suspicions.

'Luke? You know something. *You do*,' I said, swinging my legs off the couch.

'No. It's nothing. I don't.'

'What's nothing?' I put my glass down next to a particularly horrific ornamental swan. 'You can't dangle something like that in front of me, not if,' I said, reaching over and grabbing his discarded fedora, 'you ever want to wear the hat again.'

'Don't!'

'Speak then…'

'Oh, for God's sake,' he sighed. 'Right, you know how you always bump into your ex when you least expect it? Well, you're off the hook. I bumped into George for you.'

'When?'

I was sober in seconds. All I could think of was *My George*. It's not fair that Luke should see my George while I was slowly forgetting the minor details of his face, trying to piece together my favourite times with him into memories.

'I'd been researching how writers work, what inspires them, and, who'd have guessed it, it all boils down to drink and drugs. I couldn't get hold of any opium or absinthe, like the greats, so it's a lowly mojito for me.'

'Okay, so let's skip to the part when you see George?'

'I was in the spirit aisle, wondering what my Spanish detective would fancy, when this guy comes round the corner...'

'George?'

Luke nodded.

'Flowers. Chocolates. And I'm thinking, Date Night. He wheels over to the champers. The good stuff. And then I notice, it's him.'

I was transfixed, trying to read Luke's expression.

'I got to the checkout. No sign of him. Thought he must still be in the store. Next thing, he's walking past, into the car park, right in front of me.'

I took a drink, but could barely swallow.

'This next bit's, well, it's probably going to sound a bit... I don't know —'

'Luke!'

'I followed him.'

'You did *what?*'

'It was in the heat of the moment,' he explained. 'This Spanish detective thing. This character, I swear, he's taken over my life.'

'But you *followed him?*'

'It was research! I was in character, and if you're going to make me feel bad for basically acting on your behalf, I'm not saying another word about it,' he said, snatching back his hat.

We both sat, sulking for a few seconds, before I caved in.

'I'm sorry,' I said, steadying myself against the missile I could feel heading straight to my heart at any second. 'I won't make you feel bad.'

'Okay.'

'So?'

'So, I'm going to say this very quickly: She was there. The ex-wife.'

My heart plummeted to somewhere beneath the Earth's core.

'So?'

'So, they're together.'

'How do you know?'

'Great hair. Size eight. Huge handbag?' he said, reeling off the checklist I'd pieced together from the odd photographs I'd seen.

'Well, yes, that sounds like her, but —'

'She put her arms around his neck. He handed over the flowers. Group hug with the kids.'

'Are you sure?'

'Scout's honour,' he said, giving a salute. 'So, please, move on, forget him.'

'You weren't in the Scouts,' I muttered, trying to digest the whole thing, when I suddenly felt sick to the stomach.

'Once slept with a girl who was wearing a Brownies t-shirt, so technically,' he paused for mental arithmetic, 'I was in them for about, oh, seven minutes...'

'You're a pig. I'm going to bed.'

'*What?* You haven't even finished your drink yet!'

'I've had enough to drink already.'

'Are you angry with me about George?'

'No Luke. I'm thrilled.'

'Oh, come on. Don't do that. You asked. What was I supposed to do?'

'Not tell me?' I replied, standing up and fixing the cushions back on alert, ready for Mum's early morning sofa inspection.

'What? And sit here knowing you're making yourself feel bad, thinking about him, when he's basically a bastard?'

'Here's a throw,' I said, passing him Mum's TV blanket. 'Do you need pillows?'

'I can't believe you're actually going to bed,' he said, pulling off his shoes. 'You still haven't looked at *The Spanish Detective* and I'm not even tired.'

'Well, I am. I'm tired of you being completely insensitive. I'm tired of pretending every stupid thing you do is fine, while you seem to take great delight pointing out every mistake I make. And, while you're actually listening for once,' I got into my stride as Luke looked on in astonishment, 'here's something else for you to think about: maybe it's time you listened to your Dad and did the one thing you're actually good at, which is cooking. Rather than wasting your time pretending to be a writer. *The Spanish Detective* has to be the worst thing I've ever wasted my time reading. *That's right.* I read it, but I didn't know how the hell I could lie about it to your face, so unless you meant for it to be a comedy, don't put it out there.'

I stormed out into the hallway, tears filling my eyes, sadness building inside my chest, as the final facts hit me: the family photograph George said was still on the fireplace to make things easier for the children; the expensive lotions inside the bathroom cabinet, never removed; the convenient way he said she insisted on moving back to her mother, with two kids. Nothing permanent in terms of moving on. As someone currently living with her parents, there's no way anyone in their right mind would choose that option.

Not unless you were on some sort of weird break you both knew was fixable, or your husband was a disgusting liar, basically having an affair in your bed while you worked on things. My mind raced with increasingly sinister possibilities. How often was I actually at George's place? If I opened that second wardrobe, would it even be empty?

The only person who had the answers to my questions was George, which meant I'd probably never know the truth, not unless I demanded he tell me, but even then, how could I trust a single word he said? I mean, were they even divorced? Should I have asked him to produce legal paperwork over our first candle-lit dinner-for-two?

The only thing I knew for sure was they were back together. Or incredibly friendly.

My mental rambling was driving me insane, and to make things worse, Luke knew. Luke knew before I did, which made the whole thing even more humiliating, if that were possible. And now I felt terrible about the things I'd said to him, but if he could be so blunt, at least I didn't have to pretend to like *The Spanish Detective*.

I lay on top of the bed covers, thankful that Sir Lancelot and 'Princess' Marian had finally left Camelot, as I stared out into the darkness.

Chapter 12

Lara

My eyes opened as if flicked by a switch. I'd dreamt of Tom, back at Wiltshire Hall, riding horses, for miles and miles. Past, present, and future, mapped out before me, but everything seemed so different the next day.

In my case, a hell of a lot worse.

I'd slept on top of the covers, only my boots removed, which meant it obviously wasn't Barry Hogg who put me to bed, so I assumed it was my sister.

Good old sensible Jennifer, who had spent most of the previous night monitoring drinks and putting out cigarettes. The duvet was snaked around my thighs as I reached for my mobile. The direct-line to my ever-shrinking universe. I peered over the side of the bed, then felt it in the back-pocket of my jeans. Five missed calls from Silvano. One text: *Need to speak to you, Baby. Plans to finalise. Mom anxious. Me clueless without you. Call me. I love you. S x*

It was too much. *Reality overload.* My skull washed over with a heat, speeding through my body, lodging in my throat with a bullet of nausea. I visualized the walk to the bathroom. Saw it happen, convincing myself to do it, because at that moment, I didn't think I could make it. Until, finally, I opened the door.

'Are you okay?'

Jennifer. I ignored her, mostly because I wasn't in the mood, but mainly because I didn't dislike her enough to throw up all over her bare feet.

I'd managed to lock the door, forever an expert at bathroom privacy. Show me a bulimic who doesn't know how to work a bathroom, and I'll show you an amateur. It starts with running taps and ends somewhere between unclogging plugs and outstanding levels of toilet cleaning.

Jaw locked. Stomach cramping, surging, against me.

The coolness of the bathroom floor.

Jennifer knocking.

I closed my eyes.

When we were little, I'd listen to Mum's old albums with Jen. Barbra Streisand was my favourite. I'd twirl around wearing a white cotton tablecloth that was for special occasions, pretending I was wearing a beautiful wedding dress.

Jennifer would be Barbra herself, singing along, because she knew every single word. I'd pretend I was the girl in the video who Barbra was serenading.

Jennifer was delicate and sweet. She had tiny hands and feet, and dark, shiny hair that always looked perfect. My real-life dolly. Everybody loved her.

Mum sat watching Jennifer singing, smiling and clapping, mouthing along, anticipating every word, and sometimes they'd dance together. Mum called Jennifer 'Little Songbird', but I'd taken the tablecloth from the dresser drawer, and that was naughty, and now it would need to be washed and pressed.

I didn't care when I got told off. Jen would take my hand, and lead me away to play another really good game she'd thought of. I wanted to be someone else, and in my head, in the game of 'Pretend' Jen and I were so fond of, I was the sweetest one, the loveable one.

'Lara? Are you okay?'

I rolled onto my back as Jennifer knocked again.

I needed to get out of last night's clothes. Needed cold water like a baptism. I started with my jeans, pulling them over my bum, peeling each leg off with my feet. I felt better already, getting out of the layers, the coolness of the tiles like a tonic.

I leaned against the bath for a few minutes, took a breath out, switched on the shower. Showers held lots of strange memories for me, like aquatic time machines. I stepped in, remembering my first shoot, over in Montauk.

I'd been doing kids' magazines back home, but then we, that's Gerry, my former agent and me, took my book across to New York, and I met Tissy Lance, the best booker in the business.

She sat on top of her desk and lifted my hair, tilted my head back, and she just loved me.

'Lara,' she said.

'No,' I corrected her, looking across to Gerry for permission, worried that maybe I shouldn't speak directly to Tissy, like he'd said. 'It's *Laura*.'

'Not any more, sweet,' she said, swinging off the desk and back to the heavy, leather chair behind it. '*Lara's* younger, fresher. Like you,' she smiled. 'Stand over there,' she pointed to the opposite end of the room. 'Let's take a look at you.'

The hardest thing at first was learning to walk, to actually move, when you're aware that they're looking. Those eyes on you can feel as intrusive as fingers, pinching and pulling you into shape.

'Shoulders back, Lara,' Tissy instructed from beneath a steadfast gaze. 'She's a little heavy on the hip, Gerry.'

'You think, Tis? She looks tip-top to me,' he grinned.

She came over and undid my jeans, pulling them down to mid-thigh in one, quick, motion. 'Here,' she said, her fingers pincering a centimetre of spare flesh. 'Right here, needs work.'

I'd felt my eyes fizz with tears, ashamed that Tissy had found fault with me.

'Lara? Sweetheart?' She met my eye with a smile. 'They say you can't improve perfection? Well, you know, it's my job to do that. If I didn't, I wouldn't be helping you to do yours.'

Three weeks later, I was on a beach shoot for *Chic!* magazine, modelling Galloway's spring/summer collection. I'd dropped five pounds as Tissy instructed, but all I thought about was food. I literally dreamt about calories, I was completely distracted by anyone eating, even when Gerry needed me to pay attention. It was everywhere, but I had to be better than that if I wanted to make it. *Discipline.* That was the difference between me and every other girl who wanted to make it, he said.

It's not like it was anything new. I was just used to indulging first, rejecting later. The first time, I was so greedy, I almost ate a whole chocolate cake that Mum had made. I was devastated by the weight of it in my gut. I had to get it out. And, as soon as I was sick, I felt I'd apologised. The raw heat at the back of my throat, the stinging in my eyes, were worth it, to make me feel entirely empty again.

From then on, it was a constant battle between not eating the food in the first place, or needing to get it out of my body as soon as I could. My parents never suspected anything, not even when I really needed them to, and when I'd practically thrown up my dinner in front of my mother, she was furious, not sympathetic. All my life I'd been alone, had responsibilities, whether it was at home, or living up to Gerry and Tissy's demands. I used to wonder if any of them ever stopped to think what I might have wanted, but I quickly realized, I was just some ornament to be admired and passed around until people got bored looking.

After I left home, I was hot property for a long time. I couldn't keep up with the amount of bookings I was taking. I never thought I was anything special. Not really. But I knew I had the right look at the right time. I could just as easily have come along five years later and no one would have taken a chance on me. It was all about timing. That's what Gerry said. Life was about timing. Like Jennifer putting me forward for the competition. Any other time, I'd have told her to butt out, torn the page up, and slammed the door in her face, but on that day, I remember thinking it could be the way to escape; part of a bigger plan. It made sense, even if I didn't know what that plan was yet, but I think my life would have gotten screwed up whichever way I'd gone.

I cried myself to sleep most nights when I first left home, it felt as if my family occupied another planet, far, far away, in the past. I wished I could go back to the dinner table, act normal this time, share cheese crackers with Mum and Jen, hear Dad advocating the importance of eight hours sleep.

I was so tired. I went from one job to the next, surrounded by adults who told me to lose weight, loosen up, take one of these and you'll feel great again, sweetheart. My parents thought those people were caring for me. Those people made me look pretty, took nice pictures, so their daughter must be well taken care of.

I was such a lucky girl, Mum told me. This was the most important opportunity of my life, Dad said. They thought I was happy, so I told them I was.

'Jump! Arms in the air!'

My first big shoot. Patrick directing me, a very important photographer, a big name, even now.

'And smile, playful, run for your life!'

Ninety-six pounds and terrified I looked fat in my bikini. Convinced the other girls' stomachs were more hollow than mine, breasts higher, legs longer.

I ran and jumped just like Patrick said, as if my life depended on it, aware that if this went well, my agency would be pleased, and the work would get even higher profile.

Catering everywhere, but I couldn't stop to eat with the other girls watching, so I went back to the house, Patrick's home for the summer, and showered off the beach as the stylist instructed.

He offered me gum as he walked into the bathroom.

'The shoot today, it is very good. I am very happy, and you should be also.'

I nodded, frozen behind the screen, quickly reaching for the towel.

Patrick handed it to me. I was barely in my bra, getting dressed as fast as I could. He sat against the basin, this 40-something man who I was to obey, please, listen to at all costs.

'You have … movement. The energy for my pictures.'

'Thank you, Mr. Dumont.'

'No, Mr. Dumont. Patrick, for you. You smoke?'

He offered me the open pack. I shook my head.

He frowned, smiled, as I pulled on my jeans.

'Take off your bra.'

'Sorry?'

'This.'

He unhooked my bra as if we were still on the shoot. The stylist's hands yanking, clipping, loosening, tightening. I was a passing thought, an idle glimpse, behind the design. I still find it beautiful though, the amount of attention paid to each element, so many people determined to make each shot count.

I didn't know what to do next.

I looked at him, then at the floor.

It was his job to look, but then it became something else. The smell of the ocean, pressed against my face. His fingers inside me. I felt sick, scared, my body shut down, over there, in some corner, thinking of back home, thinking of sleeping in my bedroom back in England.

It hurt, but I wouldn't let myself feel it.

'What the fuck?' He smiled. 'The first time?'

He stood, panting, rinsing under the tap.

I lay still as could be as he grabbed his camera, took a final picture.

My face, sand-smeared tears, lips swollen, eyes passive, made the front cover that month.

And Mum said I looked beautiful.

Chapter 13

Jennifer

Lara appeared on the landing, looking half-drowned, thankfully after I managed to put her laptop back where I found it.

'What time is it?' she yawned, her eyes dark and hollow.

'Eight twenty-three.'

She pushed past me, adjusting her bath towel.

'Do you have to be so bloody precise? Half-past would have done,' she huffed, stomping into her room, pulling on jogging bottoms.

'My watch reads eight twenty-three. I'll contact the manufacturers,' I said. 'Tell them my sister wants them to round time up a little. It's *too precise*, for her.'

'Okay, okay,' she said, pulling down her t-shirt and getting onto the bed. 'Oh, man, I need to lie down...'

'I'm not surprised after the way you behaved last night. You do know Barry will blab it all to Mum?'

'Give it a rest. You sound about sixteen,' she mumbled.

'At least I don't *act* like a teenager...'

'Can we please do this later?' She dragged the pillows around her head.

'I was having a quick drink, and you turned it into the school leavers' ball. Why do you constantly need to be the centre of attention?'

'I feel like death,' she murmured. 'I can't deal with you right now.'

'I don't exactly feel perky myself,' I said, as Mum walked in, head full of rollers. I would have expected 'Princess Marian' to appear in a crown, but maybe that was reserved for bedtime.

'What's going on?'

'Your daughter's hungover and she ruined everyone's night. *As usual.*'

'Lara? Are you awake, love?'

'Oh, that's great. Call her love. Different story if it was me lying there on Christmas Eve.'

'Where's Luke?' Mum blustered. 'Have you even offered him a cup of tea? I'll worry about your sister,' she said. 'Go and look after your guest.'

'He's gone.'

'What do you mean, gone? This early?'

I'd heard someone in the bathroom just after six and guessed it was Luke, but I didn't want to see him.

It wasn't his fault, I knew. It would be bad enough finding out George was still with *her* myself. I just needed time to work out how I felt before I faced Luke again. I wasn't ready to pretend I was over George yet, and Luke had no time for me when I felt down like this.

'He had things to do, he said. Shopping and stuff.'

'He told me he was looking forward to breakfast,' Mum interrupted. 'He loved our pink tree. I've defrosted enough sausage to fill Hogg's Butchers. Anyway, how did it go with Barry?'

'It didn't. It never will, Mum,' I said, too tired to be polite about my mother's misguided attempts at playing Cupid. 'I wouldn't date Barry Hogg if I lost my mind, sight, hearing, *and knickers*, in a freak accident.'

'Alright, young lady. There's no need to use that language.'

'I didn't use *language*.'

'Cheek. Sarcasm. Smart mouth, whatever you call it.'

'Urgh,' Lara groaned, turning over on top of her covers. 'If I'm going to die, do I have to do it listening to this?'

'Marian?' Dad shouted from the bedroom. I was glad he'd dropped the 'Princess' bit.

'Oh, don't be so ridiculous, Lara. It's Christmas Eve,' she turned, ushering past me. 'Whatever is the matter, David?'

After finding out Dad had well and truly put his back out (however could that have happened, I *didn't* wonder, despite Mum blaming it on him moving my stuff from the hallway), Mum reacted to Lara's hangover the only way she knew how, by using innocent housewife artillery, commonly known as the vacuum cleaner, to drive pain into the very core of her daughter's being.

The vrooming went on until Lara emerged, Mum thinking she was victorious in the battle to save Christmas Eve, until we heard the car, and realized Lara had gone.

As usual, it was Dad who Mum tried to prise answers from, but as usual he was the last to know. Especially as he was confined to bed, unable to put a foot on the floor without making the kind of noise you might expect to hear in the wilderness. No one asked me anything, but I could guess there would be no driving around in tears until she ran out of petrol.

There'd be a guy. *Somewhere.* There always was.

'There goes Christmas,' Mum huffed, setting the table with her best cutlery and crystal glasses, the way she always did on Christmas Eve. 'Your sister's left home, and your father's bedridden. All we need now is for the bird to fly off, the roof to cave in, and a fire to break out.'

'It'll be fine, Mum.'

'Well, fine's not good enough. Not for our first family Christmas in years.'

I'd offered to help, but Mum launched into martyr mode, and so, keen to stop myself from calling George and demanding answers, I finally finished Lara's gift, before I popped my head around my parents' bedroom door, worried Dad might be reading *Awakenings* in a silk robe or women's underwear or something.

'Hey Dad. You okay?'

He was propped up on the bed, wearing regular, Dad-issue clothes, watching some kind of furniture restoration show.

'Been better,' he said, unable to turn his neck to look at me, 'but I'll live.'

I remembered how, as a kid, I'd always seek out his company whenever I was at a loose end at home.

'Your mum okay down there?'

'Yeah, she's fine, wrapping sausages in bacon, I think.'

'Any sign of your sister?'

I noticed an edge to his voice I rarely heard. Dad hardly ever got angry. He once told me my granddad, who I never met, had a rotten temper, and Dad had decided never to inherit the same short fuse.

'Nope. I sent her a text. No reply.'

'That's about right,' he said. 'We all have to suffer when Laura's not happy.'

It was reassuring to know how he noticed those things too. It was usually Mum letting loose on the family dynamic, while Dad remained in the background.

'Anyway, what's my girl up to?' he smiled, sitting up a little higher, pillow propped between his shoulders. 'Any plans for the afternoon?'

'Thought I might go for a walk. Need a few things from the shops.'

I still needed something for Dad. The only thing Mum suggested was yet another scarf and glove combo.

'A walk, eh? Something on your mind?'

I loved the way he knew whenever I was secretly feeling sad.

'Sort of. Not really,' I shrugged, debating how much my father really needed to know about my demolished love life. 'Just a bit fed up … with men.'

'Men? Or one man in particular?'

'One man in particular,' I smiled.

'If he's upset my daughter, he's not worth getting upset about.'

'I wish it were that easy, Dad.'

'Of course it is,' he said, turning awkwardly. 'Do you remember Bob-Bob?'

Bob-Bob was a dog that Dad had found, or as Dad had it, Bob-Bob found him, buying a newspaper one evening. Dad was buying the paper, not the dog.

Dad placed a card in the newsagents' window, but he stayed with us for about two weeks, with no sign of his owner. I loved that dog, and for a while, he loved me too. Every night, no matter how much Mum cajoled him into sleeping in the kitchen, he found his way back to my room. Bob-Bob had chosen me as his favourite, and I'd felt so special, knowing he'd given me his canine heart.

As usual, one night, he padded into my bedroom, but instead of making himself cosy, he snuffled about, until the distraction got so much, I sat up to see what he was doing. Bob-Bob was immersed in my cuddly toys, nose-first, ripping the head off my bunny nightdress case.

I begged him to stop killing bunny, but before Mum and Dad came running, Bob-Bob dropped down on his haunches, bared his long, white teeth, and growled so ferociously, I sobbed in fright, and never wanted to see him again.

'I remember you drove him to the police station,' I smiled.

'I did,' he said, sternly, all these years later. 'Anyone who upsets my daughter is no better than a criminal, as far as I'm concerned.'

'I don't think the local constabulary would agree with you, Dad.'

'The moral of the story is,' he said, one hand on the remote. 'Don't let anyone steal your heart. Hand it over when they've earned it. Because,' he said, 'I'm the first man who ever loved you, so I know better than most, making you happy should feel like the best thing in the world.'

George *had* stolen my heart, Dad was right, I thought, snuggling up on my old bed after I'd ventured out into Ingleford village. So, rather than calling and demanding answers, which I was still tempted to do, I distracted myself, scrolling through George's old texts; the especially nice ones I'd kept to show our grandchildren, or at least the man in the mobile repair shop.

I'd promised Luke I wouldn't text George, I know, but that was before Luke snooped on my ex and hit me over the head with every branch on the bastard tree. So, propelled by righteousness, and after arguing with myself over the best thing to do, other than carry on crying and wondering, I called George (also known as lying, cheating, bastard George, which is what he should have been under on my speed dial). My heart thundered with every bleep of the line. I cleared my throat, hoping not to let the shaking in my body sound in my voice.

'Jennifer?'

'Is that so surprising?'

'Well, it is a bit, yes. I didn't know whether to call you, or not.'

'Difficult getting the chance, is it?'

'Yes, with Christmas, and everything,' he said, sounding worried, which was exactly how I wanted him to sound. 'Are you alright?'

'How long have you been back with your wife?'

'I'm not back with my wife,' he said, and actually had the nerve to sigh. 'Why would you say that?'

Because you probably never left her in the first place, I thought. Or she's been in the background the whole time, waiting until he wrapped things up with me. He was lying by omission. The worst kind of lying.

'Did you ever break up with her in the first place?'

'What are you talking about? Of course I did. I'm divorced, you know that.'

'I know you're still seeing her, George. Are you with her now?'

'No, Jennifer, I'm not. Charlie — sorry, give me a minute.'

I heard him ask Charlie to put something down. Heard Charlie's protests, then Susanna's laughter.

'Jen?'

'Still here,' I said, keeping my voice strong, neutral.

'Of course I still see her. We have two kids.'

'Then, why do you … why do you have to put your arms around her?'

'What?'

'It's over with me, you got what you wanted, so can't you tell the truth? Have we been having an affair? I won't tell her, I promise,' I said, wondering if that was exactly what I should do, 'but I need to know. If you ever cared for me at all, please, I'm trying to be calm, but you have to tell me!'

'Look, Jennifer, I'm with the kids right now. It's Christmas Eve.'

And lying, cheating, George, put the phone down on *me*.

Chapter 14

Lara

Christmas carols had been blazing since Mum had woken up. While she and Dad took over the kitchen, Jen and I invaded the bathroom, getting ready until Mum summoned us downstairs, in time for *Good King Wenceslas* to provide the soundtrack to the exchanging of gifts, which always took place after we shared the Christmas morning tradition of pâté and bucks fizz. Let the performance begin…

Usually, the family Christmas Day was at least comforting and familiar, but knowing I had to tell them about the wedding, the whole thing felt horribly staged. We were all trapped in some cheesy editorial shoot for *Housewife Monthly*.

'Are you wearing the same dress?' Mum stood up, giving a clap.

Silvano had surprised me with a pale grey, chiffon mini dress, adorned with pearls around the cuffs and neckline.

'I doubt it, Mum,' Jen said, sharing a conspiratorial eye-roll with me.

'Well, good taste must run in the family,' Mum grinned. 'You look like sisters all over again.'

Mum was still fixated on Jennifer and me resembling each other in even the smallest of ways. I couldn't help but wonder who she would have chosen as the prototype daughter?

'Don't start with all the sister stuff, Mum,' Jen smiled. 'Lara grabbed all the best genes. Let's face it, I got what was left from the bargain basement of your DNA.'

'Do you mind?' Dad said, shifting in his seat, trying to get comfortable. 'There's no bargain basement in my genes. Both of my daughters are beautiful,' he added, smiling warmly at Jennifer.

Mum pulled her pout-face, happily playing along in good festive humour, especially since Dad had made it downstairs, spending the night on the bedroom floor, hoping to straighten out his back in time for the morning.

'You know, Lara, I wasn't sure about you having all your hair chopped off like that when you first arrived,' Mum said, having another sip of Bucks Fizz, which seemed to have already taken effect, 'but I really like it now.'

'Hmm,' Jen said, stroking her fingers through her shoulder-length locks, 'I was thinking of having something similar done myself.'

'Oh Jen,' Mum tutted, 'it wouldn't suit you that short. You'd look like a funny little man, like you did at school.'

'Merry Christmas!' Jennifer announced, presumably to change the subject. She disappeared into the dining room, returned with an oversized gift bag. 'Here come the presents, folks!'

As usual, she jumped the queue. I was relieved, for once.

'Okay, Mum.' She handed over the first package. 'And, Dad, be careful. It's very delicate.' She kissed him on the cheek. He rubbed his thumb across her chin, the way I always remembered him doing when we were kids. 'And, last but not least, for you.' She handed me what was obviously a book. 'With lots of love.'

Wow. She was really trying to hit hard with the sentiment this year, I thought, deliberately stalling as Mum unveiled the ugliest vase I'd ever since in my life. It was Mum's taste exactly.

'Oh, it's…' Mum examined the object, 'it's … I think this is mine.'

'Well, yes,' Jen said, 'that was the idea...'

'No.' Mum exchanged a look with Dad. 'It's the one I thought you'd got rid of for me, David. Look,' she insisted, pointing to the base, 'it's got the same chip on the bottom, and everything.'

Dad patted his cardigan pocket, producing his glasses.

'Did you give this to Jennifer?'

'I bought it!' Jen insisted. 'Well, technically, Luke ordered it because I had nowhere for them to deliver it to.' Mum interrupted with a sympathetic sigh for her temporarily homeless, younger daughter. 'I thought it would go in the lounge, before you redecorated. You know, your blue theme.'

'Teal,' Mum corrected, searching Dad's face for answers.

'Where did you buy it, love?' Dad asked. 'I put it on eBay, weeks ago.'

'And Luke ordered it off eBay for me. Weeks ago.'

'Well, then,' Dad said, 'nice doing business with you.' He shook her hand. 'Made a decent profit too. Overcharged you for postage.'

'David! You didn't!' Mum chided, on the verge of appalled. 'You know she's not working.'

'I didn't know it was Jen, did I?'

'No wonder I thought you'd love it.'

'Well, I did, *I do*,' Mum said.

'Open yours, Dad.' Jennifer picked up the wrapping paper from Mum's feet. 'Sorry, Mum. I'll get you something else.'

'Don't worry, love.' Mum leant across, placing a kiss on her forehead. 'If it's found its way back home, it must like it here. I'll find another spot for it.'

It was hard even watching this stuff. They were reading from the same script. I finished my drink, helped myself to a top up, trying to ready myself for the moment when it would be my turn to watch them unwrap news of my wedding.

'Jen.' Dad was clearly touched as he placed a heart-shaped glass paperweight on his palm. 'Was this after our chat?'

Jennifer nodded.

'I'll guard it with my life, love,' he promised, blinking away emotion.

Jeez.

'Your turn!' Jen turned her attention to me.

'Oh, yes!' Mum said, 'it's a special one. Your sister's put a lot of effort into this, Lara.'

I couldn't think of anything I'd mentioned on my reading list, especially as I didn't have one. I hadn't found anything I liked since *The Great Gatsby* years ago at school. I unwrapped the package: *Our Story: Sisters.*

'Is this what you've been hiding from me?' I wasn't sure how I felt about seeing page after page of our childhood, pasted together from Jennifer's rosy perspective. 'Thank you, it's lovely.' I forced a smile. Seeing the look of confusion on Jennifer's face, I quickly gave her a hug.

'Isn't it great, Lara?' Mum said, trying to usher the reaction she was expecting. 'Look.' She took the book and turned to the middle. 'Your first modelling shots! I kept them all.'

'It's amazing.' I made sure my smile met my eyes. 'I love it, really,' I assured them. 'And … I have gifts for you, too!'

At that moment, I'd have done anything to leave the room. The atmosphere was like a sweet, heavy perfume. I didn't quite know how they expected me to react. All I knew was I was expected to make Jen feel great about her gift. It had nothing to do with me. Expectations. All the unspoken expectations, as usual.

'So, anyway, here we go.' I handed them each an envelope.

Mum and Dad locked glances. Jennifer threw a concerned look my way.

'Is it more spa vouchers?' Mum could barely contain her apprehension.

'Open up and find out!'

Mum was the first to find her ticket.

'Is this real?'

I nodded, sipping from my glass, eyes darting to my father, who was now registering his ticket. After a few seconds, I felt compelled to break the silence.

'So, we're all going to New York — for my wedding!'

I gazed around the room. Blank faces. Until Dad piped up: 'This is very sudden, sweetheart.'

'Well, not really. We're getting married on January 5th. We both want you to be there. I mean, it's our wedding day, so of course we do!'

Mum gave a snigger of disbelief.

'You weren't so concerned about us being at the last one.'

'Marian,' Dad tried to rein her in for a change.

'Mum, I know what you're thinking. I know it's my third marriage. I'm well aware of that, but it's different this time. Can't you please be happy for me?'

'That's what you said the last time,' Mum rattled on. 'Why can't you wait twelve months? Make sure this is what you really want?'

'It is what I want!'

'Well, it would have been nice to *meet* the groom before the wedding. Call me old fashioned, but you can't give out wedding invitations as Christmas presents, and expect us to hop on a plane in a matter of days.'

'Of course not! How stupid of me to think you'd be excited...'

'Oh come on, Lara. It is a bit of a shock,' Dad said, still gazing at his plane ticket like it was a shuttle pass to Mars.

'No, it's a *surprise*. There's supposed to be a difference.'

'I'm sure my passport's expired,' Mum mumbled.

'Is that why you're looking at a ticket to New York like it's a final demand from the tax office?'

'I only said I'm not sure if my passport's run out,' Mum avoided my eye, clearly irritated. 'It's not my fault if it's expired. Anyway, we can't just lope off for a fortnight out of the blue. Your dad's not in any fit state to travel, not with his back playing up the way it is.'

'You always do this!' I heard myself shouting. Suddenly eighteen again. Anger powering my words. 'Why can't you ever be happy for me?'

'Because you cause us both nothing but worry,' Dad bellowed, getting to his feet. 'You disappeared off yesterday. Upsetting your mother. Upsetting the rest of us. And now, here we go again. It's not happening, Laura. It's Christmas Day. For once, you'll think of us. You'll put our feelings first.'

The room fell silent, until he clutched his back, grimacing.

Mum helped him back into his seat as I left the room.

'For goodness sake, Laura,' she shouted. 'You never fail, do you?'

As requested, I dropped the subject of my wedding so that my mother could fake her way through another Christmas Day. While sat at the table as she talked us through the bird-inside-a-bird-inside-a-bird, I realised that it wasn't me or even

Jennifer who was the demanding, attention-seeker in the family. It was our mother, who let nothing, not even my wedding, or the wellbeing of her family's collective colon, stand in the way of her moment of festive glory.

Later Jen stumbled into my bedroom, sitting on the edge of the bed with a sudden bout of hiccups, clutching a glass of wine. Neither of us spoke for a while. I'd had a couple of glasses myself, and by this point, it looked like Jen had enjoyed a few, too. I didn't blame her, especially as she had to stay in Ingleford long after the decorations had gone back up into the loft.

'They've ruined my wedding,' I said into my pillow.

'They have-ern't,' Jennifer slurred. 'Come on, you can't — hic — blame them. Mum needs two weeks' notice before — hic — the kettle boils.'

'It's my wedding day, Jen. I'll have no one there. Not Mum or Dad, or even you.'

'We never have you here, either,' she said, eyes half-mast, cheeks pink. 'You've got to see it from Mum and Dad's point of view. They've never met the guy. They didn't know about the wedding, and suddenly, it's grab your cases, in the middle of Chrishmish.'

'You always gang up on me. It's always the same.'

'What? You and Mum do nothing but bitch at me,' she said, taking another drink. 'How I look. What I'm wearing, what *disaster* I'm starring in. I mean, I already know — hic — I'm a mess. My life's just, pathetic! I know that,' she said, with a theatrical flourish. 'We *all* do. I don't need it in stereo from both of you.'

'You never ask me how I am,' I flopped onto my back. 'You've hardly even asked about Silvano. I mean, I'm engaged to him. What am I supposed to do? Keep trying to bring him up when you're clearly not interested? Everything's about *you*. Always has been. All I've heard is *poor Jennifer* since the minute I got here. What about poor Lara? Who gives a crap about me?'

'I do care about you, but you're never here,' she said, spilling wine down her hand as she gestured in frustration. 'Look at yesterday. We didn't know where you were, but we're used to it, because you never keep in touch…'

'I went back to Wiltshire Hall, if it's all that important. I needed to get out of here. I couldn't think straight,' I sniffed, 'and now my head's more tangled up than ever…'

'Oh, well, see? You just run away all the time. You just get married, turn up every few years. Disappear off again.'

'Thanks.'

'It'sh true,' she said, drying her hand on her tights. 'The most I see of you is on a box of hair dye or on some magazine in a shop somewhere. You never see me, and you don't seem too bothered when you do.'

'I am bothered!' I propped myself up against the headboard. I was going to reach for my wine, but I was too choked up, my head hurt, and Christmas Day was ruined. 'I've got no family!' I cried. 'No one. You don't even know me! I don't know you! And as soon as I come back to this house,' I grabbed the handful of toilet roll I'd cried into earlier, 'all it does is remind me how no one wants me here. My whole life, all I've ever tried to be, is more like you.'

'*Like me?*'

'Oh, you know. The good one. The nice sister. But instead, I'm always the problem. I'm always the pain in the arse.'

'No way.' Jennifer turned, shook her head a little too avidly. 'Look at me.' She swung her legs in the air for emphasis, tipping more wine over the side of her glass. 'I don't even have my own place. I'm back, just when Mum and Dad are into weird sex, and I don't even have a boyfriend. And I'm nearly thirty.'

'Weird sex?'

'And I'll probably never have sex again! And I can't even afford a vibrator. And I went on a date with Barry the Hoggster.'

'Oh, I flirted with him all night. That's worse.'

'Lara.' Jennifer leaned over and hugged me tight. 'We do want you here, I promise. I promise you, I do. You're my sister.'

'But,' I sobbed into her hair, 'you're like strangers. All of you.'

'No,' Jen reassured me. 'We're just pissed. We're all pissed. Mum's been on the fizz since first thing. She's slaughtered on the phone to Aunty Peggy. Dad's mixing brandy with painkillers, and I miss George so much. He's with his family right now, *his wife*. Or ex-wife. I don't know!' She shrugged, almost fell to one side before I caught her. 'I have no one exshept this empty glass. Empty. Like my heart. *The bastard.*'

'The bastard,' I nodded. 'Jen? Please come to my wedding. *Please?*'

'Laura … Lara.' She sat up and placed her empty glass next to mine. 'Here's a question. Do you remember real life? I haven't got a job. I know you don't understand, and you know about things I don't understand, like clothes and wrinkle injecshtions, but people,' she explained, talking to me as if I'd just escaped from the jungle, 'need jobs to *pay* for things. Things like food and electricity. I can't even afford to *daydream* about going to New York. I don't have a home. I'm living with our parents. I don't think I can *pencil in* a glamorous holiday.'

'I *do* know about real life! I haven't got a job, either. I'm old. Too old to model,' I said, blowing my nose. 'No one knows who I am any more. I'm not a name. I'm past it,' I managed a smile, dabbing tears from my eyes. 'I didn't realize it wasn't going to be to earn the big bucks forever. I was stupid. And now, I've got nothing. I can't do anything. All I ever did was stand in front of a camera.'

'Well, at least you're not poor. Or ugly.'

'Jen, I've hardly got a dime to my name. The divorce, Travis, cleared my savings,' I shrugged. 'I haven't even got an agent because I was too stuck up to take the one job I did have.'

'So,' Jen asked, eyes-wide and childlike. 'What are you going to do?'

'Get married. See what happens…'

It was the first time I realized Silvano had been the perfect distraction, but he wasn't the solution, not to anything.

'Jennifer?' I grabbed her hand. 'I need you to come to the wedding. *Really*. I can't do this alone. Your ticket's paid for. You have a place to stay. Please, promise me you'll come? If I can't have my parents there, I at least need a bridesmaid.'

PART TWO

Chapter 15

Jennifer

We arrived in New York on December 28th. I was sitting in the back of Silvano's big American car, while he and my sister caught up in the front.

I tried to keep the smile off my face, listening to the accents and excitable squeals of the radio, while my brain was racing with the fact that, only a few hours ago, I was in Ingleford, where even sheep looked bored, and now, here I was, in *New York, New York*!

I'd stared out of the window for most of the flight, open-mouthed at the sight of Boston, until we finally swooped down at JFK.

Once we had collected our bags and found the exit, Lara threw her arms around some old guy's neck.

I didn't put two and two together straight away.

'Jen.' She swung around. 'This is Silvano.' She hugged him tighter. 'My fiancé.'

That was Silvano?

'Silvano,' I managed, as he walked towards me with a warm smile.

'Jennifer.' He took my hand and covered it with his own. 'It is wonderful to meet Lara's family. Really wonderful.'

This had to be the first time I'd actually liked any of her husbands. He was charming and friendly, just like my sister had promised, with his gentle features, and 'New York City in Fall' wardrobe. But if he was straight, Lara was a virgin bride.

He wasn't the type of gentleman I'd have expected my sister to fall for. Not after Patrick, her French first husband. He only understood English when he chose to, usually after Dad asked what he was drinking, and openly groped Lara at my birthday party. Then there was Travis, the Texan cowboy-type.

'Let's get you settled in. I've set a room aside for you, Jennifer. We can't wait to have you.'

'Oh, Silv,' Lara interrupted, gazing at him adoringly, 'I already told Jen we'd go back to my place tonight.'

'Oh, right,' he frowned. 'I thought we decided you'd both be staying at the hotel? You're going to be living there soon, remember?'

'I know, but Jen really wants to see my apartment, don't you, Jen?'

I hadn't a clue what she was talking about, but I guessed she had her reasons.

'Yeah, that's right. I've never seen it. Got to see my sister's old place before she moves out and gets married!'

'Whatever you want, sweetpea,' he told her. 'But I promised my mother you'd be over to discuss the wedding straightaway. You know how she is. She's been working so hard. I don't think she can wait to have you as excited about the whole thing as she is,' he smiled.

'Oh,' Lara said, with what I could see was more of a grimace than a smile, 'that's so sweet of her. I can't wait to hear her plans.'

That was odd. Her future mother-in-law seemed pretty keen. The more Silvano told us about the arrangements his mother had been making, the more it sounded like an arranged marriage. No wonder my sister wanted me here. I was waiting for Silvano to offer me two camels for her hand.

'C'mon, girls, let's get on track,' he said, producing car keys. 'I'm having my final suit fitting this afternoon. And, don't forget,' he said, taking Lara's hand luggage, before grabbing mine. 'Your dress fitting's tomorrow at 1 p.m.'

'Ah!' Lara grinned, grasping my arm. 'And yours! Wait til you see your dress. It's not gross, I promise.'

'Well, not gross will have to do, I suppose.'

Chapter 16

Lara

I hadn't expected to be faced with Dolores quite so soon after landing, but thankfully, as if sensing my need to knock back a drink before I braced myself for another of her brutal assaults on my will to live, Henrik had arrived, insisting on mixing us cocktails.

'I hope you don't mind,' he greeted Jennifer, 'but I've been working with Mrs. Arazzi and Silvano on this recipe. It's the wedding cocktail.'

'Champagne-based, of course,' Silvano winked at me, 'and, I hope you'll both agree, completely delicious.'

'Wow,' Jen grinned. 'I could get used to this.'

Dolores arrived, instantly lowering the temperature, draped in her uniform maxi and flowing pashmina ensemble, her silver-spun hair wound in her trademark chignon.

Standing in her private dining room, paperwork laid on a grand mahogany table, she talked me through the seating plans, menus, and anything else any normal bride would have been left in peace to organise for herself.

I was glad to have Jennifer beside me, but my stomach still chilled with concern as Silvano took his leave.

'Sisters? I can barely believe it,' Dolores remarked, slowly, *painfully*, eyeing my sister from head-to-foot from behind her horn-rimmed spectacles.

'I take it *you're* not a model, so what is it you do, Jennifer?'

'Me?' Jen asked.

I watched as Dolores' interest visibly piqued as my sister gave a slight flicker of discomfort. Like a well-practiced assassin, she had sunk her psychological fangs straight into the jugular of Jennifer's self-esteem.

'Jennifer's in publishing,' I gushed. 'We're so proud of her.'

My sister looked at me as if I'd just eaten the last soft-centre in the box.

'How fascinating,' Dolores remarked, feigning interest. 'So, at least one of you *works* for a living.'

If her words could have physically hurt me, I thought, I'd be in need of medical assistance, by now.

'Anyway, as you can see, we've got everything under control,' she concluded, closing the notes on her wedding plans. 'Except, perhaps, for our bride,' she paused and looked at me. 'You seem a little distracted, Lara? Is there something, some minor detail, of my son's wedding I've overlooked, while you were relaxing at home in England?'

'Absolutely not,' I assured her, returning her smile. 'I'm just feeling a little tired after the flight. Thank you for all of your hard work. It's going to be incredible. We're so lucky, so grateful, for everything you've done. Really.'

'Silvano isn't the lucky one. He's my son,' she responded. 'I'm sure your mother would be only too pleased to have done the same for you. If she were coming, or somehow contributing, to her daughter's wedding, that is…'

She aimed a smile at the floor, with a dart of distaste as loud as the silence.

'Mum would have loved to be here, Mrs Arazzi,' Jen suddenly sprinted. 'And my dad, but as you know, unfortunately, he's had an accident. It's very sad.'

'It certainly is,' Dolores agreed. 'And I believe we'd already, rather generously, paid for their return tickets, along with your own. Anyway,' she announced, turning on her heel as Jennifer stood, nursing a verbal slap across the face. 'New Year's Eve, 7 p.m. prompt. Our guests will be arriving for the rehearsal dinner and celebrations. You'll be ready to greet them at 6.30 p.m., of course. Did Silvano mention the coverage we've had?'

'Coverage?'

'*Inside Interiors* did a piece on the organizing of the wedding. I believe a few others of those websites have picked up on your involvement.'

My involvement? I thought. *I was only the bride.*

'That's great,' I smiled, not sure how I was supposed to react as Dolores peered at me.

'Yes, I rather thought you'd enjoy the attention. Excuse me,' she announced, with a nod to Jennifer. 'I have to speak with my son.'

And off she went, leaving a faint trace of evil and general bemusement behind her, as always.

'Lara? *That woman.* She's … horrible,' Jennifer whispered.

'I thought it was only me she terrified,' I admitted, blood slowly defrosting inside my veins.

'You barely spoke. She's *bullying* you because you're marrying her son.'

'No. She *hates me* because I'm marrying her son.'

'Well, if it makes you feel any better, she hates me because I'm your sister,' Jennifer said. 'But that doesn't mean you had to lie about my job to make yourself feel better.'

'I was trying to save you from squirming. Especially when she's already trying to bad-mouth the entire family.'

'I can't believe she was so snooty about Mum and Dad. They're not interested in her money...'

'Or my wedding…'

'Yes, they are. Anyway, aren't you glad they're not here to meet her? They mightn't be rich, but at least they're nice people. She's just bitter because she looks like Quentin Crisp. If Quentin Crisp were reincarnated as Satan...'

'*Jen!* That's Silvano's mother.'

I surprised myself with such a respectful response. Maybe I could learn to love my future mother-in-law, after all.

'Sorry, sorry,' Jen agreed, walking over to study a particularly gruesome painting of a fox hunt, a hunt which I felt like I was currently taking part in. I could easily imagine Dolores brandishing a bugle, smearing blood on her cheeks, and daring me to outwit the hounds.

'Did you hear her though? "I can't believe you're sisters." And the way she looked at me with those mean, marble eyes?' She gave a shiver.

'For goodness sake, Jen, lower your voice,' I said, throwing a look to the door.

'You're right. She's probably got the room bugged.'

'Or Silvano...'

Chapter 17

Jennifer

We were driving towards West Village, to my sister's apartment, as I stared out of the car, feeling like a content British cat admiring a New York shaped goldfish bowl. The street signs had my tummy jolting and the weather report mentioned Central Park. *The* Central Park! No wonder Lara never came home, I decided, neither would I if I had all this on my doorstep.

The city was big enough to help me forget about George, especially as he hadn't called me back over Christmas, but, for a second, I admit, I wished he, or at least someone equally gorgeous, but *not* cheating on me or *with* me or whatever it was he'd been doing, could be here as the sexy co-star in my Stateside adventure.

A few more breathtaking blocks, blazing horns, and flashing lights later, Silvano pulled up outside a brick building that I correctly guessed was my sister's place.

'Baby, I'd be so much happier if you were at home, where you belong,' he said.

'Blame my little sister,' Lara smiled, with the extra-wide display of perfect white teeth she reserved for special, give-me-my-own-way-and-don't-argue-with-me moments. 'We need a girlie night...'

'Well, okay, then,' Silvano relented, giving me a warm smile that, after meeting his mother, I was sure he must have inherited from his father's side of the family. 'Have a good night. Take care of my bride!'

I admit, despite the amazing accents that echoed through the hallway, the concrete floors, graffiti-sprayed walls and narrow corridors weren't exactly how I'd pictured my sister living.

'Nice place,' I said, taking in my temporary home, but Lara had already disappeared into another room, refilling bedroom cabinets and opening drawers, as I scanned the lounge.

The room was cluttered with discarded clothes; a spread of magazines lay at the head of a big, green couch that looked almost slept on; the room was decorated with assorted coffee cups and random makeup bag items, scattered across a big, glass table. I started collecting mugs and glasses, heading into the alcove of a kitchen, which was slightly cleaner than the rest of the place, but lacking the levels of sparkle our mum insisted upon.

On the walls pictures of Lara hung among amazing photographs of faraway places. I stared at the images of my sister, so beautiful, with a grin as wide as the horizon, rustling her flaxen hair, wearing a black and white swimming costume, with her body bronzed and taut. And in another, wearing a full-length golden gown with a plunging halter-neck, back arched, profile perfect, as she lay draped across a staircase.

I scanned the room again, thinking how it was difficult to imagine the glamorous girl in the photographs living in this apartment, with the smell of damp and dust in the air, not to mention an ashtray the size of a fruit bowl decorating the coffee table like some stinky centrepiece.

I sat on the settee, taking out my mobile. Despite the whole George thing and the fact he still hadn't properly accepted my apology for criticising his story, I couldn't resist telling Luke the latest news before I'd left with Lara. He'd been nearly as excited as I was. His new message read:

Stuff about Lara's wedding on the net!

Get ready to become a society bridesmaid! #crazy

I smiled, opened the window, needing some fresh air, noticing scorch-holes in the curtains left by ghosts of cigarettes past. The air was ice-cold, but the view!

I looked down onto the reality of dreams. This city, every building, every *block*, seemed like life at its loudest, most colourful, most alive, but I always imagined my sister would somehow be more a part of it. The same amazing-looking girl in the magazines. But, surveying her place, she was still the same girl alone in a room full of secrets.

Chapter 18

Lara

I was relieved to bolt the door and head straight to my bedside cabinet. My fingers shook as I opened the little packet of white noise, grateful at the thought of the calming euphoria that would fill my head as soon as I inhaled. But then, I stopped.

I'd gone over two months without faking my brain into reasons to be cheerful. I was marrying Silvano. Susan, my counsellor, was right. There was no substitute for real happiness, but it had to be built slowly and carefully if I wanted it to be strong and steady.

Getting a 'Quick Fix' had become a shortcut. I'd treated it as thoughtlessly as popping a painkiller to subdue a migraine. Working long hours on shoots, we'd all had pick-me-ups. Everyone was at it. There were no parents. No real-life. No context. I was living in an alternative reality. And besides, it had been fun. What was the choice? Go back home to Ingleford?

I'd ignored the calls that came from my accountant after my final meeting with Bill, spent days alone in the apartment, until I'd decided I needed something to help me. Other than the huge modelling contract I knew wasn't ever coming my way again. I'd convinced myself that if I could just think without the panic, without the grip of anxiety in my chest, I'd be able to work out what to do next. So I'd put aside a little of the nothing I had left, and considered it an investment, desperately needing to lift my mood beneath the blanket of depression I was fighting against, and finally, I'd given in.

Then, when I least expected it, I'd met Silvano, but by that stage, I didn't think I'd have the confidence to step foot on the sidewalk, let alone enjoy relaxed conversation and pleasant evenings, not without a little help with my social anxiety.

Now I was back, and the wedding, *everything*, seemed so real. My sister was here, in my apartment, as Silvano's plans had become Dolores' version of history in the making. Worryingly enough, when we met him at the airport, I'd caught myself almost hoping Dolores had ended any talk of him marrying me.

Taking a deep breath out, I was on the verge of an anxiety attack when I remembered the exercise Susan taught me. I inhaled slowly, picturing all those people around me who made me feel tense. All those situations that became overwhelming. Then, I pictured myself growing taller and taller, until all those people and situations became tiny, miniscule flecks, dotted around the ground, at my feet. I was to look down upon them, pick them up one-by-one, realize how small and manageable my feelings were, how fleeting those moments of tension could become, if I just rose above it all.

I owed Silvano my life right at that moment. I knew that, and I truly adored him, but, no matter how kind he was, or how genuine his concern, I couldn't get past what had happened between us, or what didn't happen between us, to be precise, shortly before I flew home for Christmas.

I'd had enough prior warnings from the men in my life to recognize an alert when it sounded up. We'd been out for a lovely, farewell evening, and as planned, I'd convinced Silv to come back to my place.

'We'd be so much more comfortable back at the hotel. It's going to be your new place soon,' Silvano said, taking my hands. 'C'mon, let's get a cab.'

'I think it's about time I forced you out of your comfort zone, Mr Arazzi,' I replied, closing the door. 'Sit down, I'll make us a drink.'

The hotel was the last place I wanted to be. That night, I had plans for Silvano. Big plans, involving my freshly-made bed, and the new lingerie I'd bought with precisely him in mind.

'It's not too bad here, Silvano. I've got your favourite Scotch, and we're together. That's the most important part.'

'You're right,' he agreed, folding his coat over the back of the settee, and doing that little knee-pinch thing he did with his trousers before he sat down. 'But my home is your home now, at least it's going to be. I want you to get used to the place. It would be good for you to take a look around, get to know the team.'

'I don't think I'll ever get used to that place,' I smiled, fetching our drinks. 'But Henrik is lovely.' I knew I couldn't survive life with Dolores without Henrik offering a sympathetic look or a kind word when Silvano wasn't around to stem the flow of poison. 'You know, when I was a little girl, I used to dream about living in some grand hotel. Wearing pretty dresses every night, sitting in front of a grand piano.'

'Then we'll get you one. I'll play it for you myself.'

I laughed, shook my head and sank back against the sofa. I didn't know what I'd done to deserve Silvano, but I'd never been so happy.

'You're so good to me, Silv.' I set down my glass. 'And, tonight, I've got a little something for you...'

'Really?'

I took his hand and led him into the bedroom. He didn't say a word as I slipped out of the sweetheart dress he'd treated me to the day before. I guided my bra strap over my shoulder, but before I could go much further, he stopped me.

'Lara, you don't have to do that.'

'I want to.'

He pulled the strap back up onto my shoulder, eyes searching mine.

'This, all of this.' He took in the sight of me in the lemon lace I'd chosen to match our engagement ribbons. 'This is only what you think love is. This is where you've been before. You don't have to go back there again. I thought you understood?'

'But I want to love you.' I pressed my lips against his.

'Lara.' He pulled away, sat us both down on the bed. 'You know who I am. You know that's not who we are.' He worked his fingers against the back of his neck, tense, gathering the words. 'That's not what I want. It never will be...'

'Honey,' I grinned. 'I know that. I know it's not about sex. I'm just ... well, it's never been about sex. We're getting married soon. I thought, with time, we could grow closer...'

'Lara? You know we're never going to have that kind of relationship. You've always known who I am. Do you think you're going to change that?' He glared at me. 'It's not some minor detail that you can cure me of. I'm gay. Believe me, I tried burying that, many times, many years ago. *I can't.* And I never will, but it doesn't mean that I don't love you with all my heart, because I absolutely do.'

All those times I'd stayed at the hotel, I'd hoped he might come round. He was probably right, some stupid part of me thought I'd changed him. I mean, he was the one who wanted to get married. We'd even talked about children. But even when I'd been lying in bed at the hotel, a few doors away, he'd insisted I listen to my counsellor, get some rest. All those times in his Bentley, when I felt my chest was going to explode, he'd not so much as placed a wandering hand across my thigh, or made some show of wanting me. Apart, of course, when he proposed, which you couldn't help but think might be an indication that he wanted to sleep with me.

'I know you aren't ready now, and I know you mightn't be ready for a long time. I can be patient, but Silv, I know you want me. Don't you want to try?'

'We've had this conversation. Why are you doing this?'

I folded my arms across my waist, aware of my near-nakedness.

The dumb model at the party, all over again.

'Can you love me, Lara? Can you really love me without this?'

'Silvano, you're freaking me out. I —'

'You can't fulfil those ... needs.' He got to his feet, swept his hand across his head, agitated.

'I know, but, aren't you attracted to me?'

'Yes, of course, I'm attracted to you. Who wouldn't be attracted to you?' He sighed, sitting down on my bedroom chair and slapped his hands against his thighs. 'Where's that drink?' He loosened his tie.

I grabbed my robe and sat at his feet, resting my head upon his knee.

'Can I do something? Or *not* do something?'

'You're perfect.' He took a drink. 'My family's my focus, you know that. I at least have my priorities straight, and you're top of that list.'

'I do love you, Silv.'

'I love you too. *I do.* That's why every word I've ever said to you is the truth. The life I want is with you. Maybe I'm selfish,' he said, getting to his feet again. 'But I thought we'd discussed this. If this isn't enough I don't know what else I can give you.'

'But, Silv, I —'

'I haven't asked a single thing from you, not one damn thing. All I've ever done is take good care of you. That's all I've ever wanted to do.'

'I know you have, and I'm grateful, I really am.'

'Well, you know, you ought to be,' he said. 'You've spent your whole life being *used*, throwing,' he looked at me, making me feel naked again, '*all this* at men who didn't care a damn about you. Only what you could give them.'

I nodded, ashamed, silenced.

'Did it ever occur to you, just for one second, that I might actually love you? That it might be the kind of love that endures? Not the kind that leaves you picking your clothes up off the floor?' The intensity of his stare silenced any protest. 'That I love you more than *any* of that, and I always will. *I always will.* So, all I'm saying is … don't screw this up for yourself.'

He held my gaze and I found myself nodding.

'You've got it good, so please, Lara, don't screw this up.'

Chapter 19

Jennifer

The next morning, desperate not to waste another moment dreaming of the city I was actually in, I was more than ready for the whole New York City wedding thing! Even Lara was in a good mood, as we arrived at the dress designers.

'Ah, Miss Taylor. The Arazzi gown. Come this way...'

The place was incredible. It oozed opulence, sang lullabies. You get the picture. Quite heavenly, if you liked that kind of thing.

'Your dress is waiting,' she instructed, lifting the curtain on a freestanding boudoir, draped into an existence of over-flowing whiteness. 'And yours, mademoiselle, this way, please,' she instructed, as I gave my sister an expectant grin, and followed our glamorous assistant down a short passageway, snow-blind with floor-to-ceiling bridal beauty.

I was excited, but nervous. Very nervous. But there was no need: Palest pink. Floor-length. Spaghetti straps. My dress was perfect.

At least on the hanger.

And, placed on an ornate chair in the corner there was an open shoebox, revealing silk heels, which were just about the prettiest things I'd ever seen. *In. My. Life.*

'Please, let me know if you need assistance,' the woman smiled, as the drapes fell back to surround me.

I yanked my jumper over my head, pulled off my boots, and unbuckled my belt with the speed of a stranded superhero.

I slipped the shoes on first, turning to admire the ink-bottle shaped heel. They were high, but they were worth it, and so comfortable, they went against everything I ever knew to expect from such gorgeous shoes, it just wasn't right!

The dress almost stood up on its own, it was so well designed, like stepping into fondant icing and becoming a centrepiece. I'd resented having to send Lara, of all people, my actual, real-life measurements, but the waist sat perfectly against mine.

Zipping up (the ultimate test) it was even more perfect.

This dress was like a new body!

My shoulders looked delicate beneath the faint straps. The neckline was square, elegant, but my favourite part was how *long* I looked: longer, and slimmer, with curves only wherever necessary. My rounded stomach and hips were somehow lost. My beautiful shoes added four extra inches of leg, hidden beneath an A-line skirt. I was a bridesmaid who didn't look like something the Sugar Plum Fairy had cooked up after a long day 'sugar-plumming' or whatever it was she did.

Maybe I could actually do this? Get married. Become the princess one day.

'I do!' I pronounced to the mirror. 'I do take George Benjamin Adams, to be my lawful, wedded husband!'

But then I remembered I was single and George was a cheating, possibly still married, bastard.

The Bubble of Bridal floated a little further out of reach, and I made no effort to catch it.

'I told you, there's been a mistake!'

The sound of raised voices broke my daydream. I listened, not too sure, but finally convinced it was my sister.

'Mirror, mirror, on the wall?' I said, following the little pathway back to the main Bridal Room. 'Find me a groom, I don't need rich, or tall.'

'This can't be...'

Lara sounded close to tears.

'Oh,' I managed, plunging behind the dressing-room curtains, too late to hide my shocked expression.

'Exactly,' she said, face flushed. 'But,' she said, temporarily distracted. 'You look amazing.'

'Do I?'

'You look beautiful, but,' Lara started to cry, 'I look *disgusting*. And I'm meant to be *the bride*!'

'But Mrs Arazzi made these additional details on your behalf,' our assistant reassured us, all cat-eyes and lip-pencil. 'She expressly said,' she recited, from off a notebook suddenly in hand, 'off-the-shoulder, puff sleeves. It is not a design we would produce ourselves, madam,' she insisted, placing her long, manicured fingers to her chest, 'but one which we believed fulfilled all expectation.'

'I look like a cheap barmaid in an Old Western,' Lara said, turning to me for confirmation. 'I can't get married *in this*! I need to ... to swap it.'

'But, Miss Taylor, we can't make another dress to this time scale. There are hours of time already spent designing your gown.'

'It's not mine! It's not my gown! It's awful! This is not a design, it's an insult,' Lara bellowed, clutching at what was left of the skirt.

'Madam, please!'

I agreed with my sister. The plunging top flattened her bust, hoisting her cleavage up-and-over a cascade of net, which could have been donated from our mum's dining room curtains around the time when Fondue nights were still the height of sophistication. The skirt was cut away at the front, almost to the tops of her thighs, which, although slim and smooth, made a rather scandalous choice for a wedding dress. In short, the bride wore flesh and frills.

'I've already explained, Miss Taylor —'

'Yes, Dolores saw to this, personally, so you said…'

'Why did Silvano's *mother* choose your wedding dress?' I asked, genuinely surprised.

'She didn't! I chose my dress, but then she offered to liaise with the designer while I was back home.'

'She's very broad-minded isn't she? Was she a chorus girl, or something?'

'Dolores knows all about good taste and decorum. Etiquette is all she has left in place of a personality!' Lara cried. 'This is her way of saying her son's marrying a whore!'

'Please, excuse me,' our assistant muttered, leaving the room.

'You're not a whore! We'll find you another dress and Dolores can keep this one for Halloween,' I smiled.

'It's not that simple. What am I supposed to say? I get married in a week!'

'Lara,' I said, placing my hands on her arms. 'You're not getting married in this dress. Do you hear me?' I promised, not sure how I was managing to sound so confident, but knowing my sister needed me to be. 'No one can make you wear it. You'd look better in your bra and knickers. Less trampy for a start.'

She smiled, despite the tears.

'You're going to speak with Silvano, tell him you don't want to offend Dolores, but the dress really isn't your style, and it would ruin the wedding if you had to wear it —'

'But —'

'But, he loves you, so he'll understand.'

She nodded.

'And if he doesn't, I'll speak to him and tell him it looks like something a Flamenco dancer might wear to her Hen Night in Vegas, but first, budge up,' I said, shuffling across in front of the full length mirror. 'Have you got your phone?'

'Why?'

'I need a picture.'

'Of *this*?'

'Lara? This is the first, and let's get real, *the only time*, I'm ever going to look better than you. So please, grab your phone, have a heart, and let me cherish this moment for years to come.'

We stood, mobile aloft.

My sister had never looked so beautiful. Her smile, wide and genuine, her eyes filled with laughter and tears. And then, me. Not looking too awful standing next to her in my gown. Not too awful at all.

We'd left the bridal fitting with Lara in a fit, eager to speak to Silvano about the extra cash she was going to need at such short notice to replace the dress.

'I know darling, but it really is important,' Lara said, pulling a 'here's-hoping' look in my direction.

I took a seat in the lobby, wondering how it must feel to call someone other than your bank manager in the middle of a cash crisis. The Empress Hotel was so impressive. The concierge walked past the tall, glass doors with a polite nod of his head. Traditional and sophisticated, the carousel entrance swung with old-fashioned possibility. The promise of chance meetings and dramatic exits.

'Thank you, sweetheart. I'll be right up,' Lara almost sang, snapping her phone shut. 'He was in the middle of an interview, but he said he'd cut it short.'

'An interview?'

'They're making a documentary about the hotel. The director, Marcus, is making a six-part series, shooting half a dozen hotels in Manhattan. He reckons Silvano's going to become a household name!'

'Wowzers…'

'I know!' She gave a little jump. 'Listen, I'm just going to nip up and see what he says about the dress. Silvano is sending Marcus down. Why don't you two grab that coffee you've been whining about? The morning room's just across the way,' she shouted, already making her way up the imposing oak staircase.

Trust Lara, I thought. While I'd be quite happy just to stay here, she gets to marry the owner, a soon-to-be household name, no less, and call this place home.

I picked up my handbag, and meandered past a couple of businessmen chatting at reception, against the dial-tone ring of enquiries, as the lift gave a satisfying ping!

And a gorgeous guy stepped out.

I stopped in my tracks.

'You're not Marcus, as in "interviewing Silvano, Marcus", are you?' I asked hesitantly.

'You know Silvano?'

'Sorry,' I said. 'I'm Jennifer. Lara's sister.'

'Lara's your sister? *Really*? Jeez…'

He pronounced it Lah-ra.

'I know. She's very plain while I'm clearly gorgeous. Most people are a little surprised when they meet me.'

'No, I didn't mean that, she never mentioned she had a sister, that's all.'

'Oh, didn't she? Wait until I see her!' I giggled, nervously. 'I live in England. I'm here for the wedding, *obviously*.' Another round of coy giggles that did nothing to reflect my sanity.

'Seeing as we're both caught up in the Wedding of the Year, would you like to join me for coffee? Or do you prefer tea? Being British, and all?'

'I love … coffee. I mean, I'd love a coffee, thanks, Marcus,' I said, trying not to stare at his angular cheekbones.

'So, you're Lara's big sister?'

'Only in size, not in years,' I tried to laugh, wishing I'd labelled that under Thought instead of blurting it out over my face-tannoy and bringing my size 10-12, but most likely, 14, into it.

'Oh hell, I didn't mean —'

'I'm actually the younger, older-looking sister.'

'You don't look older. I don't even know why I said that.' He shrugged before taking a sip. 'I'm dumb sometimes. Say stupid things. You'll get used to it...'

He kept his eyes on me, and if it wasn't for the small, round table between us, I promise you, I'd have fallen straight into them and dissolved like a lump of sugar.

'I don't know why I say half the things I hear myself saying either,' I replied, wondering why I sounded like my giddy aunt, of *My Giddy Aunt*-fame. 'I can only hope one day I'll go deaf, save myself the embarrassment.'

'You're funny.'

'Thanks. You're…'

I hated it when I did this. When I gave myself the start of a sentence and left myself wondering how the hell to finish it. I was a contestant on my own gameshow, and the first word that came into my head was…

Handsome.

Gorgeous.

Sexy.

Bloody *lovely.*

'It's been quite a while since I met a girl who made me laugh.'

There it was. *My epitaph.* Chisel me a gravestone. My work was done.

This man was gorgeousness made flesh and blood. Charming. Good smile. Nice aftershave. Looked great when plunging to sudden death in a huge car. *Oh, God.* I started to remember the last time I'd gone crazy for a guy in a coffee shop.

George.

My heartbeat drummed in acknowledgement of how I'd felt exactly like this, sat there with a latte, deliberately skinny, like now, to insinuate some future weight-loss, which I had no intention of ever making a reality.

'You look miles away,' he frowned, eyes blazing.

'I was. Sorry,' I said, pushing thoughts of my former life to one side as I located Marcus's face. 'I'm still a bit tired after the flight.'

'Oh, yeah, course,' he said, putting down his cup. 'So, you're here for the wedding? Gonna be a big deal...'

'Chief bridesmaid at your service,' I said, with a salute. 'Technically, I'm the only bridesmaid, but still.'

'So, you been taking in the city?'

'Yeah, it's, well, it's amazing! First time here. Everywhere I look, I feel like I'm in a movie.'

'No way! Your sister lives out here, and you never stopped by? So, she's been giving you the tour?'

'I've been to her apartment. We drove past Central Park, and this place is incredible,' I said, looking up at the beautiful, vaulted ceiling. 'I only got here yesterday.'

'But no tour?'

'The wedding stuff's pretty full-on, so...'

'I've got to give you the tour! Empire State Building?'

'No, not yet. Lara's so stressed out, I doubt she's remembered that I'm technically a tourist.'

'I'm free tomorrow afternoon? If I can show you one thing, it's gotta be the Empire State. You free?'

Was I free?

That evening, over steak at the hotel, I told Lara I wanted to take a look around the city before the big day, playing it casual so she didn't offer to join me, and before I was forced to bow-out politely in the name of sisterly duty, she said that was perfect timing. Silvano was booking her in for a replacement gown, as long as I was sure I'd be okay on my own?

Thank you!

Thank you!

Thank you!

Chapter 20

Lara

I'd convinced Silvano I needed to replace the dress, despite him constantly reminding me how much it had cost, and more importantly, how his mother had worked so hard with the design. Yes, on ruining it, I wanted to say, but there was so much going on, we didn't have time to get into an argument.

Jen had passed on a message from home. Mum and Dad knew how busy I was with the wedding, she said, which was true, but I also knew they weren't so thrilled about the marriage, or about me having the audacity to invite them at short notice. I knew, deep down, they were already distancing themselves, waiting to meet me on the other side of the break-up.

They sent their love.

They wished they could be with us.

I only wished they would call me themselves, especially as it was New Year's Eve and, more importantly, the night of my wedding rehearsal dinner at the hotel, so I picked up the phone, and called them instead.

'Hey, Dad? Mum out?'

'How did you guess?' He always raised his voice when I was back home, as if he had to shout all the way across the Atlantic. 'Left me to man the phone. Everything okay? Wedding okay?'

'Yes, good, thanks.'

'And Jenny-flower? She doing okay?'

Jenny-flower. It was a code word he used whenever he mentioned her to me or Mum, as if to remind us that she was the baby girl. The younger one we all needed to take care of.

'She's great, yes. Loving the city. I can't keep up with her. I've had to give her a spare key, so she can come and go to her heart's content.'

I'd barely seen her during the last couple of days. I was up to my vintage tiara in wedding arrangements, while Jen had been insisting on taking herself off in every direction, getting to know the neighbourhood better than I had in the last three years, by the sound of things.

'That's our Jen,' he laughed. 'Always in motion. Well, I'll tell Mum you called. Oh,' he hesitated, 'by the way. I should probably tell you, a bouquet arrived for you this morning.'

'A bouquet? Who from?'

'Well, that's the thing,' Dad said, clearing his throat. 'I'm not getting into it right now, but it's from some Tom bloke. At the spa? I'm sure I don't need to point out, your mother wasn't too happy. And neither am I. Not when you're old enough to know better, and about to marry some other bloke.'

I sat down, remembering the last time I'd seen Tom, making that deranged phone call to him on Christmas Eve. I was hungover and it seemed like the right thing to do at the time, because I'd had that dream about him, but obviously, I wasn't thinking straight. The timing was awful.

I assumed there was a message? There was, he said, clearly reluctant to read it, but I brazen out the silence: 'Dear Lara, I want you in my life. Please say you'll meet me again. Tom.'

I was relieved to hang up, but more than a little surprised that Mum hadn't been straight on the phone to me herself. Although, let's face it, she was always sweeping things under the carpet, probably terrified I'd catch the first flight home. To be honest, I couldn't blame her, because a few years ago, I would have done. I'd have declared finding Tom as my fate, put the wedding plans on-hold indefinitely, while I went off to explore other, more exotic, opinions. At least Dad had sounded confused rather than angry, because I never knew what to say to him at the best of times. I didn't have that natural way around him that Jennifer had, and he was exactly the same around me. I suppose, there was so much we couldn't say to each other, it seemed to stop us both from saying anything at all.

I jumped a little as the cell came to life again in my hand.

'Bill?'

'Yes, hi. Can you talk?'

'Sure...'

'We've received a couple of calls today. Could be a slight problem...'

Now there was a problem, it was 'we' again, I realized.

'Okay…'

'I've had calls this morning. Journalists. Wanting us to confirm or deny some online content they believe refers to you...'

'What content?'

Oh, please, not a sex tape.

'A blog.'

'A what?'

'It's posted online. A character called Lola Tyler. A model. It's supposedly based on her journal. They seem to think it's about you.'

'Me? Why?'

'There's a few details that could be linked to you, background stuff, and some edgier content. Most noticeably, there's her third wedding taking place about now, and some details about the groom. So, you haven't posted anything online?'

'Bill, I've barely sent anyone an email for the last twelve months,' I said, trying to sound relaxed and carefree, as I went into my bedroom and rifled through the semi-unpacked suitcase still lying under the window.

'Well, that's what I thought,' he said, and I could almost picture him, reclining in his big, leather seat, 'but I think you need to take a look at this stuff. I'll send you the link. Probably some loser with an over-active imagination. I'm not too concerned.'

I'd hung up, putting some makeup and jewellery into a small holdall I'd need to get ready at the hotel, checking my watch with an hour to go, as I remembered some of the stuff I'd made a note of on my computer, things I'd tapped down to share with Susan at my sessions, and the spaghetti bowl of thoughts before and after. Bill sent me the link. I opened a can of full-fat soda, and logged on:

Modelling: The Ugly Truth.
The Diary of Lola Tyler.

So far, so melodramatic, and *Lola Tyler?* I admit, the similarity was incredibly unsettling, and one click later, my heart whirred into life with a propeller of anxiety:

My first husband started our romance with rape. I married him to make it better. That much I know, but only all these years later. Isn't that how life is? Revealing everything you already knew. I spent five months as his 'wife', having threesomes with models, makeup girls, stylists, whoever he wanted, pretending to be the sexy, no-holds-barred girl. Pretending we had an open marriage. We didn't. I couldn't admit he wanted to fuck everything that existed. But I don't regret it. He was no worse than the rest of them.

I was light-headed as I scrolled down the screen, stopping at various quotes. This was me. No doubt about it. My journal had practically been quoted and stuck online. Someone was so malicious, they had actually taken the time to do this, and I had no idea why. I felt sick, scared, vulnerable, so, screw what my counsellor had taught me, I did what I always did when the world moved too fast for me to keep my balance: I swallowed a couple of Xanax, telling myself this was different, this was an emergency, too much for me to cope with alone:

He's a married movie star. Two kids, famous wife, but they live in separate houses, one in America, one in Europe. I used to have his picture on my wall. Didn't tell him that!!! He tried hard, but he couldn't get hard. I didn't care. I sucked on that dead meat for women everywhere!!!

Thank God there were no names with that one, especially as he was expected to clear up at this year's Oscars. I still had fond memories of him and that one great night, so what the hell? I thought, going with the flow of the pills in my system, and still hoping the blog might be a coincidence and nothing for me to worry about.

They said my thighs needed slimming down. Amputation, I suggested! Had major nosebleed coz the coke went off like a grenade. Scared of blood, but same with smoking. Some people get cancer, some don't. Sometimes an overdose sounds like Heaven to me.

The revelations on the website weren't great, I knew that, but it was nothing Bill couldn't handle. Anyway, I thought with a snigger, I might get offered a big cosmetic deal once the white dust settled, wasn't that how it usually went with these exposés? Sure, it wasn't exactly how I wanted Mum and Dad to think of me, but model with eating disorder, taken a few drugs in her time, was hardly going to make the rest of the world gasp.

What I really wanted to know was who the hell had done this, and how did they get inside my laptop without me noticing? I never left it lying around, never took it out of the apartment. I felt so stupid, but I'd always kept diaries, they helped me to pretend, locked myself inside, where no one could find me, buried away, so I'd always have the real me to listen when things felt bad.

I carried on, scrolling down the screen:

And now, here I am, about to marry husband number three at the hotel in the New Year – even though he's not tempted by the sight of me in my finest lingerie. Think he's saving it for his mother, the unspoken mistress in our relationship. She's nothing but a world full of hate in an old woman-suit.

My brain had been x-rayed. Silvano would know it was me, for sure, and as soon as he did, we were so over. It was everything I'd discussed in my sessions with Susan. Everything I thought I'd shared in complete confidence. I got up, too wound up to sit down.

Could Susan have done this? She was the only one I'd discussed this with, in confidence. Although, Silvano had put me in touch with Susan in the first place, explaining how she was a friend of the family.

And then, it hit me. *A friend of the family.*

This was the thing she'd been waiting for, I realized. A way to show the world I wasn't good enough for her precious son, and I could make a guess she had all the contacts she needed to make this happen, to throw me under a spotlight of shame, if she chose to.

Dolores.

Chapter 21

Jennifer

It was New Year's Eve in New York. And I had a date with a gorgeous man. And no, this wasn't a practical joke.

Marcus was going to be joining me at Lara's wedding dinner rehearsal.

But even better than that — he'd kissed me.

The first time was at the top of the Empire State Building.

'Look at those tiny, yellow cabs! New York Taxis!' I'd squealed, struggling to be heard above the raging wind.

Marcus grinned his big, sexy, lop-sided grin.

'Man, I love it up here,' he said, pulling his beanie hat over his ears, huddling down inside his jacket. 'You warm enough?'

'Yes, I'm great!' I lied, my wind-scorched eyes watering kohl.

'Need a tissue?' he asked, producing a napkin from the pocket of his jeans. 'You know, you're very cute,' he insisted, dabbing away my tears.

I was frozen for a moment, and not just because of the freezing air howling around us.

'I said, you're very cute, Jennifer, from England,' he repeated against the steady breeze.

And then, I was suddenly very warm, impervious to anything apart from compliments from gorgeous directors.

'Look, there's The Chrysler,' he said, placing his hands on my waist and turning me around to face the landmark.

But I wasn't looking at The Chrysler. I was looking at him, the only sight in New York worth seeing, as far as I was concerned.

He noticed me, noticing him. His eyes darted to my mouth. He moved in for a kiss. The city melted away.

And then, the next day, there I was at The Empress, spending New Year's Eve getting ready for our rehearsal night, in the glamorous run-up to my big sister's wedding. I felt as if I'd been visited by a fairy godmother.

Following Dolores' strict instructions to be prompt, I'd arrived at 4 p.m. to get ready in my very own room. I'd decided a life spent in hotel rooms would suit me down to the ground, which either meant becoming a chambermaid or a high-profile business leader, travelling to conferences as part of my international duties, but, seeing as I was as completely useless at compiling spread sheets as I was at ironing bed sheets, both options seemed highly unlikely.

Anyway, the room was divine. I'd kept a straight face as Henrik, the guy who made me the cocktail when I arrived after the flight, showed me to my quarters. The moment the door shut, I jumped straight onto the bed, a regal-looking four poster with pillows as plump and firm as a set of Kardashian buttocks.

My next stop, as any girl could guess, was the ensuite. A gleaming, sharply-lit, marble-expanse, filled, and I mean filled, with gorgeous products I couldn't usually afford to smell, let alone buy, even in sample size. I ran my hand across the thick, white towels, wondering how they kept them so soft and fluffy, when after one spin in the machine, mine could exfoliate the hide of an unkempt elephant. And, I'm sorry, but this shower cubicle should never have been called a shower cubicle. That was an insult to the cylindrical glass case of modern art before me — I only wished I had something more eye-catching than me to display in it. My phone sounded up, and I reluctantly left my fairytale bathroom, to find Mum on the other end.

'Jennifer? Is that you?'

I didn't know who else she was expecting. Ever since I'd arrived in America, she always seemed surprised to find I answered to the same mobile number.

'I've missed your sister. She left a message with your dad. Everything alright?'

I'd updated her with the latest pre-wedding goings on. Every detail censored so as not to worry her. Things such as how lovely Silvano's mum was; how cool and impressive my sister's apartment had been; and how much I was enjoying sightseeing with Lara.

Meanwhile, she had big news herself. There'd been highly shocking ructions concerning Ingleford's least eligible bachelor, Barry Hogg, since we'd last met. Even Mum didn't call it a date any more, not after what she had to tell me:

'*Dogging*. I mean, how anyone could do *that* to an innocent animal. It's sickening,' Mum gasped.

'No Mum, they don't do it with the dogs,' I explained, taking in the view of the opulent avenue beneath the hotel. 'They do it with people, in cars, while other doggers, or whatever they're called, watch them.'

'What?' Mum croaked. 'They make the poor animals *watch*?'

'No, Mum,' I explained. 'There's just perverts. No dogs.'

'Such a shame,' she sighed. 'Thought he might have been someone nice for you.'

Apparently, Barry had been caught spread-eagle on a car bonnet on Hollet Hill, so the local community were boycotting Hogg's Butchers in protest. Mum said the whole thing had seriously made her consider going vegetarian. I smiled, realizing how much easier it was to be sympathetic to the latest goings-on in Ingleford, when I was in the world's most amazing city.

Even that morning, hitting the streets like a native, I'd never felt so excited to be alive as I skipped my way out of the door, letting the city sweep me up in every direction. There'd been no sign of Lara, despite us making plans, but undeterred, and secretly enjoying having to rely on my independence in a strange city, I'd taken myself off shopping at the local market, which was nothing like the kind of market I'd been expecting, being a fabulous Chelsea market, bustling with New York accents and sexy New York goodies. Although, to be fair, I was so in love with the place, they could have offered up jellied eels in plastic tubs, and I still would have swooned and paid full price for my quota.

Later, happily ensconced in my beautiful hotel room, I hung up my dress for the evening, glad I could actually justify putting it on my credit card. I busied myself with moisturizer and bronzer. Plucked my eyebrows, back-combed my hair, and separated lashes. And then I saw it.

At first, I thought it was a trick of the light. On closer inspection, I'd been right the first time. There was a single, white hair, sticking straight up from the top of my head like an aerial for old age, alerting the universe to the final year of my twenties. I secured it between thumb and forefinger. A thick, wiry, spiral, signalling the advent of home dye jobs, with boxes promising 'shades' but actually only delivering a choice of two; putrid, reddish-brown or unnatural wig-black. And besides naff dye jobs, I nearly fell faint at the prospect, but, let's face it, I was going to sprout *white pubes*.

In a race with my own mortality, I parted my hair in every direction, terrified that other old-age aerials were hiding, planning to steal my youth in the night. Life was passing me by. Here I was, at twenty-nine, and I hadn't even been engaged once, let alone married twice, like Lara.

Finally satisfied, but sadly unable to fully check the back of my head, I was driven to *do something*!

It was New Year's Eve in New York — and here I was with a big, grand, rehearsal wedding dinner to go to!

Marcus had kissed me!

My hair wasn't grey yet!

Stroke of midnight — brace yourself!

One last look in the mirror, and I was ready to head downstairs. Hair pinned up with diamante clasps to add some suggestion of glamour to my usually lank locks. Unfortunate streaky-looking tan, which I'd assured myself would blend out under the right lighting, but at least, thanks to my pre-Christmas credit card spending spree, a new dress that would always remind me of my amazing adventures in New York City.

I'd also put on the pretty bra and knicker set Mum had bought me, saying, 'You don't have to wait for a man in your life to make an effort, Jennifer.' Presumably because she'd insisted on doing my laundry and had seen the amount of depressed-looking knickers and saggy-backed bras trying to drown away their miserable existence on a cold wash.

Anyway, no miserable existence for me tonight!

My sister's rehearsal dinner was as close to an Oscars moment as I was ever going to get, and this was the best I could do at short notice — at least without a genie and three wishes.

I tried to stay upbeat, but my nerves were jangling as if I was about to take a walk down the red carpet. Even the 'rehearsal' bit was freaking me out. What was it we were rehearsing? *Eating*? I'd seen the menu. Five-courses which got steadily more fattening and unpronounceable as you worked down the page. 'Rehearsing' the eating bit tonight meant I wouldn't be able eat it all again on the big day, not unless I wanted to explode out of my beautiful dress.

I took a breath and checked my mobile. Still nothing from Lara and I could already guess that first half-hour of tonight was bound to offer the usual reaction. I steadied myself for the inevitable whenever I was introduced as Lara's sister. The mental arithmetic taking place inside people's minds, as they divided my backside by Lara's and subtracted half her leg-length, to find me the sum of none of her parts. The thought of leaving the hotel room felt even more difficult without a reassuring word, or a hand to hold. Even Luke's would have done, I thought, when suddenly, my mobile buzzed back to life:

Happy New Year in advance. G x

George. My heart pitter-patted through my dress. It was about 11.30 p.m. back home, and the last time I saw him, I realized, was about to become 'last year'. My time with George was fading into history, and that thought made me feel so sad.

You might be thinking I was biased about these things, but I wish you could have seen him that last night we were together, looking scrumptious as he opened the porch, with Bixby, his husky by his side.

'Hey Bixby,' I said, trying not to protest too much as he slobbered all over my wrist, pretty much removing my perfume with one sweep of his tongue.

'What's the occasion, sweet thing?' George asked.

'Nothing,' I blushed, glad he recognised two long hours of determined slog when he saw it.

'You look gorgeous, but I haven't booked a restaurant, you know...'

'I know,' I smiled. 'I just felt like getting dressed for dinner.'

'Dressed for dinner?' He pulled me towards him. 'I'm more interested in getting you undressed for dinner…'

That's exactly what I'd been thinking. I'd have happily skipped straight to dessert myself, but seeing as he'd gone to the trouble of cooking, we went into the kitchen instead.

Life wasn't so bad after all, I thought, watching George at the stove. There I was, getting into a state about finding a job, and buying gifts, and applying false eyelashes, when, sat at the table, I realized I could watch George forever, like one of those documentaries Dad was addicted to, when you got to see rare species in their natural environment. And George was a rare species. Handsome, kind, funny, and rather fond of me.

'It was the first thing we found,' he said, stirring the saucepan while I talked him through a far less excruciating version of my failed job interview. 'Something will turn up. Maybe even something you've never really thought of before.'

I'd decided not to mention the Christmas job. Not only because the idea of telling my grown-up man that I was practically working in a grotto was beyond embarrassing, but because I still hadn't decided whether to stay in London and take up Luke's offer of a temporary flat-share, or, move back to Ingleford to earn a bit of money delivering Christmas trees for a fortnight. Plus, I noticed George had said it was the first thing 'we' found, and that was so nice to hear, I didn't want to spoil it.

The food was lovely, but I knew he would never have invited me over if his kids had been around, and it kind of spoilt my appetite. The only witness to our relationship couldn't talk, I thought, peering over at Bixby, snoozing contentedly in his bed.

George went to take some bread for himself, then gave me a brief glance, before holding up, two shiny sultanas, which on closer inspection, looked just like my stick-on nails.

'Erm, Jen? Are these yours?'

I glanced at my right hand to check.

'Sorry,' I said, taking them while he pretended not to notice the stubby, bald fingernails which had replaced my former talons. 'I'm not very good at being glamorous, am I?'

He cleared his throat, abandoned the bread, and changed the subject.

And that was it.

Looking back, that was the moment that determined what happened next.

I wanted him to see the funny side. Say something like, 'You're perfect the way you are,' like the handsome love-interest said to the unlikely heroine in romantic movies. But in real-life, I sat there wishing I'd worn jeans and not tried to have long nails and look sexy for him, because it was for him, so it was his fault he'd made me feel stupid.

Okay, now I know, I'd blown the whole thing out of all proportion, but at that point, there was no turning back. And then, from the assortment of wrong things he could have said, I decided he had definitely said the wrong thing:

'So, what's my lady of leisure got planned for the week ahead?'

'Lady of leisure?'

He dismantled pasta, oblivious to my pounding, unemployed, heart.

'Looking for a job,' I said, sounding, if not on my high horse, then definitely saddling up a Shetland pony. 'And handing in the notice on my place.'

'On your flat?' he asked, as if the thought had never occurred to him.

In fairness, it probably hadn't. He probably expected me to have grown up savings and a backup plan.

'Where are you going to move to?'

Maybe it was the casual-sounding enquiry, when what I wanted to hear was concern. To be honest, I don't really know why I did what I did next, but I did it anyway.

'I'm staying back home, after Christmas, until I sort out what to do,' I replied, no mention of staying with Luke, not now I'd decided George didn't deserve the effort.

'Your parents' place?'

At least he had the decency to look a little shocked.

'I can't afford to stay at the flat, and I've got a better chance of getting some sort of temporary job down there.'

'So, when will I see you?'

'I'm not sure. I'll try to get back as much as I can, but I'll have to borrow Dad's car, and I'm not sure where my next job's going to be based.' He looked a little concerned, but said nothing. So, I continued: 'And it's not as if I could have stayed here, with you.'

'Well, no, it's…'

'It's what?'

'It's not ideal…'

And then. He sighed.

That sigh was so annoying. It was the most annoying sigh of my life, which is when I said: 'Why? Because of Helen?'

'What's that supposed to mean?'

I wasn't sure, but I can see now, I was prepared to bring up anything remotely irritating until he took the bait, so I went with: 'Why do you act like we're having an affair?'

'You're being ridiculous,' he said, putting down his fork.

Yep, I was, but ridiculous felt perfectly reasonable by that point.

'I'm being ridiculous? Well, then, are you ashamed of me? Is that it?'

'No! Of course I'm not.'

'Then why don't you want to tell people we're together?'

'I *do* tell people we're together.'

'Except the ones who matter! I've been seeing you all year and I've met your kids five times,' I said, instantly regretting holding up the hand that had two stick-on finger-nails missing, for emphasis. 'A handful of times,' I said, placing it out of sight.

'Stop exaggerating. We go out with the kids once or twice a month, but Susanna gets upset, you know that!'

'Yes, but I'm sick of being some "friend from work". So what are you going to do? Make me feel guilty until she turns eighteen?'

'No, but —'

'And you seem fine with us splitting up...'

'Who said anything about splitting up?'

There was nothing I could do about it. The tears came.

'I said I was going to live with my parents, and you just sit there. Do you know how that makes me feel?' I sniffed, wiping my eyes with my napkin, not caring about how long I'd spent blending eye-shadow and waiting for eyelash glue to go tacky enough to apply. 'Luke offered to let me stay with him because he knew I was upset at spending less time with you. Meanwhile, the thought doesn't even occur to my boyfriend!' I gave my nose a blow for good measure. 'And I'm sick of pretending I don't have feelings, because I do, and if you don't like it, and you don't want your kids to know, then maybe we shouldn't be together in the first place.'

'It did occur to me,' he said, pushing his dish away. 'But I have the children every weekend, and as you pointed out, they don't know about us yet, not in that way. What am I supposed to say? This is Daddy's girlfriend after all, and by the way, she lives with us now?'

'I didn't expect to move in! I didn't expect to move in at all, but you could have offered!'

'I didn't know you wanted me to! I'm not a mind reader!'

'No, but you're happy enough with me staying over a couple of times a week, with my knickers in my handbag, and not even my own...' I tried to think, 'not even my own *bathrobe* or so much as a *toothbrush*, here —'

'You have got a bathrobe here!'

'You call it, The Guest Robe! You never say it's mine. It's a bathrobe that I happen to use the night before and the morning after we have sex. Like, the spare toothbrush. You may as well buy me a Relationship Kit that I can pack up with me whenever I leave, then there'll be no trace of me at all.'

'Look, I know you're upset about the interview —'

'Stuff the interview! I fell downstairs in front of my old boss, with my boobs hanging out, and sunglasses on indoors!'

'What?'

'See? You don't know *any* of this. You act like a boyfriend, but you're...'

'Jennifer? Hold on a minute, your —'

'I'm what? Over-reacting?'

'No, your —'

'I don't want to hear it. I shouldn't have come here tonight.'

'Hang on. I'm trying to tell you,' he said, leaning towards me, 'that —'

'You love me?' I stood up, throwing down my napkin like I was throwing a tantrum, which I suppose, technically, I was.

'I do love you, but I can't take you seriously when —'

'*Don't*. Don't tell me to stop acting like a child. You treat me like a child, so maybe that's why I'm acting like one.'

'Look, just sit down and we can —'

I picked up my bag, grabbed my coat, and headed straight out of the front door. It wasn't until the taxi driver turned to collect his fare that I had a hunch about what George had been trying to tell me.

'Didn't realise I 'ad Hitler in me cab, love,' he chuckled.

'Who?'

''Itler. You know, German bloke, invaded Poland?' he said, handing me my change. 'Been to a fancy dress, 'ave we?' he asked, pointing to his top lip.

I took my mirror out of my handbag, and saw my false eyelash stuck firmly under my nose.

But, that was then, and there would be no embarrassing malfunctions tonight, I reassured myself, shutting the door to my hotel room.

I made my way to the elevator, not risking the polished stairs in heels, and as the floors counted down to zero, I felt the weeks melt away, so, for the sake of *Auld Lang Syne*, and because, to be honest, I wanted him to know I was spending New Year in New York with my sister, I texted George:

Happy New Year from New York. Jennifer xxx

I missed him, and still felt cheated out of our first New Year's midnight kiss, but then, as if my fairy godmother did actually exist, the elevator doors opened, and I saw Marcus standing in the lobby, perfectly bound in a black suit — waiting for me.

Chapter 22

Lara

I'd worked some tough shoots, stepped into some tense backstage scenes, but that was nothing compared to arriving at the hotel to find Silvano prowling the foyer on his cell.

'Oh, so *here* you are. It's 6 o'clock,' he said, tapping his watch.

'Yes. Here I am,' I grinned. 'An hour early.'

Henrik suddenly appeared, giving Silvano a nervous look.

'Can I take your coat, Miss Taylor?'

'Henrik!' I said, as if greeting an old friend. '*You're* still speaking to me, aren't you?'

'Of course, Miss Taylor.'

'You were meant to be here hours ago!' Silvano insisted, struggling to keep his voice down. 'I've been calling you all day. Where the hell have you been?'

I'd been speaking to Bill, confessing my worries, and having my life reduced to a trashy exposé, which no one could reassure me would be in the bottom of tomorrow's cat litter tray, as it was posted online for the world to read, indefinitely.

'Busy,' I said, handing Henrik my coat.

Tonight, I'd come as myself. As Lara — successful model, who could still wear a thigh-skimming sprayed-on dress, without a suggestion of sag or cellulite.

'What do you think, Henrik?' I asked, smoothing down my skirt and giving a flick of the hip. 'Good enough?'

'Are you drunk?' Silvano interrupted, as Henrik gave me a polite smile and disappeared back into whatever closet they kept him in.

'No! I've had a drink. But I'm not drunk. There's a difference...'

I was almost telling the truth. I'd had one Xanax, three glasses of vodka and two generous lines of coke with each drink, finishing off the last of my stash, since I'd visited my 'website'.

The more I read about 'Lola Tyler', the more the old, familiar panic grew. It was true, my life was a series of nasty secrets. I was a bad person, destined to live with nothing but badness around me. No one had ever really cared about me. I didn't even care about myself, just went from one disaster to the next, hoping something, or most likely, someone, could make me feel good about myself again. If I'd looked the same way I felt on the inside, people would have avoided me on the street. There'd have been no love affairs, no attention, just pity, at best.

Despite it being New Year, Bill wanted us to meet up and put together some sort of statement, until I explained that Silvano was expecting me.

'So, you're actually going to marry that guy?'

'Looks that way.'

'I can't leave you alone for five minutes without you accepting a marriage proposal, can I?'

'I guess not...'

'Do you even know what you're doing? You do know he's gay, I take it? You haven't convinced yourself you're going to *cure* him? The same way you were gonna transform Travis into a human being.'

'He's good to me, Bill.'

'Jesus, Lara. I'm good to you. He's probably counting on you to get that inheritance from his mother.'

'No,' I replied, but without a trace of confidence. 'It's not like that.'

'It's another dead end, Lara, but the least of our worries, right now.'

Bill hung up, his words still raining in my thoughts, so I decided to brazen it out the only way I knew how. I'd ignored Silvano's calls, debating whether to be a no-show, terrified he'd soon hear about the blog and see all the things I'd told Susan.

'You need to sober up.'

'What I need,' I said, wrapping my arms around Silvano's neck and gazing into his eyes, 'is for you to get me upstairs, and give your fiancée a nice, warm, welcome,' I kissed his neck, 'so then, I can at least say you screwed my brains out once this year…'

'Straighten yourselves up,' Dolores hissed, suddenly appearing in the foyer.

'Mom, I can handle this —'

'Can you now? For a *lifetime*, Silvano?' she asked, glaring at me through her glassy eyes.

'What's that supposed to mean?' I demanded, as she ushered us both into the staff cloakroom, too high on my cocktail of pick-me-ups to be intimidated, even by her.

'Lower your voice,' she spat, closing the door. 'If you can't consider me, at least consider our guests,' she instructed, looking me up and down. 'I assume you're eager to get upstairs to find an appropriate gown for the occasion?'

'Gown? Isn't that what they wear in hospital? For surgery?' I asked Silvano. 'No, Dolores, I won't be changing into a *gown*,' I snorted. 'Not unless you're planning on removing my heart with your bare hands? God knows you could use one,' I laughed, noticing the stole, draped across her shoulders. 'Is that real fur?' I asked, wiggling the tail. 'Did you kill it yourself? Hunt it down with the hounds?'

'I warned you about this,' she barked at her son.

'Oh, you warned him, did you?' I grinned. 'I wish he'd have warned me about you. About what you're capable of. Are you happy now, Dolores? Did you enjoy playing private investigator, you wicked old witch?'

'You're a disgrace to my son,' Dolores said, burning Silvano with a look as she took her leave. 'Get her tidied up and inside. If you must...'

'Oh Silv,' I said, putting my hand to his chest as his mother slammed the door behind her. 'Please don't wither in front of your mother, like that. Do you know how much of a turn off —'

He interrupted me with a slap so hard, I thought he'd split my lip open.

'I hosed you down from nothing,' he shouted.

'And what are you?' I screamed. 'Some fag, trying to convince *Mummy* she's going to have grandkids to pass her cash on to!'

He grabbed me by the shoulders, the air escaping my lungs in shock, as he shook me.

'There are appropriate clothes in your room. Here,' he said, shoving the door card in my hand. 'Get changed. Sober up. I'm expecting you in the main dining room within the next hour.' He turned and opened the door, 'I'm sorry I hit you, we'll put this down to pre-wedding nerves, for both of us. Hopefully my mother will agree, but, whether you like it or not, you better get sobered up, and start showing my family some respect.'

I wasn't nervous by the time Silvano led me around the dining room, greeting Dolores' friends.

I was numb.

Numb with the realization of what I was about to do, and of how much Silvano was already doing for me.

I smiled. I nodded. I even laughed.

Henrik had made coffee, issued water, and as I got changed, I felt the old Lara slowly releasing her grip, until I settled back into the present. My heart was still beating with a chemical clockwork, alcohol still lightened my limbs, but I peered out from inside my head, and I was determined not to let Silvano down.

The blog was nothing to do with his mother. I was being ridiculous, *paranoid*. I tried to think: the only time that laptop had left my sight was back at home. Back at home? Who would have even been remotely interested? And then, it suddenly dawned on me, as I saw my sister, chatting in between courses.

'I need to speak with you.'

'Lara! Where've you been?'

'None of your business,' I said, erasing the smiles of people gathered around her, hanging off her every sweet, inoffensive word.

'What's up?' she enquired, confidence draining. 'Marcus has just been telling me about filming the wedding. Mum and Dad will get to see it after all — on TV!'

'I said, we need to talk,' I insisted, taking her by the elbow, as her new friends exchanged curious expressions. '*Now*.'

'What are you doing?' she asked as I led her out into the foyer.

'When did you read my diary?'

'What diary?'

'Don't try and act innocent. The diary I keep on my laptop.'

Her expression plummeted. Jennifer was never a good liar.

'Jennifer?'

'I know I shouldn't have touched it, but Luke was nagging at me to look at something he'd put online,' she admitted, face flaring scarlet. 'I just saw it.'

'So you posted it all over the internet?'

'*What?*'

'I'm not stupid, Jennifer. Did someone *pay* you? Are you that desperate for money?'

'No one's paid me anything. What are you talking about?'

'Jen?' Marcus walked over, full of casual concern. 'Are you okay?'

'She's fine.'

'She doesn't look fine to me.'

'This has nothing to do with you.'

'Okay,' he said, raising a hand in acquiescence. 'Jen, I'll wait for you inside.'

'Our wannabe *expert* in *digital publishing* thought she'd pin my life up for everyone's entertainment, did she? Well done! It's gone viral. My life is trashed for everyone to see. So, congratulations, I'm finished. I hope you're happy…'

'Lara, I don't know what you're talking about, but whatever it is, it's got nothing to do with me.'

'There're *reporters* calling my agent, you little snake! How do you think Silvano's going to react once he sees it? We may as well get the divorce finalized now!'

'Reporters? Lara, I don't know what you're on about.'

'A website,' I explained, trying to regain my composure, 'published my life on line. Except I'm called Lola Tyler…'

'Lola Tyler?'

'Oh, save it, Jennifer. The least you can do is admit it was you. Did you even think about how this could destroy my life, you bitch, or did you miss being at the centre of everyone's universe as usual? Just desperate for attention, as ever.'

'I'm not at the centre of anything,' she muttered, shell-shocked.

'Oh,' I smiled, 'but you are now, aren't you? How could you *do* that to me? How could you write those things, as if I'm *nothing* to you? As if I have no feelings! It's my life! My work! My reputation!'

'I didn't put anything online, I swear, I didn't.'

'So, what happened, Jen? You're the only person who read it, and then it magically appeared online?'

'Where was it posted?'

'I told you, it's all over the internet!'

'Well, I mean, do you know where it came from?'

'Well, I'm not likely to forget it, am I? Some dumb writing contest site. Yourstory.com. Why?'

'Lara.' She took a step past me, as I noticed Marcus waiting in the wings. 'I think I might know what happened, but we shouldn't talk about this now. Not here.'

'Don't tell me what I can or can't talk about.'

'It's your rehearsal dinner. People are looking...'

'So, let them look. I said, I'm not finished,' I shouted, grabbing her by the arm.

'Get off me! You're drunk!'

'Don't you dare walk away from me,' I screamed, and, not knowing what else to do, my temper reaching boiling point, I threw the rest of my wine in her face.

Chapter 23

Jennifer

My dress was ruined and the humiliation, in front of Marcus, *perfect Marcus*, was crushing. I didn't care about the five-hour time difference. It was half-past two in the morning in England, but I knew Luke would pick up.

'Hey! New York City, girl! Happy New —'

'Luke, did you put my sister's diary on yourstory.com?'

'What?'

'Did you put it on that stupid website?'

'No!'

'Oh, thank you!' I placed my hand on my chest, hoping my heart would stop racing.

'Well…' The pause alerted my pulse all over again, 'yes. Sort of. Why?'

'Oh, my God,' I grabbed my chest again, stomping around the room. 'My sister's got *reporters* bothering her, because the whole thing's gone bloody *viral*.'

'*What?*'

'She's just flipped on me. I'm standing here, drenched in red wine,' I told him, kicking off my shoes, 'because she thinks I've deliberately ruined her life. She's never going to speak to me again. What the *hell* were you thinking?'

'Jen, I didn't plan it,' he stuttered. 'You went to bed. I had her computer. I was re-reading my stuff, you know, the unintentionally hilarious first instalment —'

'You shouldn't have been snooping through my sister's computer!'

192

'Oh, says the person who did exactly that! If you hadn't already told me about it, maybe I wouldn't have been tempted to read the damn thing!'

'I read some of it, Luke. I didn't stick it all over the web.'

'I didn't stick it all over the web. I put it on yourstory. Yes, that was bad of me, but I rewrote most of it. I changed her name. I didn't think anyone would guess who it was about…'

'*Lola Tyler*, Lara Taylor? It's not the cleverest of pseudonyms, is it?'

'I didn't know anyone would be that interested. Hardly anyone read my stuff, and the deadline's nearly up on the entries and, well, you don't understand how much pressure I've been under! My dad's going to throw me out of the apartment unless I start working in the restaurant with him,' he said. 'I just thought, if I could prove to my parents I could do this —' he scrambled for words. 'Oh Christ —'

'What?'

'I've just found it online. It's had hundreds of reposts. I can take it down, but —'

'I know. It's too late. Lara already said it's all over the place,' I huffed. 'First you ruin everything, telling me about George, then you do *this* to my sister.'

'Jen, I promise, I'll sort it out.'

'You were the one telling me not to read someone else's diary, then you sit there, reading it yourself, and do *this* to her?'

'I know, I know. It was a terrible, stupid, thing to do, but I promise, I never thought for one minute any of this would happen. It's because of the wedding I think,' he said. 'It looks as if people have seen reports about the wedding, and someone's put two and two together, and now, well, yeah, Lola Tyler was a bit of an obvious choice…'

'So, hold on. How did you get it from her laptop?'

'I...' he sighed. 'It sounds bad, but I copied the document, all of it, into my email account —'

'You what? What the hell did you do that for? You do realise you sound like a complete creep?'

'Okay,' he said, slowly taking a deep breath. 'Since I'm trying to be honest: I didn't want you to read Lara's stuff because,' he paused, clearing his throat. 'I was worried, and I wanted to check it.'

'Check what?'

'Check if ... if I was in it...'

'In Lara's diary?'

Silence spilt between us.

'Luke?'

'I, we ... we slept together —'

I slumped onto the bed, heartbeat now audible inside my head.

'I didn't want you finding out about it. Jen? It was years ago...'

'You and Lara?'

'You know the way she was hinting at stuff between me and her, flirting a bit, in the pub? I was worried in case she'd put something in there. You said there was some list of blokes she's slept with. I thought you might find out, I just wanted to see if I was in there somewhere in case you read any more of it...' he moaned, drunk on a cocktail of self-pity.

'How could you sleep with my sister and not even tell me?'

'I didn't know you then. She came to my place, to get you, that morning, remember? When you stayed at mine, after I'd interviewed her? And then, we kept in touch, and she stayed over a few times. You know what she was like back then, always needing a place to crash, and, then, we slept together. It was ages ago, okay?'

Well, no, not okay. I couldn't begin to tell him all the ways this wasn't okay, especially the part about me not knowing. And then there was the secret part. The part that felt hurt that all those times I'd stayed over at his place, not once had there been a flicker of electricity, not a chance of a glance in my direction, and then, there goes my sister, leaving a trail of marriage proposals and broken-heart confetti behind her.

I said something about talking to him the next day, being too tired to think, and hung up, just as I heard a knock at the door.

'Jennifer?'

It was Marcus.

Oh, please, go away, I thought, which shows you how upset I was, with a famous man at my door, and no desire whatsoever to see him.

'Are you okay?'

'Yes, I'm fine,' I shouted, perched on the edge of the bed.

'Does that mean I can come in?'

'No!' I was dyed crimson, from embarrassment and wine. Rehearsal dinner road-kill. 'No, I'm a mess…'

'Well, then,' he announced, with a sudden slump against the door. 'I guess I'm going to have to wait here until you clean yourself up…'

'I can't see you right now.'

'That's because there's a wall between us…'

'You know what I mean...'

'Come on. Let me in. Please?'

I got up, a quick glance in the mirror confirming it was too late to care. Reluctantly, I unclicked the lock and retreated.

He stood in the doorway, assessing the damage, before closing the door and disappearing into the en suite, quietly emerging with a towel.

'This is what friends do,' he said, slowly unpicking the clips from my hair, unclasping my necklace, removing my earrings. 'Stand for me.'

I took his hand and he pulled me to my feet.

'You need to shower,' he almost whispered as he reached behind my shoulders and unzipped me. The straps of my dress followed his hands down along my arms, until the dress fell at his feet.

'And this is what I'm going to do.'

I remember the bitter-sweet smell of him before he whipped his tongue between my lips. Next, my bra. The release of hooks. I was shaking now, with fear, with fever.

'I'm going to make you feel better...' he promised, leading me to the bathroom.

At this point, I was feeling about as 'better' as I ever had in my life, but thankfully, for once, I said nothing to ruin the moment, as he turned on the shower, stood aside, and beckoned me beneath the cascade. I looked at him, unsure, before he wrapped one hand along my jaw, tilting my mouth to his, kissing me deeply, before, too nervous to speak, I was sleep-walking into the moment.

'Shower for me.'

He stood on the other side of the glass, watching as I slowly took the gel and started with my hair, letting the bubbles trail down my body. I didn't know what to do next. Wasn't sure what he was expecting. My mind raced with possibilities, until, finally, I turned to face him, his eyes darkening, offering silent instruction.

I'd never felt so vulnerable, but infallible, in my whole life. I realized, this was incredibly ... well, *sexy*. In fact, I was pretty sure he found *me* sexy.

He walked to the other side of the cubicle, placed one hand against the glass, stalking his prey. Following his eyes, I pulled down my pants, hoping he noticed they were nice ones that matched my bra, before letting them drop to the floor, casting a quick glance to my abdomen, checking I was free from any taunting white whispers of impending old age.

Willing myself to forget he was there, I traced my hands across my body, which felt worth far more than my criticism under his attention. I ran my hands through my hair, felt my breasts tighten under the cool stream, let the water christen my body in a baptism of Marcus.

Don't let it go, I told myself. Don't get nervous.

He's not there. It's all a dream. You can be anything in this dream.

Be his. Be his in this dream.

Thoughts racing across my mind, he opened the door, kissed me hard, insistent. I was dizzy, off-balance, and forgot the first rule of great, sexual highs — I looked down. His hard-on was full and straining perfectly along the seam of his zipper.

Don't look down.

'Take off my shirt.'

Don't look down.

White cotton, becoming transparent as I worked from collarbone to navel. Tight muscle against my soft curves. I grabbed him now, both of us in contest, as he placed kisses on my neck.

Up against the wall of the shower, my hands quickly undoing his buckle, his hands finding me, frenzied fingers exploring flesh.

Just right, my pleasure met his fingertips.

My spine slipping against the tiles as he broke, hard and fast, into me, heaving me upwards, pushing me back down again.

The water rained over us as I forced myself onto him, again and again, his hips insistent, force unfolding, until I forgot there was any other way to feel.

The 2nd of January arrived and my sister still hadn't replied to a single text or answered her phone. Luke, on the other hand, was desperate to talk. He'd taken down the blog. *Lola Tyler* was no longer posted on yourstory.com, and while I appreciated the gesture, we both knew it wasn't quite as simple as that, not now it had been copied and discussed by people curious as to the identity of this supposed real-life model, who had everyone talking about the 'dark side' of the industry.

'Jen? I need to tell you something else. And, before you put the phone down, because I know you already hate me, and I'm not really supposed to tell you this, but I have to tell you, because I'm trying to make everything right...'

'If it's about you and my sister, I don't want to know.'

'No, it's not that. *It's worse.* No,' he corrected himself, 'not worse, but, maybe bad ... but it was supposed to be good.'

'Luke? You're still drunk. Stop rambling.'

'Yes, I am. I've been drunk all year so far, which means I'm keeping my resolution, and topping up my glass is a far better way to spend the day than with a hangover, especially as I'm having lunch with my parents,' he mumbled, 'but, I'd want you to tell me, even though I said I wouldn't, and George takes stuff like that, really seriously...'

'George?'

'That's what I'm trying to tell you. He's, err,' he cleared his throat, 'he's coming to see you.'

'*What?*'

'He's flying to New York. To see you.'

I was speechless.

'Jen? Are you listening?'

'Of course I'm listening. I've got the phone to my ear, haven't I?'

I wasn't listening. I'd just arrived back at my sister's, thankfully empty, apartment, after a stint of non-stop sex with Marcus. My thighs ached. My arms were weak. My stomach muscles, (that's right, I could feel actual stomach muscles) were tight with a healthy, sexually-inflicted, pain. I'd found my body's vocation. The best way to exercise. The kind that made you work through the night, and toned you up all over.

'George is coming here?' I shrieked. 'As in, *here*, to see me?'

'Finally, we have lift off...'

'But he can't! I don't want him to! What's he thinking? He's got a wife!'

'No, he hasn't. Well, he has, but she's definitely the ex-wife. And he's definitely not interested in her. She's sleeping with some sales exec, for a start.'

'How do you know all of this?'

'I went to see him, on Christmas Eve, after I'd told you about following him back from the supermarket.'

'I don't believe this! Why do you keep —'

'Just hear me out! I went to see him, and we got talking, and, anyway, he was feeling really down at New Year, so he called me. Said he'd texted you and you'd replied, and did I know you were in New York?'

'I don't care. And I don't care who his wife's sleeping with!'

'*Ex-wife.*'

'Whatever! I'm ... I've met someone.'

'You *met* someone? When?'

I'd done more than meet him, I smiled. On New Year's Day, we'd left the hotel early, I'd dropped off my wine-stained clothes at Lara's apartment, and spent the day, and night, with

Marcus … becoming a person controlled by my own body. And unlike the previous twenty-nine years, this year, I wanted to do more than pleasure myself with food.

It wasn't food I craved. In fact, I'd lost my appetite.

I couldn't think straight, couldn't concentrate. Everything screamed: *Sex!*

Every time I dressed or undressed: *Sex!*

Each time I stepped into the elevator (a much sexier, American word than 'lift,' I thought): *Sex!*

Every time I thought of Marcus: *Sex!* It was everywhere. Everything I could think of. It took all my willpower not to graze, what Marcus called my 'sexy little ass' against inanimate objects. I breathed differently. Felt the touch of things. Smelt the scent of things, *differently*.

I was *in sex* with Marcus!

I didn't care about the inches you could pinch on each of my pear-shaped hips.

In fact, all flesh was good! Good and sensitive, and alive. No more worrying if my stomach sprung a spare inch of tummy at the top of my knickers, or concern that my breasts were taking a road trip to visit my naval. *I loved my body!* It was a translator of joy. Actual joy, called *Sex*. The common language between Marcus and me.

'Oh Luke,' I said, conveniently forgetting how he'd possibly ruined my sister's life and secretly slept with her, now that I was desperate for someone to confide in. 'You wouldn't believe what's happened to me. *I'm in sex!* I'm so in sex, I can't think straight. Have you ever been in sex, Luke?'

'Jennifer? Is that you? Who are you in … who are you sleeping with?'

'Oh, there's no sleeping!' A banshee laugh I'd never heard before screeched from the chambers of my throat. I tossed back my head, a woman possessed. 'There's no sleeping, just me, Marcus, and *hours* of it.'

'Jen, you're scaring me now.'

'I'm scaring myself! Isn't it amazing?'

'Who's Marcus?'

'Marcus is a documentary filmmaker. He's working with Lara's fiancé.'

'What are you going to tell George?'

'No, no!' I interrupted. 'What are *you* going to tell George, you mean.'

'Me?'

'You should have stopped him. Or at least mentioned it to me before he boarded a plane! What's he thinking?'

'He loves you.'

Reality slammed the door in my face. The door to Marcus, and having my wrists tied to his big, brass, bed.

'Oh. Does he?'

'He does. And that's me, saying that. He loves you. If you could hear the way he talks about you. Jeez,' he huffed. 'He makes me want to find someone. I mean, real deal, Jen. *Real* deal.'

'I feel sick,' I said, sitting on the floor now, back in my real life. Back to George.

'What do I do?'

'Nothing. Don't do anything for now, and don't tell him I told you.'

'How am I supposed to act surprised?'

'You won't have to act, believe me...'

'Why?'

'I mean, when you see him. Just, trust your gut, go with it.'

'I don't have a gut. I don't eat. I just have sex.'

'Will you please stop saying that?'

'Luke? You've been dying for me to do something remotely interesting for years, and now you're telling me to stop? Since when do you not want to hear this? I'm having the best —'

'Don't say it!'

'What?'

'*That.*'

'Sex?'

'I said, don't say it! *Don't do it!* At least, not with that guy.'

'Are you having a stroke?'

'He's going to propose, Jen! I saw him today, okay? George is going to propose. I've seen the ring. Tried it on my little finger and everything.'

Chapter 24

Lara

I'd stayed at the hotel since the New Year's Eve rehearsal, mainly to please Silvano, but also to try and sidestep the centrifugal force at work beneath my feet.

I was grateful for every last hour of freedom, holding on before the storm hit. It was inevitable news of the blog would reach Silvano any minute, but I didn't get drunk and I didn't get high. The open wound of hurt had begun to heal into a bruise, without any of my usual excuses for bad behaviour, but each time my phone rang, my heart darted through the door. Every time I heard Dolores' laughter, I was sure I'd been discovered, and every night in bed, despite reminding myself how lucky I was, how incredibly grateful I should be, I longed to go home, and the night before, I'd been dreaming of Tom and Wiltshire Hall.

Bill had agreed to reign in news of the blog as best he could until after the wedding, and I'd agreed to sign off a press release as soon as I was Mrs Arazzi.

Mrs Arazzi.

Silvano's mother's name; the emblem of my future. Every time I thought about my new title, I worried that in thirty years' time, I'd be just as bitter, despite the love of a good man. Dolores tolerated my presence, although, staying under her roof at The Empress, I was afraid she might put a pillow over my face while I slept — or even worse, while I was still awake.

Luckily, she spared my life, but made her feelings quite clear during our latest tryst.

'It's about time we caught up, don't you think?' Dolores asked, casting a knowing look to the floor, her brittle smile in place, as she sat down, perched on the edge of a gilded chair, hands clasped, legs tucked elegantly beneath the seat.

Her room, the day room, was offset by chalk-grey walls, and rich, mahogany furniture, which shone with pride and purpose.

'What I don't know about my son isn't worth knowing,' she shared pleasantly, as Henrik served tea from a silver tray for one. 'What I do know about you, I'm rather anxious to forget...'

I straightened my back, offered Henrik a gracious smile, and wished Silvano could hear his beloved mother in action, but of course, I guessed, she was far too well versed to be caught out like that.

'I'm sorry you feel that way, Mrs Arazzi.'

'Are you? Are you indeed?' she gave a humourless laugh. 'I very much doubt that, Lara. I'm sure you'll agree, I know Silvano far better than you do, or indeed, ever will. My only son, *and heir*, is more precious to me than life itself, but he has his faults — as we all do,' she said, casting a look at Henrik, standing at her right-hand side. 'Thank you. That will be all.'

'M'am,' he said, with a nod. 'Miss Taylor,' he added, with a smile of condolence.

She took a sip of tea as Henrik left the room, her gaze never leaving mine, before setting the cup down and giving me her undivided attention.

'Silvano has always been weak, known to let emotion override his better judgment. Let's beautiful, *broken* things run away with his heart. Those worthless antiques he insists on collecting, unwanted *strays* he insists on feeding. And you, my dear, the prime example of his penchant for rescuing unwanted mongrels from the street,' she smiled so sweetly, I almost doubted what I'd just heard.

I was determined to keep my cool, remain calm, no matter what the provocation.

'Silvano and I —'

'Please spare me the declarations of true love. We both know this a business arrangement, and a poor one, at that.'

'You think this is about money?'

She laughed, seeming genuinely amused.

'My dear, what isn't about money? Everything is an exchange of goods between parties, except, my son forgets too easily, his inheritance is not in his possession to flitter away. Not quite yet.'

'I don't want your money.'

'Yet, you're growing accustomed to spending it. I believe the wedding dress alterations *I paid for* were not to your liking?'

'No,' I cleared my throat, trying to find my most confident voice. 'They weren't.'

'I was surprised Silvano supported your decision to purchase a replacement, *at great further cost to me*, might I add, especially since it was his idea to model your gown on my own wedding dress, of which I was rather fond.'

'You modelled it on *your own* wedding dress?'

'Yes, a bridal gown which I believe you found a little vulgar?'

'Mrs Arazzi, I'm sorry if —'

'A dress is only as vulgar as the woman wearing it, my dear. How ironic that you manage to take what is of great value, and cheapen it. Now,' she added, 'where were we?'

'If it's a pre-nup you want, I'm happy to sign one.'

'We both know Silvano better than to think that he would ever agree to such a sensible arrangement.'

'Silvano doesn't need to know.'

She raised an eyebrow.

'Ah, dishonesty. Such a fine trait in a future wife.'

I stood up.

'Sit down, sit down, let's not resort to amateur dramatics,' she said, finishing her tea while I was seated again as instructed.

'Mrs Arazzi, I've no idea what you want, apart from the fact you seem determined to ruin your son's marriage.'

'Ruin it?' she raised her cut-glass voice. 'I've done nothing but focus on his wedding since you skipped off home for the holidays. I've worked every second to ensure the very best for my only child, which is why I'm not about to let *you* make a mockery of him.'

'I said, I'll sign a pre-nup.'

'Any lawyer worth his merit can rewrite one of those damn things. I'm afraid you're missing the point, my dear. There won't be a pre-nup. And, as Silvano has already informed me, there certainly won't be any grandchildren, not unless you plan to adopt, which I'm afraid, I really must insist that you do. I'm sure the process would appeal to my son's interest in charity work, another lost soul for him to rescue...'

I'd told Silvano in confidence about the failed attempts with Travis which had led to consultants who all told us the same thing: I had little chance of conceiving, more than likely caused by several abortions I'd had over the years before we met.

The first time, Patrick made it sound as run-of-the-mill as having my period. Did I want a child, aged eighteen, starting out in my career? Of course I didn't. Would we have children together in the future? Of course, but for now, Patrick would make the whole thing go away.

And, no, he didn't want me to take the pill, putting all those chemicals into my body, controlling my hormones and interfering with my shape; making me gain weight, inflating my non-existent breasts, popping out my stomach, giving me acne.

He listed the potential side effects, explaining that, after all, it was only invented in the 1960s. The women taking it were practically guinea pigs, he explained. And sometimes, he couldn't manage to get the condom on in time because he was just too excited. It was my fault for being so sexy, so irresistible to him.

And I listened to this well-rehearsed crap, and I believed him. Until I'd had abortion number three and spoke to a nurse who assured me Patrick might just be a complete and utter selfish creep.

Travis didn't quite see it that way. I was damaged goods. Surely I'd known I couldn't have kids? I must have been able to tell if I was all messed up inside? I'd lied to him, he said. Tricked him into thinking we could have a family, because no one else would want me now. The arguments blazed and my guilt grew. So, when he complained about studio contracts, I set him up with his own record label, Wild One Records. When he said he wanted us to set some real foundations in the world, seeing as I'd never bear his children, I bought us a fifty-acre ranch in Colorado. And I kept buying, and he kept complaining, and I started drinking almost as much as him.

So, you can forgive me for not wanting to inform my parents that I was desperately unhappy, that I knew my husband didn't love me. Growing up, keeping quiet and learning to cope alone became second nature. I was the girl destined to have an easy life. The confident one: so independent, and ambitious.

But, the truth was, I was none of those things. That was how my parents needed me to be, for their own sake.

Meanwhile, Jennifer, sweet, silly, sensitive, Jennifer, was the little girl who never grew up. The one who needed them most, and they convinced themselves of this, in order to let me go. I was an astronaut, drifting between two entirely different planets, knowing deep down that I'd never be able to settle in either atmosphere, so I kept on searching for a family of my own.

'It's pre-wedding nerves, that's all,' Henrik insisted, closing the curtains after I asked if it would be okay to take supper in my room as Silvano was tied up with business.

'Probably,' I sighed. 'I should know. I'd been married enough times...'

'Third time lucky?'

I looked at him, not expecting humour from the ever-respectful Henrik, of all people.

'Tell me, Henrik,' I said, toying with my Caesar salad, 'will Dolores ever accept my existence?'

'I'm sure she will … *eventually*,' he said, heading to the door. 'She's learned to tolerate mine.'

'Not just me who gets a hard time from her, then?'

'No. Not at all.'

'Please stay?' I asked.

He stopped, hovered at the door.

'I'd love some company. This place is so *busy* all the time…'

'I'm sure they can spare me for a few minutes, Miss Taylor.'

'Call me Lara.'

He gave a polite smile.

'Have a glass of wine, please,' I insisted. 'Silvano said I should spend some time with you.'

'Did he?' he asked, genuinely curious as he pulled out a chair.

'I guess he knows I feel a little lost here...'

'I can understand that,' he nodded, filling our glasses with Chardonnay. 'I think we all get lonely. Sometimes, in the biggest crowds.'

'Yes, that's right,' I smiled.

'But, I've made my home here, as you will make it yours.'

'I can't imagine The Empress ever feeling like home. I can't even believe we're getting married in two days' time.'

'To your continued happiness,' he raised a glass. 'To you and Silvano,' he toasted.

'Are you okay, Henrik?'

He nodded, but I couldn't take my eyes from his face.

'I hope you and I,' he muttered, 'will become friends. Never enemies.'

'Enemies? Why would we become enemies?'

'I think you should speak with Silvano.'

'About Dolores? He wouldn't hear it.'

'No, not about her.'

And, without a word, deep in my heart, I already knew.

Chapter 25

Jennifer

I tried to contact George, but his phone was switched off. Maybe he was somewhere across the Atlantic, too late for me to stop him, or cancel my date for dinner with Marcus that evening. I had no idea what to do. My mind was playing, *'George: The Director's Cut'*, meanwhile, I was in Marcus's apartment.

'I think it's too dark. Hey? Are you even listening?'

'Hmm, yes. Maybe it is too dark.'

'Are you okay?'

'Me? Yes. Why?'

'You're blushing,' he said, putting down the tray, tracing his hand across my cheek.

I found it hard to concentrate when he was next to me. All I could think about was how he should take off his clothes and help me decide whether to get under him, or over him.

I know. Listen to me. I was awful.

I shut my eyes, unable to tell him how my ex-boyfriend was about to propose, flying out to see me right this second because his wife had started having it off with a salesman.

I convinced myself Luke must have got it horribly wrong for the hundredth time, and who was to say if George wasn't some crazy philanderer? Things still didn't add up, like why was he wining and dining Helen, and hugging her in the street, and buying her expensive champagne and flowers. Plus, unless he was crazy, how did George plan to tell everyone we were engaged, when his own children didn't know we were together in the first place? So instead, I breathed in the scent of Marcus's paint-stroked hand, hoping the fumes might bring clarity. Or a legal high. Talking of which…

'Jen?' he smiled. 'You're unreal. You want it again, don't you?'

We'd done it twice that morning. I hadn't even thought of breakfast. Marcus was all I needed to set me up for the day. Blinds closed, room bathed in sun-shadows, I shivered into semi-consciousness, overwhelmed by his constant insistence on pleasure.

Next, I'd attempted to dress, but he'd undressed me again. I wrapped my arms around his neck as we devoured each other. And now, here I was, a seeker of pleasure, unable to lift my head without thinking of some ecstasy I was moments away from. Well, that and the fact George was *en route*, but before I could get anxious again, Marcus put down the roller. Next, he took off his t-shirt.

Oh, dear God, thank you!

'Lay down on the floor.'

Not a question did I ask. No protest whatsoever did I make, even though I had my best skirt on and his floor was covered in flecks of wet paint.

I stared at the ceiling, stifling a squeal as he knelt between my feet, grabbed my ankles, spread my legs, and eased his hands along my inner thighs.

'Is this what you want?'

I couldn't speak, could only nod as the buttons of my blouse were slowly, expertly, undone. The same way he'd unfastened my mind into his way of thinking, and doing things I never knew existed.

'Tell me what you want, Jennifer.'

I searched for something, but I'd forgotten how to shape sounds into language. I was a Stone Age sex-mute, reduced to communicating in grunts and pointed fingers.

'Come on, Jennifer,' he insisted, hands under my skirt, hooking his thumbs under the sides of my knickers and slowly pulling them down. 'Tell me.'

'Please...' I swallowed. 'Don't ... stop.'

He took the scarf from my neck (technically, Lara's scarf, but I think once you've been intimate wearing an item of clothing, even if it is someone else's, morally, it becomes yours), and lifted my head as he blindfolded me.

I mean, really, what chance did I have?

We didn't make it out to dinner. Instead, Marcus was fixing us something to eat as I stepped out of the shower, his computer waiting for me as promised.

I hadn't told him about the blog. I'd done enough damage, and now that I was online, I could see just how much. *Lola Tyler* was everywhere. Discussed in forums. Praised on Tumblr. Suspects posted all over Pinterest.

'That's the blog? The one you posted, like Lara said on New Year's Eve, right?'

'I didn't post it,' I explained, reading the comments about my sister on one particular website, which practically spelled out how the whole thing must be about her. 'I'd never have posted it. My friend, Luke, wrote this thing, *The Spanish Detective*, and put it on that yourstory.com site, the writing competition. He decided to increase his chances of winning by posting Lara's diary, under the name Lola Tyler. Then, the whole wedding thing made it all so obvious, he may as well have put Lara Taylor and saved us the hassle.'

'Hey, you don't mind me doing this, do you?'

I turned to find Marcus holding his camera.

'What are you doing?'

I found his face, or rather, the lens.

'Turn it off! *Turn that thing off!*'

'Okay, okay,' he said, slowly lowering the camera to his hip.

Curious as to why he'd want to video my reaction to the stupid blog, we got into a 'discussion' about the documentary he was making. The one about Silvano, which, he explained, had 'kind of' become about my sister.

'Kind of?'

'Look, Jen. Your sister was a massive deal —'

'She's still a massive deal.'

'You know what I mean. You can't expect me to ignore all of this. I'm a video-journalist, and this thing with Lara is like, blowing people's minds. I'm here, taking it down, right as it happens.'

'What does that mean?'

'It means, I can't edit reality to suit you. Lara marrying Silvano isn't the lead story any more. This is guaranteed airtime,' he said, holding up the camera. 'Everyone's going to want this story.'

'So you're going to sell it?'

'Hey, don't do that,' he said, turning away. 'This is my *job*.'

'What? Ruining people's lives? Spying on them?'

'Hey, I never spied on anyone. I had full permission. I never planned any of this. Sometimes a story just develops.'

'It's not a story! It's my sister's life. It's my family.'

'Don't blame me, Jen. Blame everyone who ever made a cent from being in the public eye.'

I left Marcus's apartment, and after getting through to my sister's voicemail yet again, I'd decided to skip that and leave a message at the hotel reception instead:

You're my sister. Please call me. I'm stupid and I'm sorry.

But, no matter how many times I checked my phone, there was still no word. And, while Luke had technically detonated the whole bombshell, and I was still furious with him, I had to admit: I missed him. He was the one person I could be myself with, who never judged me if I ran out of teabags, or had a bad day at work, or accidentally put brown eye-liner pencil around my lips instead of lip-liner. Really needing to talk to someone, I called him.

'I didn't think anyone would read it. *The Spanish Detective's* had less than forty hits. Meanwhile, *Lola Tyler* goes global...'

'Don't remind me. Lara still hasn't replied to my calls. She'll never trust me again.'

'Don't say that...'

'Do you know what's going to happen once Mum and Dad find out?'

His silence spoke volumes.

'Exactly. I can't even think about my mum without feeling sick. Meanwhile, everyone is clicking on the link as if it's a TV show, but it's not, it's my sister's life. Her feelings.'

'I'm sorry. I'm so sorry about the whole thing, and I'm still here for you, Jen. You're still my closest friend in the world.'

'But you slept with my sister...'

The hovering waitress slowly chewed her gum, offering welcome disapproval, before she took her leave.

'I know. I should have told you, but it never came up. There was never a good time to tell you. And, to be honest, I didn't think it mattered any more, not after all this time.'

'Well, it does matter, obviously. It matters to me.'

'Why? Tell me why. I don't need a list of all your former lovers.'

'This is completely different! I thought you were my friend, not her ex! And —' I stopped myself before I denied it, because I'd had enough of other people's secrets to last me a lifetime. 'Maybe I'm a bit jealous. Maybe I thought you were one of the few people who didn't care that my sister's beautiful, and perfect, and exciting. I didn't think any of that mattered. I thought you were just my friend, and now I find out you're just as wrapped up with her as everyone else.'

'I'm not wrapped up in her! This whole thing started out because I was scared of hurting you. I was worried you'd find out, but it's years later, it doesn't matter anymore!'

'Well,' I stuttered, a balloon of self-pity inflating inside my chest, 'I shouldn't be surprised, because you sleep with anyone that'll have you, anyone who gives you five minutes of their time —'

'Look,' he muttered, lowering his voice. 'I didn't hit on you, because I'd already slept with your sister. Even I'm not that morally reprehensible.'

'I didn't want you to hit on me, you moron!' I insisted. 'I just thought you were one of the few people who cared about me. Anyway,' I said, not giving him a chance to defend himself, 'I've got to go. My sister's getting married tomorrow, although I'm guessing she won't need me as a bridesmaid. Even though,' I bit back disappointment, 'that dress is the only thing I've ever actually looked good in.'

'Well, maybe one day, if you and George —'

George. I was trying to put him out of my mind. I didn't think I could take any more drama in one week, not after Luke said he was due to arrive in New York any minute.

'Look, no matter what he says, George was last seen hugging his wife, planning a romantic meal for two. Have you forgotten? Maybe he's changed his mind,' I sniggered, 'brought Helen with him for a romantic trip away from the kids...'

'It wasn't his wife. That was his receptionist,' he said. 'He said he was going to explain it all to you himself. I thought he'd call you over Christmas. Turns out he's been mulling over how to propose to you instead…'

Elise? I'd met her one time. She fitted the description, apart from being about ten years older than George's ex.

'So, you got that wrong as well?' I hissed into my mobile. 'Why did you have to play around with my life? You should try sorting out your own before you start messing around with other people's!'

'That's what my dad said. They're doing it. They're kicking me out of the apartment,' Luke sounded almost hopeful, as if by sharing his own piece of bad news, we'd be able to find neutral ground again. 'Dad said unless I find a proper job, he's not letting me live there for free anymore.'

'That's hardly the end of your world, is it? At least he hasn't disowned you in the middle of New York. Anyway,' I said, 'I've got another night to spend alone in the most amazing city in the world, that is unless George turns up to propose on my doorstep…'

Chapter 26

Lara

I was restocking the kitchen for my last night of freedom, as Jen let herself in to the apartment.

'I'm sorry I threw red wine all over you,' I said. 'It was a terrible thing to do.'

'What I did was worse,' she said, closing the door behind her, dropping her bag at her feet. 'I had no right to go through your things like that —'

'Well, you weren't the one who put it online,' I told her, drying my hands. 'Yes, I'd rather my life wasn't all over the web, but Bill reckons it's already starting to die down. Some people think it's about me, no one knows for sure, but to be honest, I really don't think anyone's that interested in me anymore.'

'But, I thought you said Bill —'

'Believe me, people are probably hoping it's about someone they actually recognize. One of the newer girls. Most of the kids reading that stuff won't remember who I am, some of them weren't even born when I started out,' I assured her, the same way Bill had explained it to me, and both of us knew there was a bigger point to be made. He'd been right all along. I wasn't the big name I'd thought I was, not anymore.

'Well, I just want you to know, like I said on the voicemail, Luke didn't post it to hurt you,' she said, picking up the pace. 'He did it because he was panicking about getting a job, and thought some dumb writing contest was going to get his parents off his back,' Jen said, fixing her hair behind her ear.

'But I told him about it. Because I'm a snoop, and I'm so embarrassed! I just,' Jennifer stuttered. 'If I wasn't so stupid, none of this would have happened.'

'Believe me,' I said, opening the fridge, 'it's not the worst thing that's ever happened to me. You read my stuff, you should know.'

'Not much of it, I promise.'

'Anyway,' I said, taking out a bottle that had been chilling for nearly an hour since I got Jennifer's message at reception, and decided it was now or never. 'This,' I said, popping the cork on the champagne Silvano had donated, 'is my Hen Night. You're my sister, and tomorrow, you're my bridesmaid. So, we're having that Girl's Night we never got round to.'

It turned out to be the best Girls' Night we ever had, especially since last time we had worn matching nightdresses, shared trifle, and stayed up late watching the latest *Disney*, we were supervised by our mum.

Jen went doe-eyed talking about New York, and I pointed out she'd turned into our mother, as she said: 'I love New York. *The Big Apple*. The city that never sleeps!'

We screamed laughing about Barry Hogg's recent arrest; and Jen shrieked as I revealed Dolores had actually got married in an exact copy of the 'Flesh and Frills' wedding dress, which apparently, only looked tarty on me.

Finally, one bottle down, we danced around until I thought I'd pulled a tendon trying to 'twerk' to Kylie, so we opened a couple of face masks and lounged about in the over-sized I Heart N.Y. t-shirts she'd bought for us both.

It was only as I was about to serve our cake that, even through a layer of deep-cleansing mud, I noticed Jennifer's expression turn from goofy to glum.

'What's wrong?' I asked, giving her a playful nudge of the elbow. 'It's meant to be a little party…'

'Are you still doing drugs?'

I shrugged, 'I've been seeing someone about it. Someone Silvano knows who's treated *many* people with *many* problems before I came along. And, I haven't had any since New Year's Eve, I promise.'

'Wow! A whole four days…'

'Well, right now I have to count each day as some sort of victory. It's been tough, but despite Mum nearly pushing me over the edge, I didn't touch anything over Christmas either. …'

'Except for drinking the house dry and chain-smoking, you mean.'

'I didn't drink the house dry!'

'Try telling Mum that. I want to know you, without snooping through diaries. I want to know things about your life, and I want you to care about mine,' she said, eyes misting over, as she pulled up her thermal socks, knees under her chin, as if she were ten-years-old again. 'And I wish you weren't always running away, or running off with some bloke, because it's like you're trying to run away from us all the time.'

'That's exactly what Susan, my counsellor, says,' I smiled, my own eyes stinging with tears.

'I just want to get to know you, that's all.'

'Ask me anything,' I said, giving her foot a rub, before grabbing a cushion and propping myself up at the other end of the settee. 'What do you want to know?'

'Why did you sleep with Luke,' she said, biting her lip as if biting back the words. 'And why did you never tell me?'

'Oh, that, well,' I said, caught slightly off-guard. 'That was another lifetime ago. I didn't want it to become some big issue between the two of you guys.'

'He said that's why he read your diary. In case he was in it, and I read some more and found out,' she said, deep in thought, 'I just feel like ... why do you have to have sex with every man I meet?'

'I don't have sex with every man you meet! I cared about Luke. He cared about me. It was way before you two reconnected.'

'Well, okay, then, not every man I meet,' she chattered. 'But, now I know about Luke, and you already slept with my first boyfriend.'

'Jen, I —'

'Oh shut up! I know you slept with Elliot. He told me. You turned up, knowing he was DJing, and draped yourself all over him.'

'He was all over me!'

'Great. I feel so much better now. He was *my boyfriend*. We were living together. I couldn't even tell Mum and Dad,' she said, words caught in her throat. 'I was so hurt that you would do that to me. And I kept thinking about why that happened, and I kept telling myself it was just because you could. It was just because you have to keep reminding me that you're so much better than I am, but I already know that anyway. I don't need reminding.'

'I didn't do it to hurt you,' I said, knowing how stupid that sounded. 'And I don't think I'm better than you, not at all. I was just *screwed up*,' I admitted. 'Anyway,' I snapped, embarrassed. 'He wasn't right for you. It's not as if I was the only girl he cheated on you with.'

'See?' Jennifer looked at me, strangely calm. 'What did I ever do to you?'

'Nothing,' I said, knowing my sister had never deliberately hurt anybody in her life. 'And you barely spoke to me for a year after all that, remember?'

'Do you blame me? But I still didn't tell Mum what you'd done, just like I knew it was you who put that toffee in my hair! I did the same thing, protected you, never told Mum, not even after I had to have all my hair cut off, and everyone laughed at me at school.'

'I didn't put it in your hair! I, well I, kind of put it on your pillow, and —'

'Why did you always hate me so much?'

'I never hated you.' I shook my head. 'But, I don't know, I think it was because they loved you more,' I admitted, slumping against my seat. 'Mum and Dad always loved you more.'

'No they didn't,' Jennifer said, grabbing hold of my hand. 'You never liked yourself, that's why you were always so horrible to me, and Mum and Dad.'

'You sound like my therapist,' I said, fighting tears.

'But even though you were so moody, and secretive, and acted like you hated everyone, I could still never compare to you, no matter what I did.'

'Believe me, I was the one who didn't compare.'

'That's not true,' Jen insisted. 'You were always the favourite.'

'I don't think so, Jen.'

'Well, I'm telling you. Mum and Dad were so sad after you left. I was completely invisible. I could never make them happy, not the way you did. They missed you so much when you left, but you don't see what everyone else sees. And it's all good, I promise. If you'd just give us a chance, you'd know it's ridiculously good.' She smiled. 'We love you. We do.'

I nodded, too sad to speak.

'But please, promise me you haven't slept with anyone else I don't know about? I mean, you and Barry The Hoggster, that was some serious chemistry...'

'Well, I know, but sometimes you have to try and fight these things,' I said, giving her hand a squeeze. 'Anyway, it's supposed to be a fun night. Look at the state of us.'

'We've cracked our masks,' Jennifer pointed out, picking a piece of clay mask from off her cheek. 'We look like a pair of suicidal mime artists.'

She pulled one of the roses from my vase, placed it between her teeth, both palms in the air, pretending to be trapped against an invisible wall. Once she had me laughing, there was no stopping her. Dressed in her tourist's t-shirt, face covered by the remains of her face mask, she pulled herself along on an invisible mime-rope towards the kitchen.

'Are we eating this cake, or not?'

I could already hear her grabbing plates.

'Yes! New York cheesecake, from the hotel. Freshly-made today.'

'So,' she said, wandering back with our slices. 'What's Silvano up to tonight?'

'Quiet one, I think.'

'With his mum?'

'Probably,' I admitted, taking a mouthful, and trying to swallow my thoughts down along with it, but then the words were left, right on the tip of my tongue: 'He's gay.'

'I thought so...'

'You thought he was gay but you didn't say anything?'

'I just thought you were his Moustache, or something.'

222

'You mean Beard.'

'Well, he is ridiculously rich, and that's the biggest rock of an engagement ring I've ever seen.'

'It's not about that.' I shook my head. 'It's not about the money. Silvano treats me better than anyone I've ever met, he really does. Every guy I've ever been out with wanted to get inside my knickers after the first hello. I thought Silvano was kind of, romantic,' I told her. 'And uncomplicated. He seemed loyal, like he'd never hurt me, or cheat, or lie. And I could use some of that. He was just, kind of old fashioned, I guess,' I said, putting my plate back on the table. 'But, I don't know. I don't know whether I can trust him, either. I should have known something wasn't quite right when he was hanging around with porn stars…'

'*Porn stars*? What porn stars?'

'Marcus and his never-ending documentary.'

'Marcus?'

I noticed my sister's expression turn to stone.

'Yes, Marcus. Kinky Kleff. Former porn star. Don't tell me you've got a crush on him? He's definitely not crush material for my little sister.'

'He's not a crush…'

I untucked my feet, studying my sister's face, as it dawned on me.

'You *shagged* him, didn't you?'

'No, I…' She could barely swallow her biscuit base. 'Yeah, I did. Loads of times.'

'You've been shagging *Marcus*?'

'Oh my God, Lara. I've done it with a porn star,' she said, covering her face in her hands. 'And my ex-boyfriend's here, probably on his way to propose, except he's not even answering my texts, and surely if you wanted to marry someone, the least thing you'd do is text back?'

I sat back in my seat, and listening to my sister, my own life didn't seem quite as messed up as I thought.

Chapter 27

Jennifer

My sister's hair was beautifully arranged around her face, diamond earrings catching the light, making her look like a proper movie star.

'You look amazing.' I smiled. 'You always look perfect, but today, you look so beautiful. Don't cry,' I said, scrambling through the array of bridal beauty kit lying on the bed, trying to find a tissue. 'That wasn't supposed to upset you.'

'I'm allowed to cry. I'm the bride.'

'The bride doesn't cry! I think that's the guests' job, isn't it?'

'I haven't got any, remember?'

'Well, you've got me.'

'Don't!' she said, blowing her nose. 'Jennifer, be honest. Do you really think I should marry Silvano? Seriously…'

'You love each other. That's all that matters?' I said, realizing I was asking a question rather than making a statement. 'Oh, I don't know,' I said, taking a seat. 'I just want you to be happy. I mean, do *you* think you should marry him?'

'I don't know…'

'Lara?' I got up, placed my hands on her shoulders, trying to find the right words, needing to be reassuring. 'Whatever you want to do, I'm on your side, okay?'

'I can't be divorced three times.'

'I think you're getting a little ahead of yourself.'

'Exactly. Why? Because it's all wrong again.'

'Oh God, Lara,' I said, her panic becoming contagious. 'It's your life, but he's gay!' I cringed, 'and there're people arriving any minute for the wedding.'

I admit, that wasn't the most encouraging thing to say to a bride with cold feet, but I thought I was being quite diplomatic, considering she'd only decided to lift the veil on her husband-to-be the night before.

'For Christ's sake,' she said, riffling through her handbag, finally clamping her perfectly made-up pout around a cigarette. 'Have you got a lighter?'

'A lighter? No. I don't smoke, and I haven't got pockets. I'm the bridesmaid not the bartender.'

'It's fine,' she huffed. 'I've got matches somewhere...'

I looked at my sister, bereft in a beautiful wedding gown, ransacking the suite for the sake of a smoke, and knew I never wanted to get married. Ever.

Not even to George. And definitely not to Marcus, whose porn career I was far too scared about to even Google.

'Are you sure you're allowed to smoke in here?'

'Of course not,' she said, dragging her voluptuous cream train over to the window. 'I'll stick my head out. Don't worry, I'll try to resist the urge to jump...'

You could hear the steady commotion outside as she opened the window. Cars arriving, people gathering. The morning of a wedding, I thought, not sure if there was actually going to be one.

'*Oh shit!* My veil!'

A split second of misplaced fag later, and there was a singed, tennis ball-shaped hole right in front of my sister's face.

And then came a knock at the door.

'Miss Taylor? Your flowers have arrived...'

'Oh, you get it ... I was saving it for you anyway.'

I opened the door to Henrik, who stepped into the room wearing a tight smile, while I took delivery of the bridal bouquet, a fresh offering of stalks and white roses.

'Miss Taylor, you look stunning. Mr Arazzi is a very lucky man,' he said, giving us a small bow as he left.

'I can't breathe,' she gasped, steadying herself at the dresser.

'Relax. It's a wedding, not a contraction,' I said, passing her the flowers, not sure how I was going to calm her down before the ceremony. 'Here, let me see what I can do with this,' I said, finding a tube of eyelash glue, which I'd learned first-hand could be pretty firm stuff, and dotting it along the burnt edges of her veil.

'There'll be no contractions,' she snorted. 'There'll be no kids. Not for me. Even if Silvano were a red-blooded heterosexual, it wouldn't work. It's me. I've been there, had the tests, cried the tears, broken my heart.'

'You can't have children?'

My sister shook her head.

'We could adopt. It's what his mother wants, after all. In fact, it's practically in the contract. She'll probably choose one for us,' she said, growing pale. 'And the poor kid will be stuck with a dad with a secret life, a crazy grandmother, and an infertile, deranged mum, but at least that way, there's a small chance it won't be as screwed up as either of its parents. And,' she stutter-laughed, 'we can always rely on Uncle Henrik to babysit. Oh God,' she gasped, 'I need to see Silvano.'

'You can't see him now. It's unlucky!'

'Unlucky? I think it's pretty *fucking* unlucky to realize your groom's in love with the maitre d' on the morning of your wedding.'

'*Henrik*? He's in love with Henrik?'

'Yes, he bloody well is!' she said, clutching at her skirts, and heading straight out the door.

A swift glance down to the lobby confirmed the heads of waiting guests. I saw Silvano, chatting and shaking hands among them. Noticed Marcus, busy with his camera, before I heard the voices of Henrik and Lara coming from around the corner.

'Dolores begged Silvano,' Henrik was explaining, visibly shaken, as my sister listened intently. 'It wasn't until he lost friends, you know, in the fashion industry, that he worked with her, lived the life his mother wanted for him. And then, we met,' he said, clutching at his hands nervously. 'Delores found out, of course. She explained the family had experienced this problem with *men like me*, before. When she met his father, he was to be cut out of the family estate, despite his considerable influence in the hotel. He brought the place to life, she said, but there were no pretty *girls* catching his eye...'

'So,' Lara interrupted. 'I was going to be part of the family tapestry, another keeper of secrets, just like his mother?'

'Dolores persuaded Silvano it was for the best, for the hotel, for the family-name,' he explained, 'but she wasn't sure if you would keep his secret. If you could display the same loyalty as she had to his father, her own husband. There was no love in her life, I think,' Henrik contemplated, 'until Silvano was born.'

'I think I'm going to be sick,' Lara said.

I walked over, put my arm around her, as Henrik looked at her sadly.

'Lara? Silvano loves you,' he reassured her, 'he does. But if he marries you, I can't stay here, not without your consent. I asked him to tell you. I didn't want us to go behind your back. He was scared you wouldn't understand, but I told him it was wrong to trick you like that. I thought, maybe, if I was honest with you, we could all learn to live with each other,' he confessed. 'I'm so sorry, Lara. I really am, but I love him.'

'I need to speak with Silvano,' Lara decided, eyes glazed. 'I knew about his *preferences*. I thought I could cope with that, both of us being celibate, I mean, but now he's cheating on me? I can't believe he wants us to live like that! It's disgusting!'

And before I knew what was happening, she was gone.

'Lara!' I shouted. 'Can't you just call him? Or text? A quick text?' I shouted, trying to rein her in, as she prepared to descend the sweeping oak staircase. 'Lara, *please!*'

I saw her miss the step.

Stopped in my tracks as one long leg stretched out into thin air

Held my breath, too shocked to scream, until she slammed down onto her hip, then onto her elbow, as the wooden staircase took the full force of her weight.

'Lara!'

I raced behind her as she scraped down a couple more steps, leaning dangerously forward, grabbing hold of the banister, while I managed to snatch at her veil, pulling it from her head, savaging the remaining voile, instead of saving her.

The gathered crowd gave a collective gasp.

'Baby! What happened?'

I was helping Lara to sit up as Silvano reached the bottom of the staircase. Marcus standing behind him with his stupid camera pointed right at us, as blood trickled down my sister's leg, quickly reaching her beautiful shoe.

Then I saw her face. Also red.

Nothing infuriated Lara more than embarrassment.

I could feel her shaking, but even I didn't expect the torrent she unleashed next.

'What happened?' she screeched, and in a flash, she pulled off her shoe, sat back with a thud, and aimed the Louboutin right at his head. 'You happened! That's what happened. You and him!' she roared, turning her attention to Henrik, standing at the top of the staircase. 'I find out you're dating the maître d'! Cheating on me before you've even had the decency to marry me. And, if my cheating, gay fiancé wasn't enough,' she said, pointing an accusatory finger at Marcus, *you've* been shagging my sister! Kinky Kleff, A.K.A. James Bondage, star of For Your Thighs Only!'

Dolores appeared through the sea of bystanders.

'What on earth?'

'And I'll tell you what else happened,' Lara said, turning back to Silvano, who stood clutching his head, as well as the bridal shoe. 'She did! Your mother!' she screamed, brandishing her bouquet above her head. 'This bloody wedding nearly happened! There,' she said, launching the bouquet at Dolores. 'Catch the bouquet! I hope you'll both be very happy together!'

And it was then that I saw him. Looking up at me from beneath the candelabra. Luke. And before I could gasp his name, George appeared behind him.

I called his name as he turned back against the tidal wave of well-dressed bodies surging towards the chaos of my sister, Silvano and Dolores.

'George! *Wait!*'

I dropped the veil, and despite having seen the dangers of a high heel on a polished floor, I ran after him, following him through the carousel doors, suddenly on the sidewalk, shivering in my bridesmaid gown.

'Is that true? You and *him*,' he asked, pointing back to the foyer of The Empress.

I stood, speechless, partly through guilt, and partly because he looked so handsome when he was appalled.

'You were hugging your wife!' I ranted, reminding myself of why I'd fallen in sex with Marcus in the first place. 'Shopping for a romantic meal for two.'

'That wasn't Helen!'

'Yes, well,' I stammered, 'I only found that out yesterday!'

'I explained all of that to your good friend, Luke,' he said. 'After he turned up, snooping around my house. At least I'd already dropped the kids back with their mother, so they weren't there to see him, peering through the porch in some ridiculous hat,' he shouted, gesturing to his head, 'like Freddy Krueger doing Trick or Treat.'

'Well, how was I supposed to know it wasn't Helen?'

'I don't appreciate being spied on.'

'He wasn't spying,' I stuttered. 'There's a difference between a spy and a detective, you know?'

'Oh right,' he said, gritting his teeth in temper. 'You mean, like James *Bondage* or whatever that guy calls himself?'

'I didn't know about that,' I mumbled. 'And, just so you know, I don't appreciate running around with my heart in my handbag for most of last year. And I don't appreciate that you never even tried to get me back...'

'Are you kidding me?' he said, clearly astounded. 'I called. I sent texts. You told me to leave you alone. You never wanted to hear from me again, that's what you said.'

'I didn't mean it, everyone says that!'

'No, they don't. You do, because you don't know what it is you want. You told me it was over, ran off wearing a fake moustache, remember?'

'It was an eyelash!' I explained. 'See? You're always making fun of me. I lost my job, George. I lost my home.'

'And I was trying to help you to relax. Take your mind off things.'

'How? By pretending everything was fine, cooking me fancy dinners, and hiding me from your kids?'

'I never hid you. I was being a responsible parent, is that so terrible? We'd been going out since February. I have two children. I couldn't ask you to move in overnight. It's their house, too.'

'Then why are you going to propose? If it was too soon for me to move in, why would you want to get engaged? You barely called me when I was staying an hour down the road with my parents, so you fly to New York, and gate-crash my sister's —' I stumbled over the word, 'wedding' now that there wasn't going to be one, *'Big Day*, with an engagement ring instead? Are you mad?'

We looked at each other, and I knew it was finally, definitely, over.

'Now that I'm here, knowing how quickly you've moved on, I agree, Jennifer. I must have been mad...'

I watched him as he walked over to a waiting yellow taxi, which quickly pulled away from the kerb, with my heart held hostage on the backseat.

'He didn't propose, then?'

Luke appeared, putting a cigarette to his lips.

'What the hell are you doing here?'

'I wanted to be here, seeing as I've managed to do nothing but upset you recently. I wanted to tell you I was here last night, on the phone, but George swore me to secrecy,' he explained, lighting up. 'I thought we could all celebrate your engagement together. Plus, I told my parents there was a publisher here, interested in *The Spanish Detective*, so Dad's dropped the whole topic of putting me to work in his rustic kitchen, for now, anyway...'

I hit him as hard as I could across the shoulder.

'You're an idiot. A selfish, bloody idiot — and a liar,' I said, jaw chattering with cold, as my sister flew through the doors in a bridal tsunami, loaded with bags, heading straight into the back of a waiting limousine, before disappearing off, the way she always did when she was in the middle of an imploding drama.

'I know,' Luke said, taking off his coat. 'So the least you can let me do is save you from hypothermia,' he said, placing his jacket around my shoulders.

I had no intention of risking seeing George at their hotel, so Luke and I headed back to Lara's apartment, hoping to find her there.

'So, I guess I'm not getting engaged after all,' I said, nursing a coffee.

'I thought you said this morning's put you off marriage for good?'

'It has.'

'Well, there you go then,' Luke said, finishing another cigarette.

I pulled a face, got up and opened the window.

'You still haven't given those things up, I see?'

'What do you expect? I've been totally stressed out...'

'Me too, but you don't catch me inflicting second-hand smoke on anybody. And could you please explain why you're spending so much time with George these days?'

'I knew I'd upset you,' he said, tilting back his head and slumping against the chair. 'So, the first time I went round, he explained everything, about the receptionist...'

'And you didn't tell me? You just went home, instead?'

'He told me to keep out of it, said he was going to speak to you himself. I wasn't trying to piss anyone off.' He closed his eyes and sighed. 'I went home that afternoon, after I'd slept off our night in Ingleford. My father was as pleased to see me as ever. Launched into this huge speech about me needing to grow up, get a job, stop all this bullshit writing, and you were so upset with me. I went to see George. To confront him, make sure I was right, after everything I'd said to you. We spoke for about an hour. I went back to my parents' place, left him to it. Since then, well, he knows how much I care about you. I suppose he wanted to talk to someone who knows you as well as I do, and, like I said, I still think he's mad about you.' He paused, and I couldn't help but roll my eyes. 'As for all the other stuff, that's complete history. It was over in weeks, not even a month, I don't think. Lara broke my heart. End of story.'

'She breaks everybody's heart,' I said, heading to the spare bedroom. 'Anyway, I'm sick of hearing about it, and by the way, whose idea was it to turn up to her wedding?'

'You did say you'd never looked better than in that dress...'

'Yeah, well,' I shouted, pulling on jeans and a sweater. 'I don't think George really noticed how nice I looked, do you?'

I put my beautiful gown on a hanger, clipping it against the back of the door, knowing I would never be That Girl. The one who was pretty, and happy, and got to wear fancy dresses and go to the ball. And as for the Prince, the best I could manage was a porn star.

Just as I pulled on my socks, I felt my mobile vibrate inside my pocket. *Mum.*

What's going on? Haven't heard from you. No wedding???

'*Dear God!*' Luke's voice interrupted my thoughts. 'Jen? You need to get out here, right now…'

I walked into the living room, phone still idling in my hand, as Luke lurched forward, raising the volume on the TV.

There we were on the television screen. Me and my sister. Her, slumped on the staircase, screeching obscenities, as I clutched the veil.

The clip ended and zoomed out to a news show. The presenter came in to shot:

'The shocking footage of the Arazzi wedding that never was, comes just days after an anonymous blog appeared online, bearing a striking similarity to key events in the life of former model, Lara Taylor. Twice-married Miss Taylor has yet to comment on the blog, originally posted on the yourstory.com website.'

'That was me,' I said, stumbling backwards, practically falling onto the settee.

'Uh-huh,' Luke managed.

For a few seconds, I couldn't understand how something I'd done this morning was playing out on a TV screen. And not just mine, I realized, but everyone else's TV screens too. Then, all became clear. *Marcus*. Marcus and his *lead* story.

'Kinky Kleff!'

'Sorry?' Luke said, still fixed on the screen as if I might pop up again at any minute.

'Marcus. He was filming it. He told me Silvano wasn't the big story any more. It was my sister, because of that bloody blog thing you posted. He's sold the footage.'

I grabbed the remote, flicking through the channels like a couch potato on a caffeine-rush. Ten seconds in, there it was, the tail-end of the clip on another show:

'I think we can all agree, she looks fabulous, yes?' A shiny-looking guy in a bright green suit sat in the middle of huge, purple couch, surrounded by co-hosts. 'Lara Taylor is a woman who knows how to fall down a staircase. Jilting the groom on the morning of her wedding…!'

The co-hosts collapsed into giggles beside him.

'And I don't know about you, Enzo,' a wafer-thin woman with a quiff as high as her heels, chimed in, 'but her almost-bridesmaid is just adorable, in what we think, may be a Clarrisa gown, palest pink, featuring spaghetti straps.'

Heads nodded, mumbled in agreement, as Enzo put his hand to his earpiece.

'We believe that adorable bridesmaid might well be sister-of-the-almost-bride, a Miss Jennifer Taylor, but her identity has yet to be officially confirmed…'

'This is surreal,' Luke muttered.

'I can officially confirm,' I nodded, 'this is absolutely crazy.'

Chapter 28

Lara

'Kill me now.'

'I admit, the thought had occurred to me.'

I was sat with Bill in front of the 60" screen embedded in the wall of his office.

Within minutes of me phoning from the hotel, Bill had received a call from Multi-Media-Magnets, who had acquired footage from my wedding, hotly thought to be connected to the mysterious blog on the yourstory.com website.

Several calls later, and no surprises, Bill identified Marcus Kleff as the purveyor of the footage. Marcus had promised them the blog was based on my journal, although Bill had successfully distanced us from confirming anything until he and I had finalised a statement.

'The shocking footage of the Arazzi wedding that never was, comes just days after an anonymous blog appeared online, bearing a striking similarity to key events relating to former model Lara Taylor...'

'*Former* model?'

'Ssh!'

'Twice-married Miss Taylor has yet to comment on the blog, originally posted on the yourstory.com website.'

'We have to respond as soon as possible. I've put something together...' Bill was saying, but the full impact was only just sinking in as I flicked through channels.

'They're covering it on *Model Behaviour* too?' I said, hitching up the yards of voile around my feet.

'I think we can all agree she looks fabulous, yes?' Enzo Ronsinni was enthusing, sat in the middle of his famous couch. 'Lara Taylor is a woman who knows how to fall down a staircase. Jilting the groom on the morning of her wedding...!'

'Oh,' I said, hanging my head, gazing down at my bloodstained wedding shoe. 'Jilting the groom? Is that what I did?'

'The big coverage is coming up over on Channel Fifteen,' Bill said, taking the remote from my hand and clicking over.

'If you've just tuned in, stay with us as we're joined by international super model, Amber Rhodes. Thanks Amber, you've been gracious to join us at such short notice...'

'I get former. She gets international?'

'Ssh!'

'Amber's currently known as the face of Alexis Home Shopping...'

'Only after they offered it to me, first!'

'And you turned it down,' Bill reminded me.

'Well, you didn't exactly sell it to me!'

'Amber, a lot of the comments on the blog, show the fashion industry in a pretty dark light. You've been modelling since you were sixteen, is that right?'

'That's correct, Jim.'

'See, *she's* older than I am!'

'Lara, can I please listen?'

'Oh man,' I admitted, 'she still looks great though...'

'And, does any of this negative spin resonate with you? Travelling the world, enjoying the finer things in life, is that the worst thing to happen to a beautiful, teenage girl?' he sniggered.

'I think that's the idealized version, Jim. It's a fantasy, which is probably why so many young girls and their families regard modelling as a positive opportunity.'

I was starting to like Amber Rhodes.

'Well, it certainly was for you, Amber. One of the highest paid models in the business,' he said, checking his notes, 'isn't that correct? Model of the Year, three consecutive years during the last decade, and, your own clothing range launching this spring.'

Her own clothing range? I couldn't even afford to buy pieces from the designers whose clothes I'd modelled since I was a kid, not any more.

'That's right, Jim. I've been very lucky, very blessed, but —'

'So it's fair to say, if this website has come from a, shall we say, inside source,' Jim said, elbow resting on his knee, trying to look casual as he toyed with the pen in his hand, 'the problems, the drug taking, for instance, can't be blamed on her good fortune?'

'Oh, yeah, like good old Jim's not known for his drinking? This is a joke!'

'Lara! Pipe down…'

'From the outside looking in, I understand people are going to have little sympathy for these young girls, but —'

'Surely, drug taking, in these circles, is down to an excessive lifestyle, not because of abuse, poverty, or deeper issues?'

'In my experience, self-medication was almost compulsory. Substances, from nicotine to stimulants, were given to me by adults, people in authority, who I trusted.'

'Hold on, Miss Rhodes, you're actually saying you took illegal substances, drugs —'

'I'm saying these were distributed to me, freely, when I was a vulnerable, young girl, living away from home. The same way a caring mother might give her child a couple of vitamin tablets and a glass of milk with breakfast, these pills, substances, were encouraged as part of my everyday life.'

'Well, presumably you were old enough to realize you were taking drugs...'

'No, not until it was too late, by then, I already had a problem. These things were given in the form of capsules, like something you'd get from a doctor. They looked like medicine. All I knew was that when I was tired, they got me through a shoot. When I was hungry, they took my mind off the need to eat —'

'And these people in authority, giving you these drugs, are you saying these were people working in the industry?'

'I'm saying,' she said, swallowing back emotion, 'they were adults I trusted and never dared question. I was under tremendous pressure, trying to be mature, trying to be professional. Trying to make my parents proud.'

'But you could have returned home at any time, and instead you understood you had the ability to earn quite substantial amounts of money —'

'I was too young to understand money!' Amber said, raising her voice, adjusting her jacket. 'Other people, older people, were the ones who concentrated on that side of things. I was trying to please these people who told me great things were happening to me, but they didn't feel so great. I was abused —'

'Abused is a very strong term —' Jim cautioned.

Amber locked her hands around her knees, stared into the camera: 'I was raped and sexually assaulted on a number of occasions throughout my career. I found myself at the mercy of adults who were wrongly trusted with my well-being. I was pressured into removing my clothes. I was pressured into accepting drink and drugs as part of my life, and either coerced, or forced, into sexual situations I barely understood, and had no desire to be in. So yes, Jim,' she said, turning her attention back to him, 'abused is a very strong term, and one I'm very familiar with, as a woman who has been bought and sold in the name of fashion.'

'Holy shit,' Bill said, falling back against his seat. 'We're issuing our statement. Now.'

After the Jim King interview, Amber Rhodes was dropped from every lucrative contract she had, except for *Alexis* mail order, who stood by her as an organization "which encourages women everywhere to be heard". And, to spend money — without hesitation, I thought, cynical *former* model that I was.

In a stroke of genius, Bill had been one of the first to contact Amber directly. He had an idea, a business proposition, he said, which could potentially change the lives of myself, Amber, and hopefully, countless other models.

It was — ta-dah! — Taylor-made Models.

Since the networks had run with my wedding footage, our phones had rung off the hook. Interviews were courted; statements were coveted. And for the first time in my life, I wasn't ashamed of the truth any more.

I respected Amber's bravery, and I didn't want to pretend. I wanted my life, my work, to be real. I needed them to be, and I knew if I were strong enough, Mum and Dad could be, too. I'd been modelling my whole life, I realised. Trying to be the model daughter had ruined my childhood. Trying to be a professional model had nearly destroyed my grip on reality. And I'd wanted to be a model wife only because I thought reinventing myself would save me — but now, I knew, the only way to save myself was with affirmation. The truth of who I really was, with no apologies, or secrets.

My first reaction had been to hide from the TV clip, deny the blog, but instead of running away, I'd been forced to become stronger.

I felt like me for the first time in my life.

Silvano rejected my calls, and I can't say I blamed him, so I called the main desk and was put through to Henrik instead.

'Please, let Silvano know I am so sorry. From the bottom of my heart. Humiliating him was never my intention but, Henrik, I could not consent to living a lie again. I've been living that way my whole life, and it's poison.' I spoke into silence on the other end of the line. 'Silvano was like my guardian angel. He saved me when I was looking to be saved. He's an incredible man, and if I could wish anything for him, it's his happiness. If that means you being with him, please, make him see sense.'

'Lara, I can't promise Silvano will forgive you, but thank you. Thank you for acknowledging my existence,' he said, clearly emotional, 'and for respecting my feelings. I will explain to Silvano my part in all this, and I wish you happiness also.'

That day was a revelation. They say the truth hurts, but it also heals. I wanted to back Amber, to agree to every interview, give them all what they wanted, and what I needed to do, but Bill made me hold back.

I could almost hear the cogs turning as he zoned out at his desk, reading the thousands of comments posted beneath the yourstory.com blog.

Sitting over a carton of noodles and ice cold beer, Bill and I agreed that the contents of the blog, namely my journal, and Amber's interview, had raised two issues: the exploitation of younger models, and the early retirement of the more, shall we say, experienced cover girls, like myself.

The younger girls, and their families, needed professional reassurance about their welfare. While us older girls deserved steady work — we'd earned it!

During that twenty-minute conversation, the press release, which had started out as a response to a blaze of bad publicity, became the launch of a new approach to the industry.

'*Taylor-made Models*,' Bill had written on a notepad, sliding it towards me with a grin, 'because it's all thanks to you that our models will have a stable present, and hopefully, a lucrative future.'

The idea was two-fold. Amber and I would mentor the younger girls, assign chaperones to accompany them on shoots; physical trainers and nutritionists would monitor their well-being; while we'd use our experience to nurture their talent, only working with those whom we trusted.

We were both convinced, this could be successful, revolutionary even, and once we released our statement, we knew Taylor-made Models was destined to happen:

To All My Friends and Fans,

Since the contents of my private journal became public, I've been touched by your comments.

Initially, I felt fear. Now, I've become driven by a real need within the industry to ensure the career of younger models is nurtured, to ensure young girls starting out in this amazing industry never have to keep the secrets that I, and countless other models like me, have kept for so long.

And, as an experienced model, I want to ensure their careers continue to develop, regardless of age, size, or ethnicity.

Today, I'm proud and delighted to announce the advent of Taylor-made Models. A modelling agency Taylor-made for the 21st century model.

With Love, Sincerity & Great Excitement,

Lara Taylor xxx

Within minutes, we announced Amber Rhodes' collaboration, and within hours, Bill had lined-up half a dozen legendary names, who not only related to our brand values, but were eager to start living them. Unfortunately, the next call I received came from my least favourite, muck-racking, English journalist, former co-passenger on my flight back home, Dan Chatterton.

There was a book deal on the table.

My life story.

Either I collaborated, he said, or I'd have to trust his integrity to write it without my involvement.

Four days' later, I was back in the UK, only this time, I made sure I wore my sunglasses through arrivals.

Chapter 29

Jennifer

I admit, I was hoping 'drinks with George' would become more like a date with George. Luke had spoken to him. He didn't want to leave New York before he'd spoken to me again. We owed each other some explanations, he said.

I'd arrived before him, sat rearranging my hair, checking my lipstick, with one eye on the door. And then, there he was, searching the room, until his gaze found me. My heart was resuscitated. Lungs filling with a deep breath as I took another sip of wine.

'Thanks for coming,' he said, taking a seat.

'Thanks for asking me.'

It all felt so horribly formal, as if I'd never been his girlfriend, or borrowed his toothbrush, or seen his appendix scar before.

'I think there're a few things I need to clear up. Stuff I probably should have explained months ago, but no one realizes these things until it's too late, do they?'

'I know that feeling.'

'How's your sister?'

'Back home. All over the papers.'

'And,' he smirked, uncomfortably, 'how's fame treating you?'

'You saw the clip?'

'Oh yes,' he said, looking slightly stern. 'Who hasn't?'

I paused as we both remembered what came next.

The whole Marcus thing.

'George, I'm sorry —'

'Don't be sorry. I shouldn't have turned up like that, trying to, I don't know,' he said, lifting his hands off table, placing them back down again, 'be romantic.'

'It was,' I said. 'It was romantic, George. And I ruined it.'

He took a drink.

'I thought there was something going on with your wife. None of it made any sense. Everything was always so —'

'Listen, I get it. I do, which is why I thought we should speak before I left.'

Oh God, I thought, realizing this might be the last time I ever saw him.

'The whole misunderstanding with Elise? It was nothing. She collected the children from school for me. I needed to pick up some toys I'd ordered for Christmas, without Susanna and Charlie investigating every package in the back of the car. While she did that, I picked up a few things to thank her. The "romantic meal" was for her to take home to her husband. That's it.'

'But,' I said, feeling utterly stupid, 'you can understand how it looked to Luke and me.'

'I can. If one of my friends had followed you around New York, I'm sure things would have looked a little ropey too, with you and, what's his name...'

I grabbed my glass, swallowing down the guilt with Shiraz.

'Anyway, that's not why I'm here.'

'No?'

'No. I wanted to explain my stuff, with the kids, with Helen,' he cleared his throat. 'You always said I was hiding you away. I can see that now, and for that, I apologise,' he sighed. 'Susanna and Charlie are adopted. I think, looking back on how I was with you, that it made everything far more complicated when we got divorced. We went through so much to get those kids in the first place. Susanna always seemed to pick up on things not being that great between Helen and me. She started asking if she could go back to live with her *real* mummy and daddy. It broke Helen's heart. And mine. So, when I met you, I wasn't exactly in a rush to tell the kids that I'd met someone else. I thought it would make things more difficult, not easier, in the long run.

'I can see now, it was stupid, putting it off like that. But, no offense, when we first got together, I didn't know if things were going to get serious. By the time they did, I couldn't work out the best way to tell the children, other than gradually letting them get to know you, without the pressure of introducing you as a girlfriend. You know,' he met my eye. 'Susanna's not easy at the best of times. If I'd come out and said it, she wouldn't have given you a chance. That's my honest opinion. I thought, let them get to know Jennifer first. By the time they both think she's great, they'll be fine with it,' he said. 'That's the best way I can explain...'

I nodded.

'The big thing was, Helen wanted to adopt another child, but they won't consider you over forty. She got *obsessed* about it. I didn't think it was right for any of us, never mind the children. I was happy having two. Susanna and Charlie are biological siblings. I thought introducing a third child would be too much for them, too much for us. Helen never forgave me. She moved out of my parents' place —'

'Your parents' place?'

'My place now, my house? It was my parents' place. We moved in there after Dad retired to his apartment. Helen and I split up shortly afterwards. She said it never really felt like our home to her,' he said. 'Not that it matters, but that's what happened. Does my life make any more sense to you now?'

'I wish you'd told me all this at the time.'

'I know, I know. But, this is all new to me. Dating again. With two children and an ex-wife. It's a lot to expect someone to take on board. I'm getting used to it myself.'

'But, I think I would have.'

'I know you would, which is why,' he took a huge breath. 'I was planning on arriving here. Sweeping you off your feet with an engagement ring.' Oh, you still could, I wanted to say. You still could and we could forget about all the other stuff, 'Which has got to be the most stupid thing I've ever *nearly* done,' he finished his wine.

'George, all that stuff, *with him*, it's not real. It was a fling. A moment of madness. I thought you'd lied to me. If I'd have known —'

'Look, you're over here. I was the bad guy. You don't owe me anything. I get it.'

Hope blossomed inside me.

'But, the thing I can't get past. Not only the fact it was all over the news,' he half-laughed. 'I could never have done that to you. Not so soon. Not the way I feel about you.'

Hope threw a lasso around my heart, and dragged it off into the distance.

We said our goodbyes, and as we did, I realized he wasn't mine to kiss or hug goodbye any more. Instead, he wished me well and put me in a taxi. I sat, crying, all the way back to Lara's apartment.

Chapter 30

Lara

Five days since the wedding that never was I was in the kitchen, back in Ingleford, scanning the newspaper Mum had been saving for me.

'There's been a man, a reporter, some journalist bloke, wanting to speak to us. Says he knows you,' Mum said, handing me a business card.

'Daniel Chatterton? Don't tell him anything. He doesn't know me. We were on a flight together once.'

'Says he's writing a book about you.'

'No, he's not. He wants to write a book about me, that's all.'

The report Mum had saved was more of his handiwork, presumably trying to drum up publicity for, what he thought, was his forthcoming book:

Model Behaviour?

EXCLUSIVE: Sam and Wendy Knowles recount their school days with meltdown model, Lara Taylor. By Daniel Chatterton.

'Lara was gorgeous even then,' recalls Sam, 34.

'But she always smelt disgusting. Of sick. Because she threw up her school dinner all the time,' Wendy, 33, revealed.

'He knocked on this door,' Mum said, noisily taking a pan from the cupboard. 'To tell me my daughter's said terrible things, *private things*, about her own family. On the internet. All over it, he said.'

I still hadn't explained to my parents why I'd suddenly come home. I didn't know where to start, but I knew it was a race between me and Mr Chatterton to drum up the right kind of headlines.

Unfortunately, it looked like I'd lost the first round.

'I didn't say anything, Mum. What did Daniel say?'

She turned from the stove, tying her apron at the waist.

'Only that it must be difficult, for me, having a daughter who walks out on yet another marriage. A drug addict. A...' She double-knotted the apron. 'A tramp!'

'Is that you or him talking?'

'What's it matter?' She steadied herself against the counter. 'I take it you've run off from America so you can come back to that Tom? And I'm telling you now, that can't happen, because he —'

'Mum, I'm not going to be the bad guy any more...'

'And who is the bad guy?' she gasped. 'Me, I suppose?'

'I'm not going to be your secret any more, Mum,' I said. 'I just want to be your daughter.'

She looked at the floor in silent disagreement.

'Don't make anything for me,' I said, pulling on my jacket, folding up the newspaper. 'I'm going out for dinner.'

'Out? Out with who?'

'With our new friend, Dan Chatterton.'

Daniel booked a table at W, the glass-enclosed restaurant within the Wiltshire Hotel.

'Nice choice,' I smiled, as the waiter showed us to our seats.

'Glad you approve, Miss Taylor,' Daniel smiled. 'I've been staying here.'

'A short stay, or should I be worried?'

He laughed as the waiter retreated.

'That all depends on tonight,' he said, opening the menu. 'I've been looking forward to seeing you.'

'I hear you've already met my parents.'

'Just your mother, actually. She was very sweet.'

'Really? Shame you upset her so much, then. I saw the article with, Sam and Wendy, was it? Who I barely remember from my school days...'

'That's strange. They said they bumped into you over Christmas. You notice, I kept both your rather sleazy stint on the karaoke,' he said, 'and your mother's obvious distress at the tantalizing blog she knew nothing about, out of the paper.'

'You want gratitude?'

'Look, I'm not here to upset anyone. Especially you.'

'That's right. You want to work with me.'

'That's right. On our book. Your chance to set the record straight.'

'Set it straight? You mean after you've bent my life out of shape with some more trashy newspaper articles? I've already issued a press statement.'

'Taylor-made Models. Smart move.'

'It's not a move, Mr Chatterton. It's something I feel very strongly about.'

'Dan, please. And I feel strongly that people will want to hear your story.'

'Buy it, you mean. You want to make yourself a quick profit at my expense. Let's not pretend you're doing this as some act of public service.'

'Maybe I'm as interested in your life as everyone else,' he said, as the waiter took our orders. 'Wine?'

'Not for me, thanks. And why's that, Daniel?'

'I can't resist a beautiful woman.' I rolled my eyes. 'But I admit, a beautiful, *interesting* woman, brave enough to stand up for what she believes in? You're not the average bimbo, Lara Taylor.'

'Just a, what was it you wrote, *former* model?'

'Let's make that a *formidable* model, shall we?'

'I'll take that as an apology for that atrocious piece you wrote after our flight.'

'It could have been worse, and you know it. Like I said, I'm not trying to upset anyone.'

'You say that a lot. Used to having to apologize to people, I guess?'

'No. Just doing my job. I'm good at it.'

'Me too. Except you don't have to put up with strangers knocking on your parents' door or interviewing people you went to school with nearly twenty years ago, in the hope of damaging your reputation.'

'I've never tried to damage your reputation. I've only reported your actions.'

'Reported my actions? Village tittle-tattle from my school days? Most of which was complete trash, and has no bearing on who I am, whatsoever. Great journalism.'

'It was a little low budget, I'll give you that, but I knew it would help to strike up a conversation between us. And so, here we are. I wanted you to see how much better it would be to get involved, rather than leaving me to fix puzzle pieces together.'

'I'm puzzling to you, am I?'

'Yes, very,' he smirked. 'I can't figure you out, but I thought it might be fun trying, which is why I'm so committed to this project.'

'What's to figure out?'

'On the flight, you were obnoxious. *Rude.* Then, I read the blog. Did some research. Saw your er —' he smirked again, 'no offence, but your wedding day? *The clip?* Next thing, you've set up an agency and become an ambassador. *Of sorts.* My sister says you're a feminist icon.'

'That's very kind of her. What does she say about you?'

'About me?' he asked. 'She probably thinks I'm a bit of a prat.'

'She's very astute.'

He grinned.

'Miss Taylor, please forgive me,' our waiter interrupted as he served the starters. 'I'd no idea you were a guest of Mr. Reeves.'

'A guest of Mr Reeves? No, no, I'm not,' I gestured to Daniel. No way could I call him friend, and wouldn't give him the satisfaction of naming him as some sort of business partner. I could see he was loving every minute, amusement hovering across his face as I paused, 'My associate is staying here.'

'Mr Reeves insists you enjoy our hospitality. Please, enjoy dining on us.'

'Oh no,' I looked at his name badge, 'Roger. That's really not necessary.'

'Mr Reeves won't hear of it, madam.'

Tom Reeves suddenly came into view, chatting with waiting guests.

'In that case, please, tell him thank you,' I smiled.

'Problem?' Daniel asked.

'Not at all,' I said, unfolding my napkin.

'You didn't mention they knew you here.'

'I sometimes take a horse out, use the spa occasionally.'

'Anyway,' he smiled. 'We need to work out how we're going to get started.'

'How this works, Daniel, is that you contact Bill Staniss who discusses potential projects with me,' I explained, cutting into a smoked salmon pancake.

'I understand,' he nodded, demolishing his crab starter.

'And then, we consider other avenues which may be open to us.'

'Okay,' he said, meeting my eye. 'Such as?'

'Such as, I'm already in the process of discussing a book deal.'

'*Really*? Well, that is interesting.'

'It is,' I said. 'I'm very excited.'

'And,' he said, meeting my eye as he lifted his glass. 'Will it be a tell-all, or a tell-less version, of your fascinating life?'

I smirked, refusing to let him see my discomfort as I finished my plate.

'You seem to think it's rather more fascinating than it is, Dan.'

'Oh, I disagree.'

'Why's that? Because there's a quick buck in it for you?'

'I told you. I find your life very interesting. And, yes, fair enough,' he scrunched his napkin onto the table, 'I think it's worth spending time working with you.'

'People have grown tired of the blog. The wedding clip will be forgotten about in a week. You wrote yourself, after my flight home for Christmas, about how I'm a former model. An old name. I really don't see the interest, do you?'

'Depends on the angle, doesn't it?' he said, as the waiter removed our plates. 'There's always more than one way to look at these things. Take Mr Reeves, for example. Your relationship with him, I find very interesting.'

'I don't have a relationship with Mr Reeves.'

'Don't you? Tom seems very keen to bridge the gap. After I explained I was here to see you, he told me so himself. When I interviewed him this morning...'

'How dare you pry, you —'

I stood up.

'Oh, come on, Lara. I've been honest from the start. I said, if we weren't going to work together, I'd go it alone.'

'My life. That's what you said you were working on, not destroying other peoples' lives.'

'Like I said, it depends on the angle. If you work with me, we can look at things … from a different perspective.'

'Well, let's think,' I said, grabbing my handbag. 'How about you see how comfortable you are, with taking your angle, and shoving it up your arse.'

I heard footsteps as I approached my car, and assumed at first it would be Dan, still trying to blackmail me into collaborating with him.

'Lara? Aren't you going to say hello?'

'Last time I dropped by, you weren't so interested,' I said, fishing the car keys from the bottom of my handbag. 'Do me a favour, Tom. Stay away from him. That reporter staying with you? He's bad news.'

'Dan Chatterton? He said he was working with you. On your book, with your express permission. Said you were coming here tonight to discuss it.'

I hesitated, not really wanting to hear the answer to my next question.

'What have you told him?'

Tom's eyes met mine, and, not for the first time, I recognized myself in them.

'Everything,' he said, looking concerned. 'I told him everything.'

Chapter 31

Jennifer

'The thing is,' Luke raised an eyebrow. 'I've sold *The Spanish Detective*.'

'You've sold it?' I asked, as surprised as I was excited. 'When did that happen? When you were out doing the tourist thing with George, while I was stuck here on the phone to Mum?'

'George was fine at MoMA. So, I met Marcus…' he cringed.

'*Marcus*? You sold it to that —'

'I know! I know! Let me explain. He contacted me, sent me an email. He knew I'd posted Lara's blog. I think he was fishing for more information about her, but I ended up explaining about the site and *The Spanish Detective*, so he read the stuff, and he loved it, thinks it's got real potential. Look, I don't like the guy any more than you do —'

'I doubt that very much.'

'He says he's going to turn it into screenplay.'

'A screenplay?' I studied Luke's face, and as soon as he met my eye, I'd worked it out. 'It's not going to be a dirty movie, is it?'

'Not a dirty one, no,' he muttered. '*Erotic*. There's a difference.'

'*Is there?*'

'Mine has a story, remember...'

'Oh, yeah. I forgot about the *story* part…'

'Look, I'm having nothing to do with it, okay? He bought it for $5000 —'

'$5000 dollars! *For that?*'

'Yes,' he said, slightly defensive. 'He thinks it's a good concept. Reckons he's going to turn it into an erotic six-part series.'

'I've had enough of Marcus's erotic parts to last me a lifetime...'

'Well, that's why I took the money and ran. Anyway, how did your date go?'

'It didn't, I mean, it wasn't a date, but it was fine. It was good to see him.'

'And he explained everything? About the kids?'

'How do you know more about my ex-boyfriend than I do?'

'I told you. We've been talking. I like the guy. And he's still on our flight tomorrow...'

'There's nothing else to say.'

The whole thing with Marcus had ruined everything. Despite him buying Luke's awful work, I was beginning to wish he really had driven off that cliff in a Cadillac.

'Here's to broken hearts, shattered dreams, and scandal,' Luke said, raising a toast over the tapas he'd made for us.

'You're an amazing cook, Luke.'

'Better cook than a writer, then?'

'Much better,' I said, slicing through another piece of *tortilla*. 'Sorry.'

'I agree,' he said, clinking his glass against mine. 'So now, for my big news,' he said, reaching for the *Patatas Bravas*. 'I didn't want to hear it from mi padre,' he admitted, 'but I belong backstage, in a kitchen.'

'*Really*?'

'I've spoken to Mum. Going to give it a shot, but only as long as I get to adapt the menu, and *shoosh*! the place up a bit.'

'You'll be the star of La Cocina, the leading man who puts bums on seats.'

'You think so?'

'I know so.'

'Well, I can always count on you to book a table, can't I?'

My phone rang and I saw it was Lara. 'Jen, I think I've found you a job,' she bleated, without the briefest hello or how you doing.

'Please tell me this doesn't involve our mother or Home for All Seasons.'

'Not exactly. It involves you writing my autobiography.'

'*What*?'

'Your Christmas present, the scrapbook thing, got me thinking,' she said. 'There're two publishing houses interested in commissioning my story. One already has a writer attached. The other one's interested in having you head things up.'

'Why me?'

'Why not? It'd be great for marketing since everyone saw you on that video clip. Bill thinks it's a pretty cute idea.'

'Really? But that's only a scrapbook.'

'You'd have support. I'd be working with you. You'd have an editor. You've got an English degree, worked for God knows how long in a dead-end book store job, which you don't have any more...'

'Okay, okay...'

'You can't afford to turn this down, Jen. I don't trust anyone else to do this. And, let's face it, you need the break.'

'Well, if you think I can do it...' I said, already nervously biting my lip.

'I know you can. Better than anyone else ever could.'

'So, what happens next?'

'Bill needs to finalise things. I've told him you fly back tomorrow. He's going to arrange a meeting for you back in London with Azure Publishing.'

Mum and Dad came to collect me at the airport, already in a spin as Mum had got the flight times mixed up, glancing over at 17:00hrs and having a seven o'clock arrival in mind.

Then, Dad picked up my suitcase, let out a yelp, and gripped his lower back, dropping the case back onto the pavement in defeat.

'I'm okay, it's fine,' he grimaced, as Mum rubbed the base of his spine.

'Can I give you a hand?'

I recognized the voice straightaway, but couldn't quite believe it.

George was standing there. With my parents.

'Oh no,' Mum insisted, giving the radiant smile she reserved for handsome strangers. 'We're fine. My husband's not getting any younger, that's all,' she joked.

'Mum? Dad? This is George,' I said, realizing how odd it would sound explaining that he was my ex-boyfriend, so I added nothing else to the introduction.

'I'm a friend of Jennifer's,' George smiled, 'just got off the flight. Luke was desperate for a smoke,' he explained. 'He's wandered off somewhere.'

'Oh right,' Mum said, giving me a pointed look. '*George*. Of course. Jennifer's told us so much about you.'

Yes, I thought, like how we split up two months ago.

'Likewise,' he smiled, grabbing my suitcase and loading it into the boot for me. 'Well then,' he said, looking at me. 'Take care. I'll hopefully see you sometime.'

And that was it.

I wanted George Adams, but all I got was this lousy I Heart New York mug, I thought, as Mum stood at the kitchen sink, still in her dressing gown and slippers, with Lara at the table, Dad by her side, a newspaper spread open in front of them.

'Anyone like a drink?' I asked. That's when I noticed the look on my sister's face, and my eyes had been drawn to the headline in front of her. I re-read the paragraph, words swimming before me:

EXCLUSIVE: Lara Taylor's Secret Brother Reveals Lifetime of Lies!

Tom Reeves on shock discovery as half-brother of formidable model.

By Daniel Chatterton.

'I had no idea who she was,' admits Tom, 30, who shares the model's striking green eyes. 'On Christmas Eve, she turned up and told me she was my half-sister. She said she couldn't bear keeping her mother's secrets anymore.'

'It's the guy who wanted to do the book. The little creep won't leave me alone,' Lara said, searching our mother for signs of life.

'Are you surprised when you're off having dinner with him?' Dad said. 'Goes out with a reporter. Then complains when he's writing about her? Do you not think you've brought this on yourself? *On us?*'

'It was too late,' Lara muttered. 'He was already sneaking around, making stories out of nothing.'

'This isn't nothing!' Dad grabbed the newspaper. 'You couldn't bear to keep your mother's secrets, that's what it says here. Maybe this Chatterton thinks he's doing you a favour, in that case?' Dad was moving around the room as if searching his own thoughts. 'All of this, going to see,' he said, unable to say the word, '*him*, there,' he said, batting the newspaper with the back of his hand. 'And you never thought to tell us this was going on? Doesn't enter your head that maybe we needed to know this was coming?'

'I didn't know!'

'Oh, come off it, Laura. You had a better idea than either one of us.'

'He said he wanted to work on a book, not plaster this stuff all over the paper.'

'And you meet him there, at that hotel, that your ... where you know Tom Reeves, will be?'

'I told you. When the reporter suggested it, I thought he was trying to get a reaction from me. How would I know Tom had already spoken to him? That was the last thing I thought he wanted. He practically threw me out when I told him who I was.'

'Oh yes, when you took my car without permission to drive there on Christmas Eve and destroy this family!'

'I didn't destroy your family!' Lara stormed. 'She did!'

'*She did?*' Dad shouted. 'Now listen to me, I mightn't mean a damn to you,' he said, pointing a shaking hand towards Lara, voice thundering, 'but *she's* still your mother —'

'Stop it!' Mum turned, face swollen with tears. 'Just stop it!'

'No, love,' Dad insisted, putting his arm around her. 'We need to bring this out in the open. Should have been done years ago, before anyone else had the chance. Jennifer?'

I was still stood, frozen, my empty mug in my hand.

'We owe you an apology. And an explanation.'

'You owe *her* an explanation?' Lara shouted. 'Oh, of course, *your* daughter. The only one who actually matters.'

'I have never treated you differently. *Never*,' Dad spat. 'I love both of you the best way I can, but you've made it difficult, Laura. You've made it difficult from the day you went listening in on adult conversations.'

'And why did I do that?' She asked. 'Because I always felt different,' she said, choking back tears. 'Everything was always my fault, because she had an affair!'

'I didn't have an affair!' Mum cried. 'Your Dad did!'

Dad's gaze fell to the floor. He closed his eyes for a second, as if the memory was too painful to revisit.

I swallowed back shock, feeling like a ghost, invisible, all-hearing, among my own family that morning.

'What are you talking about?' Lara asked, searching their faces.

'Your Dad and I were childhood sweethearts. Far too young,' Mum said, blowing her nose. 'Only seventeen, and he'd had his eye on me long before then.'

Dad gave a small smile despite the sorrow casting shadows across his face.

'We were inseparable, so, even though I was only twenty, and against my mum and dad's wishes, we got engaged on my birthday. Wouldn't even do what my mother asked, and wait until I was twenty-one,' she recalled. 'We had a huge party, all the family there. I had no idea another girl had caught your dad's eye.'

I stared at my dad, finding it hard to imagine him checking our mum out, let alone anyone else.

'My sister, Peggy.'

'Aunty Peggy!' Lara shrieked.

'It was a long time ago,' Mum insisted. 'We were children, really. Anyway, it caused ructions. My family wouldn't hear your father's name mentioned. I met someone else, and a couple of years after that, we got engaged.'

'Charles Reeves,' Lara muttered.

'Yes,' Mum confirmed. 'His family owned that place down the road; it wasn't called Wiltshire Hall then —'

'The Connaught,' Lara said, lost in her own thoughts.

'That's right. The Connaught,' Mum nodded. 'But I still loved your dad, and when I found out Charles was seeing someone else, that just about did it.'

'He cheated too?' Lara asked, probably wondering if being unlucky in love ran in the family. The more of this I heard, the more I was starting to believe it myself.

'His family never liked me. I was never good enough,' she sniffed, pulling out a dining chair and taking a seat. 'His mother wanted him to take up with the daughter of this family friend of theirs, plenty of money, and so he did. He didn't know I knew about the other girl. Truth was, his mother took great delight in telling me,' she smiled, sadly. 'Your dad split up with Peg after five minutes, went out with a few girls after that, but he'd never forgotten about me.'

Mum got hold of Dad's hand, a smile finally breaking through her sadness.

'We were in love. And then, we found out I was pregnant. Truthfully, I always thought you were your father's child. As you grew up, I had my doubts, especially after Jennifer came along. The older you both got, the differences seemed more obvious. But it was only when you were a small baby,' Mum said to Lara, 'that Charles got in touch. He was suspicious, but Dad and I decided not to tell him there was any doubt.'

'We wanted to be a family,' Dad explained, squeezing Mum's hand.

'Didn't want the Reeves' lot throwing their weight around,' she continued, 'and they would have,' she said, darting a look back at my father. 'I didn't want my family interfering either. My mum, your nana, didn't speak to Dad until after you were born. I'd had quite enough of that. Your dad always loved you,' she turned to Lara. 'I practically had to fight him over your night feeds, and that wasn't the way most men behaved over thirty years ago,' she reached across, grabbing Lara's hand.

'I never wanted you to think I didn't love her,' Dad lift his glasses, wiping his eyes. 'And I never wanted you to think I didn't love you like you were my own daughter, Laura, because you were my girl from the minute I laid eyes on you. Same as your sister.'

'How could you keep this a secret?' I heard myself ask, as everyone finally remembered I was standing in the kitchen, hearing all this for the first time.

'We were trying to protect our family,' Dad said, searching my face for forgiveness. 'No matter what, that was all we ever wanted.'

'Lara?' I managed. 'How long have you known all this?'

'Since high school, but it was only recently, my counsellor suggested I should try to find out more about my birth father.'

I didn't have a clue what to say, but the more I thought about it, the more it made sense. Finally, I managed: 'I'm sorry. I just wish I'd have known about all this. You shouldn't have gone through any of that, not on your own.'

'I'm sorry I exist,' she announced, tears forming. 'I'm sorry I'm this secret thing. This bad thing in the middle of the family. And I hate that we're not even a family. Not anymore.'

Mum covered her mouth, crying against her hand.

'We are a family,' I hugged her. 'I get why you were always so unhappy, and so bloody *horrible*, and angry, and sad, and all of that now. You'll always be my sister,' I reassured her, 'because I'd hate being related to someone who was more like me, and just as annoying, and dull. I can't stand her already, and she doesn't even exist.'

'Thank you,' she laughed through tears, rest her head on my shoulder. 'I think that's the first time in my life, you haven't acted like I should be happy, just because I'm a size six.'

'Six?' I said, giving a sniff and a smile. 'I thought they only did that in shoes...'

The next day I was back at the site of my previous humiliation: Azure Publishing.

I was dreading seeing my old boss. A woman so joyless, she made me want to grow a pair of testicles, just so I could retract them in her presence.

Bill organized the meeting, taking calls with Genevieve. Between the two of them, they decided that no book about Lara, whether official or some trashy, Dan Chatterton-type exposé, would hold the interest of the readers quite like the story of a beautiful model as told by her (merely-human) sister.

At first, I thought this meant we were in it together, but once I told Lara how I knew both Genevieve and Angela, she decided I could handle it alone.

'Get used to it,' she said. 'You're an author now.'

But I wasn't. I wasn't an author. I was a famous model's sister.

A former bookseller. An eternal optimist, but no author.

I'd started making notes, and Lara had given me back the *Our Story: Sisters* gift I'd made her (without any great sentimentality, I noticed) but apart from a few pages of waffle, and with only three weeks to get started since I got back from New York, I wasn't sure where to begin.

The offices were set in the same space-age looking expanse I remembered, but with a different receptionist who, thankfully, wouldn't remember me crying into a glass of water with torn trousers and an exposed breast.

'Miss Taylor!'

Genevieve strode towards me, as pointy and perfect as ever.

'It's fantastic to see you again. Just flown in from New York, I hear?'

'Erm, yes, a few weeks ago,' I said, getting to my feet, playing it safe in flat shoes and a dress that had no buttons and no chance whatsoever of bursting at the seams at any given moment.

'Super!' she said. 'Shall we take the lift?'

We chatted about her latest call to Lara's agent, Bill, as we walked into her office, where Angela sat waiting, wearing her usual head-to-toe black ensemble. A colour which usually matched her mood.

'Jenny!' she beamed, standing to shake my hand. 'Great you could make it. I'm super excited to be working on this project. You never mentioned your sister was Lara Taylor.'

'Could you get us some drinks, Angie?'

Angie? I didn't remember anyone ever calling Angela Salton, 'Angie'. Of all the nicknames she had at Brookhouse Books, I was sure that was never one of them.

'Of course, Mrs Manley,' Angela said. 'Coffee, Jenny?'

'Yes, please,' I said, 'white, one sugar. Thanks.'

And if that wasn't weird enough, she served it like a lady-in-waiting, doing everything for me except drinking the thing.

'So, we understand the genesis for your collaboration was a project you compiled for Lara?'

'Yes, I have it, here,' I said, taking *Our Story: Sisters* from my bag. 'It's photographs mainly. Starts with us as girls, but there's some amazing shots of Lara, from her early modelling days, that our mother kept.'

'Absolutely fascinating,' Genevieve mused, bringing her glasses to the edge of her nose, peering at page-after-page.

Angela shuffled around on her iPad, then got up and started pointing the thing at the book.

'Angie, what are you doing?' Genevieve asked. 'We hardly need you to *photograph* the work. Photography will be determined closer to publication,' she huffed, impatiently fixing her glasses back in place.

'Oh, right, of course,' Angela mumbled, sharing an 'oh-no-there-I-go-again-look' with me.

With me, of all people, I thought.

The person who used to be *you*!

And you used to be *her*!

'You said you'd put some notes together, Jennifer?'

'I have, Mrs Manley —'

'Genevieve, please,' she smiled.

'It's just silly, really,' I said, handing her a page of thoughts, which I now thought might be a huge mistake. She was probably expecting something serious, intelligent, *literary*, even. Something vaguely resembling a book, when all I'd done so far was scribble nonsense.

'Angie?' Genevieve said, skimming over my notes. 'Could you read these to us, please?' she said, handling the pages to Angela. 'I'd like to get a sense of Jennifer's voice.'

'The differences between Lara and I,' Angela read, with an awkward smile: '1. Lara can wear a shapeless jumper and baggy jeans, and still look like a tall, slim, gift-wrapped model in sheep's clothing. If I tried the same look, you'd think I'd borrowed someone else's clothes — either those of a rather muscular dwarf or an overweight child.'

'Oh my goodness,' Genevieve smiled, before Angela continued: '2. Lara walks into a room and all eyes are on her. This would only happen to me if I had my skirt tucked into the back of my worst, purple, slightly fraying, size 12 knickers, with yellow hearts printed all over them. And, I think you can tell by the level of detail here, this has actually happened to me. I threw the knickers away. Once I got home, obviously. Not back into the crowded restaurant. Although, from the looks I got, I may as well have done just that.'

'That happened? That actually happened to you?'

'Yes,' I nodded, as Genevieve grinned and signalled to Angie to continue, with one flounce of her slender, bejewelled hand.

'3. Lara's a winner. She passed her driving test first time, won the Face of Francesca modelling competition, and took the modelling world by storm. The only thing I've ever won is sympathy from very close friends who care enough to have a heart.'

'I'm sure that's not true,' Genevieve insisted, as Angela returned to my notes:

'4. Everyone fancies Lara. She's not even a "type", like blonde or busty, but universally gorgeous in any language. I'm definitely a "type". The short, pear-shaped type, who is incapable of getting a tan or keeping a manicure for longer than three days, let alone securing the attention of an admirer. Unless they pose a serious threat to women.'

'Oh, Lord!' Genevieve laughed, 'unless they pose a serious threat to women,' she giggled.

Angela returned to the page, gave me an approving look before reading out:

'5. Lara wears beautiful clothes, expensive perfume, and goes to all the right places. The only nice clothes I own are courtesy of the charity shop I found in a really posh area, surrounded by big, expensive houses. Any decent perfume I wear will be a gift, as I'd feel far too guilty to spend the best part of £50 on anything that evaporates, so I save it for special occasions, like seeing my boyfriend, who I no longer have. The rest of the time, I splash out on the best deodorant on the shelf, and hope for the best.'

'I save it for special occasions, like seeing my boyfriend — who I no longer have,' Genevieve shrieked, slapping her hand against her knee. 'This is wonderful! Just wonderful stuff! I love how you've made the *character* of Jennifer Taylor into a comedic figure. *The Everywoman*, if you will, which will play beautifully against the archetypal, unattainable beauty, of Lara Taylor. I admit,' she said, folding her arms, 'this is not the approach I was expecting, but it's so … *heightened*, so engaging, in a way I'm sure our readership will love. Don't you think, Angie?'

'Absolutely!' Angie said, but I could tell from the look she gave me, she knew as well as I did, that I was only telling the truth.

Chapter 32

Lara

It was a cold morning in March, and I was back in Manhattan, preparing for one of the most important days of my life, when my cell struck up with the unfortunately familiar voice of Dan Chatterton.

'So, let me get this straight. Your autobiography? Your little sister's heading up the editorial?'

'No comment.'

'Don't you think it's a little naïve, Lara, letting nepotism stand in the way of journalism? I understand your sister lost her job recently, but even so…'

'No comment.'

'Have I caught you at a bad time? I suppose yesterday's news about your former fiancé's civil partnership might have caught you off-guard. You'd met Henrik Romento, I believe? Silvano Arazzi's partner?' he asked, feigning concern. 'I take it you weren't invited to the ceremony?'

'No comment.'

'Lara? Come on. Are we going to have a conversation?'

'Goodbye, Daniel.'

I hung up, travelling in the back of the car Bill had sent, *en route* to the Taylor-made Models launch shoot, eager to meet some of our new signings, and desperate to live up to my own reputation.

Anyway, Dan was wrong about Silvano and Henrik. Henrik had sent me a text and I was even happier when Silvano called me personally.

'Silvano, I'm so sorry. I owe you so much.'

'You owe me nothing,' he replied. 'What you've done is to heal me. You've healed my heart. You've healed my family. Thank you for what you said to Henrik, it opened my eyes to my own truth. You've given me my life back.'

I'd instructed Bill to set up repayment to Silvano, but he'd declined, saying it would be unfair of him to regard our relationship as some kind of debt.

'It's a pity you don't feel the same way about our relationship, Bill,' I'd joked.

'If that's what you want, maybe we should get married?' he laughed. 'Then we'll both be happy.'

The truth was, working with Bill again, it felt as though we'd never been apart, but I suppose after all these years, it would take more than an argument to separate us, especially now that the future seemed more exciting than some of the biggest highlights of the past, although, as excited as I was for Taylor-made Models, I was truly terrified.

I was starting out again, and just as nervous as I'd been on that very first shoot. In fact, even more so, I thought, as we pulled up outside what was now known as Taylor-Made Towers.

Inside, Monroe was installed in front of a row of dressing table mirrors, as furtive glances from the young girls reflected my way.

'Here she is!' he shrieked above the noise of hair-dryers and rasp of conversation, as I walked across the studio. 'Star of the show!'

The room broke out in applause. *For me.*

'Lara!' Amber Rhodes strode towards me on legs as long as the summer solstice, grin as wide as the Atlantic, high-fiving me on the way to her shoot.

'Lara?' Bill approached, his mind on business as usual. 'We need you in hair and makeup soon as you can,' he instructed, his eyes already finding other situations which required his attention at the other end of the room. 'Jim King's people have confirmed, they need you at the studio for 5 p.m. sharp.'

The place was plugged in; buzzing with a purpose and energy I'd almost forgotten. I chatted as Mandy Le Bron, an amazing makeup artist I hadn't worked with in years, told me how honoured she was to take the call from Bill. She wanted to be part of something that empowered women, she said, boosting their confidence the same way she attempted to do with every brushstroke.

One hour and thirty-five minutes later, I finally recognized the woman in the mirror. I wasn't perfect. I wasn't young, but I was back, at the centre of it all, and happiness was written all over my face.

I took my place, lights angled along my profile, as Beverley Q, one of the best, and few, female photographers on the planet, took the shoot.

For the first time in my life, I knew who I was. I wasn't just some image, playing some part, but a person being photographed in my own right.

No drink, no substance, no lover, had ever made me feel so alive.

Under the lights in Studio Three, Jim King perched in his seat, taming an eyebrow with a lick of his finger, before the red light of live television blinked into action:

'You join me tonight with one of fashion's most famous faces. A woman with a fascinating past, yes,' he asserted with confidence, 'but all the more fascinating to us, is her future.'

'Thank you, Jim,' I managed to smile, rigid with nerves, as I pulled the hemline of my skirt over my knees, hoping I looked alright, aware of the faces in the audience, the viewers at home who had read all about me. 'You've given me quite a lot to live up to.'

'Not at all. Taylor-made Models,' he read from his notes. 'A twenty-first century modelling agency for the twenty-first century model. Would you care to elaborate?'

'Of course,' I said, trying my best to relax a little. 'Our agency is a commercial business, but we've placed our hearts at the centre of that business. We aim to ensure our models are given the best advice, looked after by caring, responsible, individuals, and that their careers are nurtured in a safe, and loving environment.'

'This, of course,' Jim said, giving his trademark concerned glance to the camera, 'is something you found sadly lacking from your early modelling days, is that correct, Lara?'

'That's correct,' I said. 'But, I have to be clear. It was an unbelievable opportunity, and I'm eternally grateful to some of the wonderful people I met along the way, including my agent, Bill Staniss, who is an incredible man, and an amazing professional.'

'You've enjoyed success, you acknowledge that,' Jim said, clearly relieved he didn't have a fanatic on his hands. 'But you've also struggled. Please, tell us.'

'Well,' I sighed, 'that's true. But show me a person who hasn't gone through some sort of personal battle,' I said, as the audience murmured in agreement. 'I might be in the public eye, but if anything, I've had a lot of privileges,' I admitted.

'Modelling is sometimes seen as a decadent existence. I certainly saw it that way, because that's the world I was invited into back then, but that lifestyle is deeply unhealthy, and not one I would ever advocate.'

'Amber Rhodes was a guest of ours recently,' Jim said, causing a ripple of applause to spread across the audience. 'I believe she's now working with you at the Taylor-made agency?'

'She is, and we are just thrilled to have such a fantastic role-model, let alone such a successful model, join us. She's working closely with our younger recruits. I don't think they could ask for a better mentor,' I smiled. 'That's the thing: Taylor-made Models is about work, hard work, but it's also about family. It's about healthy models, respecting experience, celebrating difference.'

'You mentioned family,' Jim said, looking thoughtful. 'There's been some attention,' he paused, trying to be diplomatic, 'paid to your family recently, most notably, your sister, Jennifer, and a half-brother you never knew, Tom.'

'That's right, Jim. My sister,' I paused, felt the sting behind my eyes. 'My sister is the most wonderful, sweet, talented woman.'

'And it's Jennifer, I believe, who is currently working on your autobiography?'

'She is doing such a fantastic job. There's nobody better, nobody closer to me than her. I trust her implicitly, which is why I asked her to take on the project, rather than hiring any other writer. There are no secrets, not any more,' I smiled. 'Tom came into my life after all these years. I'm not going to pretend to have a close relationship with him at this particular moment, it's all so new for both of us, and I can't tell you what the future holds, but I do know, the past is no longer

275

something unknown. And that's a huge relief, to me, and to the rest of my family.'

'Talking of family,' Jim said, recrossing his legs, revealing a hint of white sock. 'I hope you won't mind me saying, married twice, engaged three times? Will you marry again, Lara?'

'Was that a proposal, Jim?' The audience went wild, clapping uproariously. 'Because, if that's the case, you're a very attractive man, but those white socks, which I can't help but notice against your suit, just have to go!'

'Well, Lara,' Jim replied, accepting the joke graciously, and rather enjoying a frisson of flirtation, 'if that's all it takes...'

And in a moment of TV history that would be recalled whenever Jim King's name was mentioned, he slipped out of his shoes, removed both socks, and went down on bended knee.

Chapter 33

Jennifer

I'd finally finished the first three chapters, hoping the work so far was what Angela was expecting, and unbelievably hungry for lunch. Well, quite believably really, as I'd run out of butter and had to make do with a piece of dry toast for breakfast.

I stood at the window, surveying the high street, a beautiful spring morning, silently making Francine's my destination, before I reminded myself that this was my new home, and took another glance around the lounge, which even featured a vase full of fresh flowers, and matching cushions.

The fresh flowers didn't look that great, to be honest. They were in that hideous teal-and-golden-geese vase I'd accidentally re-gifted to my mother, before she decided she really couldn't live with it again, after all.

I'd watched Lara being interviewed by Jim King the day before, actually letting out a squeal of excitement as my beautiful sister made the world, and Jim King, fall hopelessly in love with her all over again.

Although I'd missed the first few minutes. Mum wouldn't stop sending texts about how great Lara looked. How good she was at being interviewed. Wasn't she so natural on television? But the moment I gave in, picked up the phone and called her, she told me off: 'I can't have a conversation with you, and listen to your sister on the television. What do you think I am? The All-seeing Eye?'

I'd finally gone to bed, and as I switched off the lamp, it hit me, not for the first time, how much my life had changed.

There I was, lying in my new double bed, in a room fitted with skylights and an en suite. I even had a coffee maker, generously donated by my new landlady. My two-bedroom apartment, (featuring a kitchen/diner and in sought-after location, don't you know), was owned by Genevieve, conveniently situated on the top floor of the building adjoining Azure Publishing.

Once I explained I was still living in Ingleford with Mum and Dad, she told me she was looking for a new tenant, as her husband was frittering their savings away on golfing holidays, and she had a much more important investment, namely herself.

'Between you and me, I could use the rent. I'm having a little work done,' she winked. 'And I've got my heart set on a place in France that'll give me the perfect excuse to show off the results.'

I loved the apartment, and once I told Lara, she spoke to Bill, who had my rent covered by a little extra in my advance. They'd made it all seem so simple, it was difficult to remember I'd been living in my childhood bedroom only two months ago. My new place was lovely, better than I could have hoped for, and so was my new job. In fact, everything about being me felt new, except for my weakness for cake, and inability to throw away my scruffy old cat slippers.

Just as I grabbed some photographs of Lara for the book, putting them in a file to scan at the office, Luke called.

'Hey, you haven't forgotten about Friday, have you?'

'Friday? Well, I know it comes after Thursday, and generally before Saturday.'

'Hah-bloody-hah,' he snapped. 'I'm up the wall! Still securing a seafood supplier, none of the new chairs have arrived yet, and the paint's barely dried on the walls, not that Dad's bothered. Every time I try and speak to him, he just goes, "Luke, I tell you, too ambitious. Madrid wasn't built in a day!" Why did I ever get involved with this restaurant?'

'Because you're an excellent chef, brilliant host, and love having something to moan about.'

'Yeah, I know,' he admitted. 'I'm loving it actually, or at least I will be, once we're on track. How good was Lara's interview last night?'

'I know,' I smiled. 'I was in tears by the end!'

'Oh, that reminds me,' he said, suddenly serious. 'Sorry to tell you, but it looks like *The Spanish Detective* is definitely going ahead. Marcus emailed me. Channel Fifty-seven's commissioned a pilot. He's taken the starring role.'

'Great. Remind me never to watch it,' I sulked, now that I was officially no longer a fan of Kinky Kleff or his dubious back-catalogue.

'Of course we're going to watch it! It's my idea! Although,' Luke admitted, 'now that Channel Fifty-seven's involved, I think it might be a bit too pervy to watch with you, and I'm definitely not mentioning it to my mum. Anyway, got to go, I'm determined to get rid of all this old, maraca-and-Sangria-bottle junk Dad's got scattered all over the place, before anyone notices. See you next Friday! Dress to impress!'

Now Luke had me thinking of food again, I decided to take a detour to Francine's before I headed over to the office. I crossed the road, and as I opened the door, there he was: George, sitting having lunch with Susanna and Charlie.

I stood at the counter, ordering my usual traditional-lemonade-and-tuna-crunch-combo to go, but as the guy behind the counter asked if I was taking out or staying in, I decided to make the most of the chance encounter.

'Jennifer?'

George caught my eye as I turned, file tucked beneath my elbow, plate balanced precariously in my hand.

'You okay there?' he asked, standing up and slipping the file from my arm before pulling out the empty seat at their table. 'What are you doing here?'

'That's my office, across the road. What are you doing here?'

'Nice day. Thought I'd treat the kids to lunch. We've just been to the bookshop down the road. Susanna loves reading, don't you, sweetheart?'

'I've got a reading age of ten,' Susanna announced, through a mouthful of pasta. 'That's two years older than I am.'

'Wow,' I said. 'That's impressive.'

'Not really,' she said, with the same world-weary tone I remembered. 'I've been reading to myself since Mummy and Daddy decided to live in different houses. They're both too busy to do story-time with me now...'

'That's not true, Susanna,' George said, clearly uncomfortable. 'I read to you both last night.'

'Yes, Daddy, I know,' she sighed, 'but that book was for babies, like Charlie.'

'I'm not a baby!'

Charlie thumped his little fists down on the table, sending a few photographs spilling out from the side of my file.

'Charlie,' George scolded him, with that authoritative whisper parents saved for public displays of bad behaviour. 'That's enough.'

I noticed Susanna peering at one of the photos, picking it up to take a better look. 'Who's that lady in the bikini?'

'That's my big sister, Lara.'

Susanna looked at me with a suspicious frown.

'But *she's* really, really pretty.'

'Susanna!' George barked.

'It's okay,' I smiled. 'She *is* really, really pretty.'

'Nah,' Charlie piped up, with his cute, round face resting on both hands, 'she's prettier,' he said, pointing at me with one chubby little finger.

'Thank you, Charlie.'

'*De nada.*'

'De nada?' I smiled at George. 'Do you know Spanish, Charlie?'

'Uncle Luke taught me.'

'Uncle Luke?' I said, looking to George for an explanation. 'As in *Luke*?'

'Hasn't he mentioned?' George said, sipping his coffee, 'I made a small investment in the restaurant, been working with him, mostly on the menu. More of a second opinion, really. It's my amateur attempt to get inside a kitchen.'

'Great,' I said, 'that's really great,' wondering why Luke never remembered to tell me anything that I might actually be interested in. Things like how he was still in touch with my boyfriend. *Ex-boyfriend*, I corrected myself, sitting there with him and his children, enjoying every minute, and wishing we could start over again.

'You'll be going to the restaurant opening, next week?'

'Yes,' I said, and even though I'd been looking forward to seeing Lara, and catching up with Mum and Dad, I was suddenly a lot more excited by the prospect.

'Maybe we can chat then?' George asked. 'Away from little ears,' he said, as Susanna abruptly announced that her pasta smelt funny, like Charlie's feet.

Listening to your mother chatting to your boss would make most people feel a little uneasy, but listening to my mother talking to my publisher about her favourite book, made me want to cheese grate myself from the feet upwards, until I was small enough to lie undetected on a side plate, praying for the dishwasher.

'What do they call it?' Mum asked my dad. 'A must-have, trend, craze…'

'A *phenomenon*?' Dad suggested.

'That's right, a publishing phenomenon!' she said, giving Dad a congratulatory arm-squeeze. 'Well, it is, it is to me,' she explained, lowering her voice, but not low enough, to confide to Genevieve. 'I said to David, I thought those days were over until I read *Awakenings*. Not anymore!' she confessed with a hearty laugh.

'Okay, Marian,' Dad said, giving a cursory look in my direction as I scratched another rogue splash of *aioli* from my skirt.

'I must admit,' Genevieve said, toying with her *chopito*, 'I took that book home to my husband, and insisted he put it at the top of his reading list, but he's far happier with Bill Bryson. I guess he hasn't quite awoken yet…'

'Well, maybe it's time to set your alarm clock an hour earlier,' Mum smiled, before she and Genevieve conspired with giggles.

This really wasn't what I was expecting for tonight. I'd pictured walking into La Cocina, Luke apologizing to the guests he was serving, greeting me — best-friend of the owner — while people wondered who I was, The Girl in the Red Dress, who only had eyes for the handsome man who couldn't stop staring at her. That was going to be George, in case you were wondering.

Instead, I'd arrived too early, and rather than V.I.P. guest, became an extra pair of hands in the evening's proceedings.

'Oh, hell!' I shouted, jumping a few seconds too late from the splatter of Spanish dip I was decanting into small, ceramic pots.

'It looks like part of the dress,' Luke prattled, distracted, as he threw me a tea towel, and wiped up the rest from the floor.

'What time's George getting here?' I asked, irritated enough to drop my plan of forgetting he had anything to do with my excitement for tonight.

'His daughter's got a temperature. He can't make it.'

Luke carried on, zipping past, as if he hadn't just ruined my appetite for seeing anyone else, apart from George. And now, there I was, with only Genevieve and my mother for company, wondering if it would be rude to polish off the rest of the *tortilla* single-handedly, while my mother boasted about her sex life.

'Top up, ladies?'

Luke appeared with a bottle of red, knowing he looked cute in his apron.

The old Luke was back, tending to the ladies, and impressing the guys with his gloriously stocked bar.

'Luke, this food! It's superb,' our former Brookhouse Books manager, Angela, drawled to my left. 'I had no idea you were such a culinary genius.'

'Neither did I. I always wanted to be a literary genius.'

'Really? I think you'd be wasted slaving over a manuscript. We need you slaving over a hot … stove, instead,' she pointed out, gazing over the top of her glass.

'Well, I promise,' he said, placing his hand on his heart. 'Anytime you need a table, your willing slave will do his best to impress you.'

'I'm impressed already, Luke. You know,' she said, 'I'd love a great cook book on my list.'

'Really?'

'Hmm,' Angela nodded. 'A real kitchen-staple. Headed-up by a chef who looks as great as his food tastes, and isn't shy in front of a camera...'

'I used to work in TV. Had my own show,' Luke said, trying to sound casual.

'I remember you mentioning that,' Angela nodded. 'I think we should talk,' she said, producing a business card from her evening bag. 'Andalusian cuisine, on the shelves in the peak of summer, could capture that enduring spirit of wistfulness.'

'Really? Well, why don't you take a look around the kitchen with me? I'll share some of my secrets.'

'I'd love to,' Angela replied, and as they strode off, I swear I caught Angela checking out more than his menu.

Thankfully, at that moment, Lara approached the table, smiling at Mum, who beckoned her over and took her hand, still chatting to Genevieve.

'Please have some of this *tortilla*,' I pleaded, catching her eye across the table. 'It's only Spanish omelette, but I swear it's tastier than Javier Bardem on a moonlit beach.'

'Am I okay to sit here?' she asked, surveying Angela's seat.

'Yes,' I nodded. 'Angela's only got eyes for Luke,' I said, watching her hanging on his every word at the bar.

'Mum seems happier,' my sister smiled.

'Still barmy though...'

'Oh, absolutely,' Lara agreed. 'I got home yesterday, she was out of breath, wearing some sort of sari. I asked her what she was doing. Said it helps her relax when she's doing her Bikram Yoga.'

'Where was Dad?'

'I don't know. Upstairs, I think?'

I raised my brows, glanced across at our parents, let my silence do the talking.

'Uh,' Lara huffed, taking a slice of omelette. 'You don't think?'

'Let's not think…'

Before I could give a shiver, my breath left my body as I reassessed the bar.

'He's here. *George.*'

'He is,' Lara said, taking my glass. 'And you need a glass of wine.'

'I've got one,' I said, not grasping why my sister had confiscated my Shiraz.

'No, you *had* one. Now I have it, and George is waiting at the bar…'

'Oh, right,' I muttered. 'I get it,' I said, taking a deep breath. 'See you later.'

'Hopefully not,' Lara smiled.

I left my chair, stopped, pulled my sister to me with a quick hug.

'Thank you.'

'Oh, please,' Luke said, back at the table. 'I preferred the two of you before.'

'Sorry, I'd have to disagree with you,' I smiled.

'Good luck!' Lara grinned.

George smiled as I walked towards him. I smiled back, glad that we were speaking again, glad that we were friends, but I admit, still disappointed that's all we were.

'You look gorgeous,' he told me, hesitating before he kissed my cheek.

I'd missed the scent of his hair, his aftershave.

'Thanks. You smell good,' I smiled, suddenly worried by how odd that might sound. 'I didn't think you were coming,' I said, quickly changing the subject. 'How's Susanna? Luke said she had a temperature?'

'Kind of,' he said. 'Teething problems. Helen's moved in with her new boyfriend.'

I hoped he was making a point of letting me know how he was fine about his ex-wife getting serious with someone else.

'So Susanna didn't want to stay with you this weekend?'

'The kids had dinner with me, but I told Helen I was coming here tonight,' he explained, leaning towards me over the chorus of Spanish music and animated chatter, 'so they're staying with their mum until tomorrow, but,' he shrugged, 'Susanna put two-and-two together, after we saw you, in the cake shop.'

'Put two-and-two together?'

He smiled, paused, gave a cursory glance around.

'She asked if you were my girlfriend.'

I smiled in return, but didn't find it funny. I'd been his girlfriend. This great-looking, great-smelling man had once loved me, and slid his hands around my waist, and thrown me down on his bed, and —

'And I told her you were,' George said, interrupting my thoughts, 'and we had a talk, and by the time I dropped her off with her mum, she was all smiles again.'

I stood, looking at him, looking at me.

'Sorry,' he shook his head. 'I know that sounds really presumptuous, but, well,' he took a breath out, 'I'm probably trying to sound confident, because I know I messed up. I over-complicated everything, trying to please everyone. Everyone except you, and, when I saw you the other day,' he paused. 'Look, shall we go somewhere where we can —'

'Oh, there you are!' Mum bellowed, 'I wondered where you'd got to,' she said, looking to me, before she noticed George. 'Lovely to see you again,' she said, miming a side-kiss at him, 'and another one,' she said, miming its twin in the other direction. 'That's how they greet each other in Europe. When in Spain!'

She was drunk. Not even tipsy, but actually zonked.

'And thanks again for helping my husband the other week, at the airport. We've been doing a lot of…'

I swear, I stopped breathing.

'Yoga,' she continued. 'Trying to keep limber,' she giggled. 'Got to keep up my new regime. My *Awakenings*,' she said, giving me a really inappropriate look.

'Oh,' George said, 'isn't that the book that all the women are reading?'

No. Please don't talk to my mother about that book, *or anything*, in fact, on the one night of the year she's alcohol-honest and too far away for Dad to restrain her.

'I think the bathroom's just over there, Mum,' I said, ushering my mother past George as casually as I could. 'Your lipstick needs doing.'

'It's a bit *sexy*,' she explained to George, 'You should borrow it…' she said, slightly bemused as she found herself in the bar-side huddle I'd just pushed her in the middle of, before I turned back to George.

'Quick, save me, before she comes back…'

'I was going to say,' George smiled, 'shall we go back here,' he said, signalling the kitchen. 'Where we can talk properly?'

It felt wonderful, following George, all lovely, six-foot-one of him, through the restaurant. And then, the best bit, he turned, and took my hand as we walked past the kitchen, with Luke's mother, Pia, giving us a wave and a smile.

'I've got something for you,' George said, heading into the stock room, taking a large parcel, gift wrapped, from a shelf, and placing it on a trolley in front of me. 'Open it,' he said, and I tore off the paper, to reveal plush, grey, fabric. 'It's that Relationship Kit you told me to get you,' he explained, eyeing me cautiously.

I held up the bathrobe. My name was hand-written across a strip of white tape, stuck to the lapel.

'I woke up one morning, in New York, and I put on the hotel robe, and I thought of you,' he said, 'like I did every morning. The way I still do every morning,' he said, looking serious. 'You said you didn't want to feel like my guest any more. So, that's your robe. For when, for *if*,' he corrected himself, 'you ever stay again. The tape's from the kid's stuff, for school,' he smiled. 'And I promise,' he said, taking my hand. 'I'll never call it The Guest Robe, or this,' he said, holding up a toothbrush with another strip of name-tape along the handle, 'The *Spare* Toothbrush, again. All this,' he said, gesturing to the discarded wrapping, 'I'm not trying to rush anything, but I'd really like us to go on a date sometime. If you still think that's a good idea?' He asked, trying to gauge my reaction.

'Not really,' I admitted.

'Okay...' he muttered, trying to read my expression.

'I think,' I said, putting my arms around his neck. 'I'd much prefer you to kiss me first, before we even think about dating again.'

He smiled, one arm around my waist, before he glanced back at the trolley.

'Only if you put on the bathrobe,' he said, grabbing the robe, and threading my arms into it.

'Oh kinky!' I squealed, before remembering Kinky Kleff and hoping I hadn't just ruined my chances with George for a second time.

'No,' he said, looking thoughtful, as he wrapped me in velour, 'not kinky. But, since your mum's offering to lend me *Awakenings*, I can think of a few things I'd like to do with you and this belt.'

Chapter 34

Lara

As soon as Jennifer told me about the restaurant opening, I'd rescheduled my workload, and told Luke I wouldn't miss it for the world. I'd spent years searching for a family I already had, and from now on, I was determined to share as much of my life with them as I could.

I'd already shared half of it with Jen, who was doing an incredible job with my autobiography. She was creating something that meant everything to me, reminding me that, for every single one of our differences, just like my parents, my sister had helped shaped me, and I didn't need biological fact, or fiction, to make us closer.

This is what I was thinking as I sat next to her, catching up over an amazing menu of tapas with Mum and Dad sitting opposite, looking happier, and more in love, than they had in years.

'Anyway,' Jennifer said, straightening up with a bunny-hop. 'How's it going? Taylor-made Models?'

'Amazing,' I said, still protective of something that felt so fragile, so personal.

Jennifer smiled, giving my wrist a squeeze. 'I can't believe you convinced me to do the book. I can't believe you even considered me. I'd defo have gone with the Dan Chatterton option, if I were you.'

I let out a groan of disgust at the sound of his name.

'No, you wouldn't…'

'Hey, he's not all that bad. What about my Good Citizen Award?' she smiled.

'That was funny. Unintentionally funny.'

Dan's latest 'exclusive' had targeted my sister, reporting the ground-breaking 'story' of her accidental role in intercepting a local robbery. Obviously peeved that she had won what he thought was 'his' role as writer of my autobiography, he included a few well-meaning quotes from Cristos, the shopkeeper, pictured holding a framed certificate addressed to Jenny for 'Good Citizenship', which basically painted her as a chocolate-dependent slob.

'Don't,' she said, giving me a shove. 'Mum's kept the article. She put a pen through Dan's name, though. She was so proud of you the other night,' she said, nibbling at a chilli-stuffed olive. 'She couldn't believe you were on a TV show.'

'Me, neither. I was shaking like a leaf.'

'You didn't look nervous. You were great.'

'Thanks. Do you think so?'

'A natural. Mum said so herself. Were you okay, talking about Tom?' she asked, her voice hesitant.

'Sure,' I shrugged. 'We've exchanged numbers, but,' I gave a sigh, 'I'm in no rush. Although,' I paused, 'he sent me a gift. A framed shot of my father. He's on horseback, laughing, and,' I smiled, 'it's so weird, you know. I've never had that before, that, looking at someone, and, no offense,' I said, 'but looking at someone, and just knowing, seeing yourself, captured in that split second, written all over someone's else's face, like that. It's pretty intense…'

'Yeah, I understand,' she said. 'The last few months have been *fairly* crazy.'

'I know,' I said, taking a mental journey through some of the highlights and lowlights. 'When I think of this time last year —'

'Don't think. That was then. You were a completely different person. You're so much more,' she paused, searching for the right word, '*chilled* now. I like it.'

'I feel it. I'm just sorry I've been such a big mess for so long,' I said. 'Let's get much better at staying in touch, not just for the book, but from now on, okay?'

'Are you kidding me? If you weren't such a mess, Mum would have got me a Saturday job at Hoggs Butchers by now.'

'And started encouraging you to go dogging on Holburn Hill after your shift with Barry,' I laughed, glancing over at Mum, who was still holding court at the table.

'Well, I'm a career girl now, aren't I? No more elf costumes for me. At least, I hope not...'

'And how's the new flat?' I smiled.

'Amazing,' she said, with a sway of appreciation. 'I just stand there, and I can't believe it's my place. Every little crack in every wall, every window I look out of, every creaking floorboard. I love it.'

'I'm going to make a move myself, I think. Time to let my place go.'

'Really? I loved that neighbourhood.'

'It never really felt right for me. I just bolted after Travis. It's full of unhappy memories. I was talking to my counsellor about it —'

'You're still seeing her?'

I nodded.

'No matter what, I'm grateful Silvano encouraged to me go and see her. If it wasn't for Susan — and you — I'd be, God knows where, probably married to Silvano, knowing we'd both made a huge mistake, and, well,' I said, rolling my eyes, 'who knows what else.'

'What did *I* do?'

'Everything! I thought about what you said, about,' I lowered my voice, '*being dependent, on something,* a man, or a substance. Running away whenever things got heavy. Now I've got you. I've got Mum and Dad, and this,' I smiled, 'is the best time I've ever had, but,' I said, 'I know, I'm going to have bad days too, and I don't want to get back to that point ever again. Correction: I'm *not* going to get back to that point ever again.'

I saw the relief on Jennifer's face, and happiness unwrapped inside my stomach.

We carried on chatting about our crazy parents, and for the first time, they did feel like both our parents, not just Jennifer's, but mine too, I thought, as Jennifer walked over to George, who arrived with clear intentions of getting back with my sister, as far as I could see.

'You know,' Luke said, smiling shyly at me, as I eyed Jennifer and George at the bar. 'I've missed you.'

'It hasn't been that long.'

'You know what I mean...'

I knew that face. The one Luke wore when wine fermented into romance.

'I had a great time with you, Luke. I really did.'

'Do you remember, once, when we...' He gave a quick glance across the table, leaned in a little closer, and whispered something that lay me right back down on that huge rug in his flat, back when I still had natural breasts and a 23-inch waist.

'How could I forget?' I smiled, a little flirtatiously, for old time's sake.

'Well,' he said, with another glance across the restaurant, 'why don't you pay me a visit sometime? I've still got the rug.'

'I bet you have,' I said, nodding slowly with amusement. 'I bet you have, and I bet it's been put to some good use since the last time we slept on it.'

'Luke! We have others here,' Ramon, Luke's father, thankfully intervened to save my blushes. 'My son wants to give only the most beautiful women in the restaurant the best service,' he said, in mock-disgust.

'What can I say, Pops? I must take after you.'

'Take after me? Your father is more charming than this,' Ramon said, taking my hand and planting a kiss on it, before he laughed warmly. 'Now, come on, Luke. *Work*!'

It was only after I reapplied my eyeliner, standing in the bathroom, that I thought to check my cell. There was a missed call from Bill from an hour ago, and I'd learned never to ignore a missed call from him. I knew better than most, anything was possible – and it turned out, I was right to think so.

'I met with Jim King's producers today,' Bill explained, still sounding as upbeat as I'd left him in Manhattan. 'They loved the show.'

'That's great.'

'It is, but there's something greater,' he paused. 'They want you to do a pilot. Six weeks. You host. Pick the guests of your choice. They want strong voices, like yours, they said. People with a story.'

'Bill, I couldn't—'

'Lara, you can do this. Sit with it. Mull it over, but, you know, if I thought you couldn't handle this, we wouldn't be having this conversation.'

'Okay, but a *TV pilot*?'

'Look at it this way. It's more original than the eponymous fashion range, isn't it? By the way, we miss you over here,' he said. 'I miss you.'

'I miss you too, Bill,' I smiled. 'Don't worry, I'll be back to work in no time.'

'That's not what I meant. I said, I miss you. Talk soon. Take care, sweetheart.'

After he ended the call, I stood for a second, wondering whether to text him that I missed him too, but you know what? Never trouble, trouble, I reminded myself. I walked back into Luke's restaurant with a smile on my face. I had a future, and every single day felt like a new beginning. I wasn't hiding from life any more. Our table was still bustling when I returned, candles flickering under conversation, wine-stained glasses reflecting the light, lipstick marked with appreciation.

'Dad?' I called. And straight away, my father turned to me.

A NOTE TO THE READER

Dear Reader,

And there we have it! You've reached the end of AWFUL BY COMPARISON. I hope you enjoyed it, and had a great time getting to know Jennifer and Lara Taylor.

While I don't have a sister myself, this book wasn't so much written about sibling rivalry, as how we compare ourselves unfavourably to our peers. Jennifer strives to be an accomplished adult, in a world where she'll always think of herself as the inelegant, baby-sister. Lara represents the voice of the media. A climate in which women are encouraged to comment and compete, on the most basic of terms. Both ideas collided and became the basis of this novel, when I read a piece about 'Celebrity Siblings', which suggested lives without fame and photoshop were lives half-lived.

This was my first published novel. This was the book which caught the attention of my brilliantly supportive, and utterly lovely, Literary Agent, Caroline. Thanks to the book making her laugh, she gave me the chance to make you smile and squirm on the Taylor sisters' behalf too. (Thank you, Caroline).

It was never my plan to write comedy, but from first to final draft, the amusement and affection I felt for these characters kept me going. So, I'd also like to thank every person who ever told me I was funny. They're the people who put the idea of writing this novel in my head. So, if you didn't find the book funny, you only have those people to blame.

If you'd like to join the AWFUL BY COMPARISON discussion, please share a review on my **Amazon** or **Goodreads** pages. You can also find me on **Facebook**, or follow me on **Twitter**. To fully delve into the Caliskaniverse, make your way over to **www.patriciacaliskanauthor.com**.

You'll find me there, working on my next book. I'm always grateful for the happy distraction, so make yourself at home, take a look around, and most of all, thank you. It's always lovely to hear from you, and as long as you keep reading, I get to keep on writing.

With Sincere Thanks, Patricia X

Sapere Books is an exciting new publisher of brilliant fiction and popular history.

To find out more about our latest releases and our monthly bargain books visit our website:
saperebooks.com

39659326R00176

Printed in Poland
by Amazon Fulfillment
Poland Sp. z o.o., Wrocław